François Rabelais

The Heroic Deeds and Sayings of the good Pantagruel

His Visit to the Oracle

François Rabelais

The Heroic Deeds and Sayings of the good Pantagruel
His Visit to the Oracle

ISBN/EAN: 9783337193782

Printed in Europe, USA, Canada, Australia, Japan

Cover: Foto ©Andreas Hilbeck / pixelio.de

More available books at **www.hansebooks.com**

The Fifth and Last Book of

The Heroic

Deeds and Sayings

of _the_

Good Pantagruel

His Visit to the Oracle

Composed by

M. Fran. Rabelais

Doctor in Medicine

London
Gibbings and Company Limited
MDCCCXCVII

CONTENTS

BOOK V

TREATING OF THE HEROIC DEEDS AND SAYINGS OF THE
GOOD PANTAGRUEL

v

Contents

Contents

PLATE

BOOK V

———

THE AUTHOR'S PROLOGUE

INDEFATIGABLE topers, and you thrice precious
martyrs of the smock, give me leave to put a serious
question to your worships, while you are idly striking your codpieces, and I myself not much better
employed: Pray, why is it that people say that men
are not such sots nowadays as they were in the
days of yore? Sot is an old word, that signifies a
dunce, dullard, jolthead, gull, wittol, or noddy, one
without guts in his brains, whose cockloft is un-
furnished, and, in short, a fool. Now would I know,
whether you would have us understand by this same
saying, as indeed you logically may, that formerly
men were fools, and in this generation are grown
wise? How many and what dispositions made them
fools? How many and what dispositions were wanting to make them wise? Why were they fools?
How should they be wise? Pray, how came you
to know that men were formerly fools? How did

you find that they are now wise? Who the devil
made them fools? Who in God's name made them
wise? Who do you think are most, those that loved
mankind foolish, or those that love it wise? How
long has it been wise? How long otherwise?
Whence proceeded the foregoing folly? Whence
the following wisdom? Why did the old folly end
now, and no later? Why did the modern wisdom
begin now, and no sooner? What were we the
worse for the former folly? What the better for
the succeeding wisdom? How should the ancient
folly be come to nothing? How should this same
new wisdom be started up and established?

Now answer me, an't please you: I dare not
adjure you in stronger terms, reverend sirs, lest I
make your pious fatherly worships in the least uneasy. Come, pluck up a good heart; speak the truth
and shame the devil, that enemy to paradise, that
enemy to truth: be cheery, my lads; and if you are
for me, take me off three or five bumpers of the
best, while I make a halt at the first part of the
sermon; then answer my question. If you are not
for me, avaunt! avoid Satan! For I swear by my
great-grandmother's placket,[1] that if you do not
help me to solve that puzzling problem, I will, nay,
I already do repent having proposed it: for still I
must remain nettled and gravelled, and a devil a bit
I know how to get off. Well, what say you? In
faith, I begin to smell you out. You are not yet
disposed to give me an answer; nor I neither, by

---

[1] The original is *mon grand hurluburlu*. And lower, in ch. 15,
Friar John says, Saint Hurluburlu. The *ehrlich wahrlich* of the
Germans, *i.e.*, upon my honour, in good truth, may have been
Rabelais' occasion to forge this burlesque oath out of the cor-
ruption of those German words, as he before had framed St
Picaud from the German *bi Gott*.

these whiskers.　Yet to give some light into the business, I will even tell you what had been anciently foretold in the matter, by a venerable doctor, who being moved by the spirit in a prophetic vein, wrote a book ycleped the Prelatical Bagpipe.　What do you think the old fornicator saith? Hearken, you old noddies, hearken now or never.

> The jubilee's year, when all, like fools were shorn,
> Is about thirty [trente] supernumerary.
> O want of veneration! fools they seem'd,
> But, persevering, with long breves, at last
> No more they shall be gaping greedy fools.
> For they shall shell the shrub's delicious fruit,
> Whose flow'r they in the spring so much had fear'd.

Now you have it, what do you make of it? The seer is ancient, the style laconic, the sentences dark, like those of Scotus, though they treat of matters dark enough in themselves.　The best commentators on that good father take the jubilee after the thirtieth, to be the years that are included in this present age till 1550 [there being but one jubilee every fifty years].　Men shall no longer be thought fools next green pease season.

The fools, whose number, as Solomon certifies, is infinite, shall go to pot like a parcel of mad bedlamites as they are; and all manner of folly shall have an end, that being also numberless, according to Avicenna, *maniæ infinitæ sunt species*.　Folly having been driven back and hidden towards the centre, during the rigour of the winter, it is now to be seen on the surface, and buds out like the trees.　This is as plain as a nose in a man's face: you know it by experience; you see it.　And it was formerly found out by that great good man Hippocrates, Aphorism. *Veræ etenim maniæ*, etc.　This world therefore

3

wisifying itself, shall no longer dread[2] the flower
and blossoms of every coming spring, that is, as you
may piously believe, bumper in hand, and tears in
eyes, in the woeful time of Lent, which used to keep
them company.

Whole cartloads of books, that seemed florid,
flourishing and flowery, gay and gaudy as so many
butterflies; but in the main were tiresome, dull,
soporiferous, irksome, mischievous, crabbed, knotty,
puzzling, and dark as those of whining Heraclitus,
as unintelligible as the numbers of Pythagoras, that
king of the bean, according to l. 2, sat. 6, Horace:
those books, I say, have seen their best days, and
shall soon come to nothing, being delivered to the
executing worms, and merciless petty chandlers:
such was their destiny, and to this they were
predestinated.

In their stead beans in cod are started up; that is,
these merry and fructifying Pantagruelian books, so
much sought nowadays, in expectation of the following jubilee's period: to the study of which writings
all people have given their minds, and accordingly
have gained the name of wise.

Now, I think, I have fairly solved and resolved
your problem; then reform, and be the better for it.
Hem once or twice like hearts of oak; stand to your
pan-puddings, and take me off your bumpers, nine
go-downs, and huzza! since we are like to have a
good vintage, and misers hang themselves. Oh!
they will cost me an estate in hempen collars if
fair weather hold. For I hereby promise to furnish
them with twice as much as will do their business,
on free cost, as often as they will take the pains to

[2] Alluding to the proverb :
  ' Quand les feves sont en fleur, les fous sont en vigueur.'
  Beans in flower, madness (or folly) in power.

4

dance at a rope's end, providently to save charges, to
the no small disappointment of the finisher of the
law.[3]

Now my friends, that you may put in for a share
of this new wisdom, and shake off the antiquated
folly ·this very moment, scratch me out of your
scrolls, and quite discard the symbol of the old
philosopher with the golden thigh, by which he has
forbidden you to eat beans: for you may take it for
a truth, granted among all professors in the science
of good eating, that he enjoined you not to taste of
them, only with the same kind intent with the fresh
water physician, Amer, late Lord of Camelotiere,
kinsman to the lawyer of that name, who forbade his
patients the wing of the partridge, the rump of the
chicken, and the neck of the pigeon, saying, *Ala
mala, cropium dubium, collum bonum, pelle remotâ.*
For the dunsical dog-leech was so selfish as to reserve
them for his own dainty chops, and allowed his poor
patients little more than the bare bones to pick, lest
they should over-load their squeamish stomachs.

To the heathen philosopher succeeded a pack of
Capucions, monks, who forbid us the use of beans,
that is, Pantagruelian books. They seem to follow
the example of Philoxenus and Gnatho, one of whom
was a Sicilian, of fulsome memory, the ancient
master-builders of their monastic cram-gut voluptu-
ousness, who, when some dainty bit was served up
at a feast, filthily used to spit on it, that none but
their nasty selves might have the stomach to eat of
it, though their liquorish chops watered never so
much after it.

[3] See the old story in the *Serées* of J. Bouchet. An usurer
had bought a cord to hang himself with, if the harvest failed.
It proved abundant, on which he hung himself, that the price
of the cord might not be thrown away.

5

So those hideous, snotty, pthisicky, caves-dropping, musty, moving forms of mortification, both in public and private, curse those dainty books, and like toads spit their venom upon them.

Now though we have in our mother-tongue several excellent works in verse and prose, and, heaven be praised, but little left of the trash and trumpery stuff of those dunsical mumblers of Ave Maries, and the barbarous foregoing Gothic age; I have made bold to choose to chirrup and warble my plain ditty, or, as they say, to whistle like a goose among the swans, rather than be thought deaf among so many pretty poets and eloquent orators. And thus I am prouder of acting the clown, or any other under part, among the many ingenious actors in this noble play, than of herding among those mutes, who, like so many shadows and cyphers, only serve to fill up the house, and make up a number; gaping and yawning at the flies, and pricking up their lugs, like so many Arcadian asses, at the striking up of the music; thus silently giving to understand, that their fopships are tickled in the right place.

Having taken this resolution, I thought it would not be amiss to move my Diogenical tub, that you might not accuse me of living without example. I see a swarm of our modern poets and orators, your Colinets, Marots, Herouets, Saint Gelias, Salels, Masuels, and many more;[4] who, having commenced masters in Apollo's academy on Mount Parnassus, and drunk brimmers at the Castalian

---

[4] See Duchat's account of these authors at large in loc. Anthony Herouet, says Duchat, was a Parisian, an excellent poet, and was raised to the Episcopal See at Digne, in Provence. Joachim du Bellay had long before said of this deserving author,

'Seu canis heroas, seu condis ἐρωτικα, verum
Nomen eroeti fata dedere tibi.'

fountain, among the nine merry Muses, have raised our vulgar tongue, and made it a noble and everlasting structure. Their works are all Parian marble, alabaster, porphyry, and royal cement; they treat of nothing but heroic deeds, mighty things, grave and difficult matters; and this in a crimson, alamode, rhetorical style. Their writings are all divine nectar, rich, racy, sparkling, delicate, and luscious wine. Nor does our sex wholly engross this honour; ladies have had their share of the glory: one of them, of the royal blood of France,[5] whom it were a profanation but to name here, surprises the age at once by the transcendent and inventive genius in her writings, and the admirable graces of her style. Imitate those great examples, if you can; for my part, I cannot. Every one, you know, cannot go to Corinth. When Solomon built the temple, all could not give gold by handfuls; each offered a shekel of gold.

Since, then, it is not in my power to improve our architecture as much as they, I am even resolved to do like Renault of Montauban:[6] I will wait on the masons, set on the pot for the masons, cook for the stone-cutters; and since it was not my good luck to be cut out for one of them, I will live and die the admirer of their divine writings.

As for you, little envious prigs, snarling bastards, puny Zoiluses, you will soon have railed your last:

[5] Margaret of Valois, Queen of Navarre, sister to Francis the First; born at the castle of Engouleme, 10th April 1492, and died in that of Audos, in Bearne, the 21st December 1549. Of all her writings, whether in prose or verse, nothing did more honour to her pen than her Heptameron.

[6] In the last chapter of the romance of Aymon's Four Sons, we find Renaud, as the first act of penance for his past life, carrying hods of mortar for the building of St Peter's church at Cologne.

go hang yourselves,[7] and choose you out some well-spread oak, under whose shade you may swing in state, to the admiration of the gaping mob; you shall never want rope enough. While I here solemnly protest before my Helicon, in the presence of my nine mistresses the Muses, that if I live yet the age of a dog, eked out with that of three crows,[8] sound wind and limbs, like the old Hebrew captain Moses, Xenophilus[9] the musician, and Demonax[10] the philosopher; by arguments no ways impertinent, and reasons not to be disputed, I will prove, in the teeth of a parcel of brokers and retailers of ancient rhapsodies, and such mouldy trash, that our vulgar tongue is not so mean, silly, inept, poor, barren, and contemptible, as they pretend. Nor ought I to be afraid of I know not what botchers of old thread-bare stuff, a hundred and a hundred times clouted up, and pieced together; wretched bunglers, that can do nothing but new-vamp old rusty saws; beggarly scavengers, that rake even the muddiest canals of antiquity for scraps and bits of Latin, as insignificant as they are often uncertain. Be-seeching our grandees of Witland, that, as when formerly Apollo had distributed all the treasures of his poetical exchequer to his favourites, little hulch-backed Æsop got for himself the office of apologue-monger: in the same manner, since I do not aspire higher, they would not deny me

[7] As did Zoilus, that implacable enemy to Homer's reputation. *Pendentem volo Zoilum videre,* says Martial.

[8] According to Hesiod, as reported by Pliny, l. 7, c. 48, the crow or raven lives nine times the age of a man.

[9] Pliny, l. 7, c. 70, says, after Aristoxenus, that the musician Xenophilus, lived 105 years. See Lucian in his discourse on long livers.

[10] He lived near 100 years, without ailing anything in body or mind. See Lucian's discourse entitled *Demonax.*

that of puny rhyparographer,[11] or riff-raff follower of Pyreicus.

I dare swear they will grant me this: for they are all so kind, so good-natured, and so generous, that they will never boggle at so small a request. Therefore both dry and hungry souls, pot and trenchermen, fully enjoying those books, perusing, quoting them in their merry conventicles, and observing the great mysteries of which they treat, shall gain a singular profit and fame: as in the like case was done by Alexander the Great, with the books of prime philosophy composed by Aristotle.

O rare! belly on belly! what swillers, what twisters will there be!

Then be sure all you that take care not to die of the pip, be sure, I say, you take my advice, and stock yourselves with good store of such books, as soon as you meet with them at the booksellers'; and do not only shell those beans, but even swallow them down like an opiate cordial, and let them be in you; I say, let them be within you; then you shall find, my beloved, what good they do to all clever shellers of beans.

Here is a good handsome basketful of them, which I hear lay before your worships; they were gathered in the very individual garden whence the former came. So I beseech you, reverend sirs, with as much respect as was ever paid by dedicating author, to accept of the gift, in hopes of somewhat better against next visit the swallows give us.

---

[11] Ryparographer, Gr. ρυπαρος, *sordidus*. Pyreicus the painter is so surnamed by Pliny, because he confined himself only to drawing ridiculous and grotesque pictures ; in which he, however, excelled in his time, as Rabelais did in his ; who by his romance, for all it seems at first sight so impertinent to many people, hath acquired him the title of a refined wit, a good poet, and one of the best French writers that has ever appeared.

ON THE AUTHOR'S PROLOGUE.—The author begins this Prologue with a question, Why people say, that men are not such fools nowadays, as they were in the days of yore? He answers it himself, by a prophecy out of an imaginary book, which he calls the Prelatical Bagpipe. Let us see if we can unriddle it.

'The year of jubilee' was in 1525, under Pope Clement VII. Then all Europe suffered themselves to be shorn or fleeced by the pardon-pedlars, the sellers of the court of Rome's indulgences, and other trumpery ware. 'Is supernumerary about [or above] thirty [or trente].' This means, that time is past, and such years of jubilee are needless, out of fashion, and cried down after the year 1530 (or, perhaps, the Council of Trent), by reason of the change made by the restoration of learning, and the reformers: so that people were no longer to be fleeced by the sellers of pardons. And, indeed, about the year 1530, King Francis I. invited the learned to come to Paris, and having procured several men well versed in various studies, fixed them in the university of Paris. Belleforest and Lambinus say, that in 1531, he established twelve professors for Latin, Greek, Hebrew, mathematics, philosophy, divinity, oratory, physic, etc. But Du Tillet, who at large relates what that prince did, and designed, for the advancement of learning, says this was 1530. And Genebrard, who was afterwards one of those professors, writes, anno 1530, *Guillielmo Budæo et Joanne Bellaio hortantibus, regios linguarum professores instituit. In Clemente VIII.* Now, those learned men, to whom Petavius gives the epithets of *litterati et pii*, purged the age of its foolishness, and very much forwarded the affairs of the reformation: so that in 1530, or at least at the time of the sitting of the Council of Trent, the reign of ignorance may be said to have come to an end.

'O want of veneration! fools they seemed.' That is, those who had been foolish enough to suffer themselves to be sheared and fleeced thus, appeared such as they were, when ignorance had been expelled; I mean, bigoted fools; neither did the veneration which uses to be paid to the church, hinder the wiser sort from laughing at them, or at least from pitying their silliness.

'But, persevering, with long breves, at last no more they shall be gaping, greedy fools.' Those long breves should be the sacred books; which may be called so in opposition to the Roman breviary, in which their contents are as maimed, imperfect, and abbreviated, as the vain imaginations of superstition are spun out there to a tedious length: at least, they mean the books written by the learned, many of which are long. So the people who appeared foolish being no more blinded by a ridiculous superstition, will no more gape after it, nor be greedy of it; being filled with sound knowledge.

'For they shall shell the shrub's delicious fruit, whose flower they in the spring so much had feared.' That is, they shall shell beans in cod; which is as if he had said, truth that lay concealed, and before was known but by a few, will be revealed to the world; and as much as at first it was hated, despised, and feared, at its first appearance, so much the sweeter and more delicious will its fruit prove, when the world shall have had a taste of it.

By these beans in cod we may also partly understand our author's work. The beans are the mystery; the cod is the emblem and outward dress: which is good for nothing but to wrap up what is within it; neither ought we to feed upon it, but solely on what it contains. So we might fix the period of ignorance, and the beginning of the new æra, or restoration of learning, at the year 1550, at which time it began to bear good fruit, and this fifth book was written, though it was not published till after our author's death, perhaps because it spoke too plain. This makes him foretell the speedy oblivion of whole cart-loads of books, that were dull, dark, and mischievous, though they seemed florid, flourishing, and flowery, gay and gaudy as so many *papillons* [butterflies]; by which he seems to play upon the word *papa*, as in Papimany, and in the sixth chapter of the Pantagruelian Prognostication, where the King of the Papillons, or butterflies, undoubtedly means the Pope.—*M*.

CHAPTER I

HOW PANTAGRUEL ARRIVED AT THE RINGING ISLAND, AND OF THE NOISE THAT WE HEARD

PURSUING our voyage, we sailed three days, without discovering anything; on the fourth, we made land. Our pilot told us that it was the Ringing Island,[1] and

[1] He that made the key to Rabelais asserts that England is meant by the Ringing Island; but he is mistaken, since, besides several other reasons, that island had already withdrawn itself from the Pope's authority, under Edward VI., when this book was written.

indeed we heard a kind of a confused and often-repeated noise, that seemed to us, at a great distance, not unlike the sound of great, middle-sized, and little bells, rung all at once, as it is customary at Paris, Tours, Gergeau, Nantes, and elsewhere, on high holidays; and the nearer we came to the land, the louder we heard that jangling.

Some of us doubted that it was the Dodonian kettle, or the portico called Heptaphone, in Olympia, or the eternal humming of the Colossus raised on Memnon's tomb, in Thebes of Egypt, or the horrid din that used formerly to be heard about a tomb at Lipara, one of the Æolian[2] Islands. But this did not square with chorography.

I do not know, said Pantagruel, but that some swarms of bees hereabouts may be taking a ramble in the air, and so the neighbourhood make this dingle dangle with pans, kettles, and basins, the corybantine cymbals of Cybele, grandmother of the gods, to call them back. Let us hearken. When we were nearer, among the everlasting ringing of these indefatigable bells, we heard the singing, as we thought, of some men. For this reason, before we offered to land on the Ringing Island, Pantagruel was of opinion that we should go in the pinnace to a small rock, near which we discovered an hermitage, and a little garden. There we found a diminutive old hermit, whose name was Braguibus, born at Glenay.[3] He gave us a full account of all the jangling, and regaled us after a strange sort of fashion: four live-long days did he make us fast, assuring us that we should not be admitted into the Ringing Island otherwise, because it was then one of the four fasting, or ember weeks. As I love my belly, quoth

[2] See Pliny for all these particulars.
[3] In Poictou.

12

Panurge, I by no means understand this riddle:
methinks, this should rather be one of the four
windy weeks; for while we fast we are only puffed
up with wind.   Pray now, good father hermit, have
not you here some other pastime besides fasting?   Methinks it is somewhat of the leanest: · we might well
enough be without so many palace holidays, and those
fasting times of yours.   In my Donatus, quoth Friar
John, I could find yet but three times or tenses, the
preterit, the present, and the future, and therefore I
make a donative of the fourth (*i.e.*, the fast of the
quatre-tems) to be kept by my footman.   That time
or tense, said Epistemon, is aorist, derived from the
preterimperfect tense of the Greeks, admitted in
variable and uncertain times.   Patience [4] *per force*
is a remedy for a mad dog.   Saith the hermit, it
is, as I told you, fatal to go against this: whoever
does it is a rank heretic, and wants nothing but fire
and faggot, that is certain.   To deal plainly with
you, my dear pater, cried Panurge, being at sea, I
much more fear being wet than being warm, and
being drowned than being burned.

Well, however, let us fast in God's name; yet I
have fasted so long, that it has quite undermined my
flesh, and I fear that at last the bastions of this
bodily fort of mine will fall to ruin.   Besides, I am
much more afraid of vexing you in this same trade
of fasting; for the devil a bit I understand any thing
in it, and it becomes me very scurvily,[5] as several
people have told me, and I am apt to believe them.
For my part I do not much mind fasting : for alas! it is

[4] The proverb in the original is, Patience, say the lepers.
Alluding to the herb patience (*lapathum*) which those afflicted
with the leprosy seek after with great eagerness, to relieve them.
[5] *Ridiculus æque nullus est, quam quando esurit.* Plaut. in
Sticho, act 2, scene 1.

as easy as pissing a bed, and a trade of which any
body may set up; there needs no tools. I am
much more inclined not to fast for the future : for
to do so, there is some stock required, and some
tools are set to work. No matter, since you are so
steadfast, and would have us fast, let us fast as fast
as we can, and then break fast in the name of famine.
Now we are come to these esurial idle days. I vow
I had quite put them out of my head long ago. If
we must fast, said Pantagruel, I see no other remedy
but to get rid of it as soon as we can, as we would
out of a bad way. I will in that space of time
somewhat look over my papers, and examine
whether the marine study be as good as ours at land.
For Plato, to describe a silly, raw, ignorant fellow,
compares him to those that are bred on shipboard,
as we would do one bred up in a barrel, who never
saw any thing but through the bung-hole.

To tell you the short and the long of the matter,
our fasting was most hideous and terrible ; for, the
first day we fasted at fisticuffs,[6] the second at cudgels,
the third at sharps, and the fourth at blood and
wounds : such was the order of the fairies.[7]

ON CHAP. I.—The Ringing Island can mean nothing but the
clergy of the Church of Rome, whose mysteries are all performed
at the sound of large, middle-sized, little, and very little bells.
They are rung at matins, mass, noon, vespers, sermons, and the
salutation to the| Virgin every day, on the eves or vigils of holy-
days, at processions and at stations ; and, whenever the priest
lifts up the wafer-god, a little bell is rung, that the people may
fall down and adore that piece of dough, which, they must
believe, made heaven and earth, though it were made that very
morning by the baker, and some of the same stamp be shown in

---

[6] The meaning of all this is, that one or two days fasting may
not do a man much harm, but three or four days may prejudice
his health, nay, be as much as his life is worth.
[7] Who had ordained the fatal (as said before) fast of the
ember weeks.

every parish. Besides, when the priest carries the viaticum, a
diminutive bell always tingles before him. Thus bells are often
rung wherever there is a monastery, church, chapel, or hermitage,
to awaken the people's devotion, summon them together, dismiss
them, and make them come again. Add to this, that as whatever is said of the Ringing Island in the following chapters, cannot well be adapted to any thing but the Popish ecclesiastics, so
those who pretended to explain these books, only by printing at
the end of some French editions twenty or thirty names, which,
without the least reason, they call a key, either never read them,
or had a design to impose on the reader more than our author ;
else they would never have said, that the Ringing Island is
England. I own there is much ringing there, and the English
are famous for making that a recreation ; but this book was
written during King Edward the Sixth's reign, at which time the
Reformation had prevailed here ; and though our author mentions the Knights of the Garter in the fifth chapter, while he
speaks of the knight-hawks of the Ringing Island, it does not
follow he meant England, since he only places the Knights of
Malta among the Roman ecclesiastics ; which was judiciously
done, because they make a vow never to marry, read the breviary,
and have livings like abbots. Even that passage proves that the
Ringing Island is not England: since Ædituus makes one of
his island's knight-hawks look wistfully on the Pantagruelian
strangers, to see whether he might not find among their company a stately gaudy kind of large, huge, dreadful birds of prey,
so untoward, that they could never be brought to the lure, nor
to perch on the glove (which may mean, that other knights
claimed a pre-eminence over those of Malta). Ædituus adds,
I am told there are such in your world, who wear goodly garters
below the knee, with an inscription about them which condemns
him who shall think ill of it (*qui mal y pense*) to be bewrayed and
conskited. So it is plain there were none such in the Ringing
Island. Then in the sixth chapter, Ædituus says, that all the
good things which they have in this island come from every part
of the other world, except some of the northern regions ; particularly from Touraine, our author's native country ; and that the
income of the duke of that country could not afford him to eat
his bellyful of beans and bacon, because his predecessors had
been more than liberal to the birds of the Ringing Island, that
they might there munch it, twist it, cram it, gorge it, craw it,
riot it, junket it, and tickle it off ; stuffing their puddings with
dainty food, etc.

The hermit, whom the Pantagruelists met, assured them they

should not be admitted into the Ringing Island, unless they fasted four days, because it was then one of the four fasting or ember weeks. As the island is the Popish clergy, none enter into it, that is, into orders, without fasting, and a great deal of formality; and it was judiciously that Rabelais made his travellers be admitted there at one of the times prescribed for the admittance of laics into the body of the clergy. Yet he shows, that those fasts (though commendable in their institution) were much abused; and many, like Panurge, are pretty apt to say, Since you are so steadfast, and have us fast, let us fast, as fast as we can, and then break fast. Thus only putting a constraint on themselves a while (or seeming to put it) to indulge them in gluttony after it.—*M.*

CHAPTER II

HOW THE RINGING ISLAND HAD BEEN INHABITED BY THE SITICINES, WHO WERE BECOME BIRDS

HAVING fasted as aforesaid, the hermit gave us a letter from one whom he called Albian Camar,[1] Master Ædituus of the Ringing Island: but Panurge greeting him, called him Master Antitus. He was a little queer old fellow, bald-pated, with a snout whereat you might easily have lighted a card match, and a phiz as red as a cardinal's cap. He made us all very welcome, upon the hermit's recommendation, hearing that we had fasted, as I have told you.

When we had well stuffed our puddings, he gave us an account of what was remarkable in the island, affirming that it had been first inhabited by the Siticines; but that, according to the course of

[1] This must have been some Jacobin, or at least some ecclesiastics with a black cassock under a white surplice. Albian, from *albus*, white; and the priests of Baal were called in Hebrew *cemarim*, only because of their wearing black gowns.

nature, as all things, you know, are subject to change, they were become birds.

There I had a full account of all that Atteius Capito, Pollux, Marcellus, A. Gellius, Athenæus, Suidas, Ammonius, and others had writ of the Siticines; and then we thought we might as easily believe the transmutations of Nectymene, Progné, Itys, Alcyone, Antigone, Tereus, and other birds. Nor did we think it more reasonable to doubt of the transmogrification of the Macrobian children into swans, or that of the men of Pallene in Thrace into birds, as soon as they had bathed themselves in the Tritonic lake. After this the devil a word could we get out of him but of birds and cages.

The cages were spacious, costly, magnificent, and of an admirable architecture. The birds were large, fine, and neat accordingly; looking as like the men in my country, as one pea does like another: for they eat and drank like men, muted like men, digested like men, but stunk like devils; slept, billed, and trod their females like men, but somewhat oftener: in short, had you seen and examined them from top to toe, you would have laid your head to a turnip that they had been mere men. However, they were nothing less, as Master Ædituus told us; assuring us, at the same time, that they were neither secular nor laic: and the truth is, the diversity of their feathers and plumes did not a little puzzle us.

Some of them were all over as white as swans, others as black as crows, many as grey as owls, others black and white like magpies, some all red like red-birds, and others purple and white like some pigeons. He called the males clerg-hawks, monk-hawks, priest-hawks, abbot-hawks, bish-hawks, cardin-hawks, and one pope-hawk, who is a species

by himself.   He called the females clerg-kites,
nun-kites, priest-kites, abbess-kites, bis-kites, cardin-
kites, and pope-kites.

However, said he, as hornets and drones will get
among the bees, and there do nothing but buzz,
eat, and spoil every thing ; so, for these last three
hundred years, a vast swarm of bigottelloes flocked,
I do not know how, among these goodly birds every
fifth full moon, and have bemuted, bewrayed, and
conskited the whole island.   They are so hard-
favoured and monstrous, that none can abide them.
For their wry necks make a figure like a crooked
billet ; their paws are hairy,[2] like those of rough-
footed pigeons ; their claws and pounces, belly and
breech, like those of the Stymphalid [3] harpies.   Nor
is it possible to root them out : for if you get rid
of one, straight four-and-twenty new ones fly thither.

There had been need of another monster-hunter,
such as was Hercules ; for Friar John had like to
have run distracted about it, so much he was nettled
and puzzled in the matter.   As for the good Pantagruel, he was even served as was Messer Priapus,[4]

[2] Dangerous hypocrites ; with Jacob's voice, but the hands of
Esau.

[3] See Diodorus Siculus.

[4] The gods having been invited by their good mother to a
feast, repaired to it one and all, even the nymphs and satyrs, not
excepting Silenus himself.   Their godships, after spending part
of the night in drinking pretty liberally, some fell asleep, others
went to dancing and other little sports.   Priapus running after
the nymphs, spied Vesta asleep.   Whether or no he knew her,
or took her for somebody else, he resolved not to miss the
opportunity, but Silenus' ass fell a-braying, and awaked Vesta,
who getting up in a sad fright, and the celestial gentry running
in, upon the noise she made, poor Priapus was discovered ; nor
could he with the skirt of his robe, had it been four times as
large, conceal the condition he was in.   It is an idle frivolous
story.   Qvid, in the sixth of his Fasti, tells it agreeably, as he
does everything else, and Lactantius after him, l. 1 of his

contemplating the sacrifices of Ceres, for want of skin.

ON CHAP. II.—When Pantagruel and his attendants have fasted after a strange sort of a fashion, they are kindly received by Albian Camar, Master Ædituus, or Sacristan of the Ringing Island. Camar in Hebrew signifies an idolatrous priest ; and St Jerome has made it *aruspex* and *ædituus* in Latin. We may observe, by that beginning, what esteem our author had for the Ringing Island, with its sacrifices and mysteries.

Ædituus acquaints our strangers with the metamorphosis of the Siticines and Sicinnists into birds. The Siticines and Sicinnists were those that used to sing mournfully on the dead, and at funerals, among the ancients. *Siticines appellantur qui apud sitos canere soliti essent, hoc est, vita functos et sepultos.* A. Gellius, lib. 2, cap. 20. Consequently, the clergy of the Church of Rome, who chiefly subsist by obits, trentals, and masses, for the repose of the souls of the dead, may well be called by those names.

We are told that the Siticines were become birds; those birds are those ecclesiastics, who raise themselves by contemplation and holiness of life (if you will believe them), soaring above the things of this earth, on which we poor grovelling laics crawl. Ædituus would make Pantagruel sensible of this, when he tells him that those birds, which looked like men, ate and drank, slept and billed like men, were nothing less than men, being neither secular nor laics.

Their spacious, costly, magnificent cages, admirable in their architecture, are their churches; which appears the plainer by reason of the bells which our author says were above them.

The variety of the feathers and plumes of those birds denotes the different orders and clothings of the Popish clergy, which distinguish them from each other: the Benedictines are white, the Austins black, the Franciscans grey, the Bernardins black and white, the Bishops purple, the Cardinals red; some knights and commanders are white and blue; and there are nuns dressed like most of those professing the same orders.

It is observable that they are all made birds of prey, clerg-hawks, monk-hawks, priest-hawks, abbot-hawks, bish-hawks, cardin-hawks, and pope-hawks; and clerg-kites, nun-kites, abbess-kites, etc.

The wry-necked bigottelloes, who had flocked thither during

Divine Institutions, n. 21. I have added a little to the thing, the better to explain our author's text, who has darkened the fact exceedingly, by having Ceres instead of Cybele, and skin instead of covering or lappet.

the last three hundred years, are the orders of Franciscan and Dominican friars. Our author, who had been a Cordelier, *i.e.*, a Franciscan, and misused by the fraternity in the convent, was well acquainted with their merit, and speaks experimentally; which makes him wish for another Hercules to root them out.—*M.*

CHAPTER III

HOW THERE IS BUT ONE POPE-HAWK IN THE RINGING ISLAND

WE then asked Master Ædituus why there was but one pope-hawk among such venerable birds, multiplied in all their species? He answered, that such was the first institution and fatal destiny of the stars: that the clerg-hawks begot the priest-hawks and monk-hawks, without carnal copulation, as some bees[1] are born of a young bull: the priest-hawks begat the bish-hawks, the bish-hawks the stately cardin-hawks, and the stately cardin-hawks, if they live long enough, at last come to be pope-hawk.

Of this last kind, there never is more than one at a time; as in a bee-hive there is but one king, and in the world but one sun.

When the pope-hawk dies, another rises in his stead out of the whole brood of cardin-hawks; that is, as you must understand it all along, without carnal copulation. So that there is in that species an individual unity, with a perpetuity of succession, neither more or less than in the Arabian phœnix.

It is true, that about two thousand seven hundred

[1] See 4th book of Virgil's Georgics.

and sixty moons ago,[2] two pope-hawks were seen upon the face of the earth: but then you never saw in your lives such a woeful rout and hurly-burly as was all over this island. For all these same birds did so peck, clapperclaw, and maul one another all that time, that there was the devil and all to do, and the island was in a fair way of being left without inhabitants. Some stood up for this pope-hawk, some for the other. some, struck with a dumbness, were as mute as so many fishes; the devil a note was to be got out of them; part of the merry bells here were as silent as if they had lost their tongues, I mean their clappers.

During these troublesome times, they called to their assistance the emperors, kings, dukes, earls, barons, and commonwealths of the world that live on the other side the water; nor was this schism and sedition at an end, till one of them died, and the plurality was reduced to a unity.[3]

We then asked, what moved those birds to be thus continually chaunting and singing? He answered, that it was the bells that hung on the top of their cages. Then he said to us, Will you have me make these monk-hawks, whom you see bardocuculated[4] with a bag, such as you use to

[2] At twelve moons a year (Rabelais, as he insinuates in the preface of this book, composing it about the year 1550) the 2760 moons he speaks of, i.e., 230 years, point out the year 1380, the times of the great schism, which was caused on one hand by Urban VI. sitting at Rome, and on the other hand, the pretended Clement VII. sitting at Avignon.

[3] At the council of Constance, when Cardinal Otho, of the family of Colonna, was made Pope by the name of Martin V.

[4] The Benedictines, or rather Bernardines, whose cowls look like the bardocucullus (or hood) of the ancient inhabitants of Saintonge, Langres, and some other Gauls. See Fauchet Ant. Gaul., l. 1, ch. 5.

strain Hippocras wine through, sing like any wood-
larks? Pray do, said we. He then gave half-a-
dozen pulls to a little rope, which caused a diminutive bell to give so many tingtangs; and presently
a parcel of monk-hawks ran to him, as if the devil
had drove them, and fell a-singing like mad.

Pray, master, cried Panurge, if I also rang this
bell, could I make those other birds yonder, with
red-herring-coloured feathers, sing? Ay, marry
would you, returned Ædituus. With this Panurge
hanged himself (by the hands, I mean) at the bell-
rope's end, and no sooner made it speak, but those
smoked birds hied them thither, and began to lift
up their voices, and make a sort of untowardly
hoarse noise, which I grudge to call singing.
Ædituus indeed told us, that they fed on nothing
but fish, like the herons and cormorants of the
world, and that they were a fifth kind [5] of
cucullati newly stamped.

He added, that he had been told by Robert
Valbringue, who lately passed that way in his
return from Africa, that a sixth kind was to fly
hither out of hand, which he called capus-hawks,
more grum, vinegar-faced, brain-sick, froward, and
loathsome, than any kind whatsoever in the whole
island. Africa, said Pantagruel, still uses to produce some new and monstrous thing.

On Chap. III.—The pope-hawk, who, like the phœnix, is a
species alone, is undoubtedly the Pope. We have there a true
account of what happened some 1760 moons, that is about 140
years, before our author wrote; only to blind this, or perhaps by
some mistake in the printing, it is made 2760 moons: I mean
the schism of Avignon, which lasted forty years. Three Popes
were seen then at the same time, Bennet the Ninth, Gregory the

---

[5] The minims, instituted by Francis de Paul, about the middle
of the 15th century, long after the establishment of the four
orders of mendicants.

Twelfth, and Alexander the Fifth. This schism ended at the Council of Constance, which began in 1414, and ended in 1419.—*M.*

CHAPTER IV

HOW THE BIRDS OF THE RINGING ISLAND WERE ALL PASSENGERS

SINCE you have told us, said Pantagruel, how the pope-hawk is begot by the cardin-hawks, the cardin-hawks by the bish-hawks, and the bish-hawks by the priest-hawks, and the priest-hawks by the clerg-hawks, I would gladly know whence you have these same clerg-hawks. They are all passengers, or travelling birds, returned Ædituus, and come hither from the other world;[1] part out of a vast country, called Want-o'-bread, the rest out of another towards the west, which they style Too-many-of-'em. From these two countries flock hither, every year, whole legions of these clerg-hawks, leaving their fathers, mothers, friends, and relations.

This happens when there are too many children, whether male or female, in some good family of the latter country; insomuch that the house would come to nothing, if the paternal estate were shared among them all (as reason requires, nature directs, and God commands). For this cause parents used to rid themselves of that inconveniency, by packing off the younger fry, and forcing them to seek their fortune in this isle Bossart (or humpy island). I suppose he means L'isle Bouchart, near Chinon, cried Panurge. No,

[1] Monks are said to be civilly dead to this world.

23

replied the other, I mean Bossart (crooked), for there is not one in ten among them, but is either crooked, crippled, blinking, limping, ill‑favoured, deformed, or an unprofitable load to the earth.

It was quite otherwise among the heathens, said Pantagruel, when they used to receive a maiden among the number of vestals: for Leo Antistius affirms, that it was absolutely forbidden to admit a virgin into that order, if she had any vice in her soul, or defect in her body, though it were but the smallest spot on any part of it. I can hardly believe, continued Ædituus, that their dams on the other side the water go nine months with them; for they cannot endure them nine years, nay, scarce seven, sometimes in the house ; but by putting only a shirt over the other clothes of the young urchins, and lopping off I do not well know how many hairs from their crowns, mumbling certain apostrophised and expiatory words, they visibly, openly, and plainly, by a Pythagorical metempsychosis, without the least hurt, transmogrify them into such birds as you now see ; much after the fashion of the Egyptian heathens, who used to constitute isiacs, by shaving them, and making them put on certain linostoles, or surplices. However, I do not know my good friends, but that these she-things, whether clerg-kites, nun-kites, and abbess-kites, instead of singing pleasant motets and charisteres, such as used to be sung to Oromasis by Zoroaster's institution, may be bellowing out such catarates and scythropys (cursed lamentable and wretched imprecations), as were usually offered to the Arimanian demon; being thus in continual devotion[2] for their kind friends and relations,

[2] M. Motteux is vastly mistaken here to say, in continual devotion for their friends. Rabelais means just the contrary :

that transformed them into birds, whether when
they were maids, or thornbacks, in their prime,
or at their last prayers.

But the greatest numbers of our birds came out of
Want-o'-bread, which, though a barren country,
where the days are of a most tedious lingering length,
overstocks this whole island with the lower class of
birds.   For hither fly the *asapheis* [3] that inhabit that
land, either when they are in danger of passing their
time scurvily for want of belly-timber, being unable,
or what is more likely, unwilling to take heart of
grace, and follow some honest lawful calling, or too
proud-hearted and lazy to go to service in some sober
family.   The same is done by our frantic inamoradoes,
who, when crossed in their wild desires, grow stark
staring mad, and choose this life suggested to them
by their despair, too cowardly to make them swing,
like their brother Iphis of doleful memory.   There
is another sort, that is, your gaol birds, who, having
done some rogue's trick, or other heinous villainy,
and being sought up and down to be trussed up, and
made to ride the two or three-legged mare [4] that groans
for them, warily scour off, and come here to save their
bacon ; because all these sorts of birds are here provided for, and grow in an instant as fat as hogs,
though they came as lean as rakes ; for having the
benefit of the clergy, they are as safe as thieves in a
mill within this sanctuary.

But, asked Pantagruel, do these birds never return
to the world where they were hatched ?   Some do,

'font continuelles devotions de leurs parens et amis,' *i.e.*, they
(the cloistered people) are continually devoting or cursing their
friends, who put them there.   What says Merlin Coccaie ?   'Est
monachæ, quando moritur, maladire parentes.'

   [3] It means obscure, little known.   Such are the Utopians,
Amaurotes, etc.

   [4] The gallows, or triple-tree.

answered Ædituus; formerly some few, but very late
and very unwillingly; however, since some certain
eclipses, by the virtue of the celestial constellations,
a great crowd of them fled back to the world.   Nor
do we fret or vex ourselves a jot about it: for those
that stay, wisely sing, the fewer the better cheer;
and all those that fly away first, cast off their feathers
here among these nettles and briars.[5]

Accordingly we found some thrown by there; and
as we looked up and down, we chanced to light on
what some people will hardly thank us for having
discovered; and thereby hangs a tale.

ON CHAP. IV.—Ædituus owns that all the birds of the Ringing Island are passengers.   There is a sort of hawks distinguished
by that name.   He adds, that none of them were bred in that
place, but all came from the other world; that is, out of the
laity, who are styled worthy men with respect to the clergy, who
assume that of divine.   One of the countries out of which they
come is called Want-o'-bread, and the other, Too-many-of-'em.
The first shows, that many will take to any thing rather than
starve; the other, that the avarice of unnatural parents makes
them compel their children, often the most defective in body or
mind, to be monks, friars, priests, etc.

Those birds who returned to the world are the monks and
clergymen, who, like Luther, Calvin, and others, left their
monastical or ecclesiastical habits; or, like Rabelais, left their
monasteries.   The feathers found among the nettles, means his
frock and cowl, which he cast off, and in general those of other
monks who apostatise—so their desertion is called by the Church
of Rome.   What the company chanced to light upon there, as
they looked up and down, for the discovery of which some
people will hardly thank them, may imply this work, which
exposes all the mysteries of monachism.—M.

---

[5] How many monks at that time did not cast away their habit!

CHAPTER V

OF THE DUMB KNIGHT-HAWKS OF THE RINGING ISLAND

THESE word were scarce out of his mouth, when some five-and-twenty or thirty birds flew towards us : they were of a hue and feather like which we had not seen any thing in the whole island. Their plumes were as changeable as the skin of the chameleon, and the flower of *tripolion*, or *teucrion*.[1] They had all under the left wing a mark, like two diameters dividing a circle into equal parts, or, if you had rather have it so, like a perpendicular line falling on a right line. The marks which each of them bore, were much of the same shape, but of different colours; for some were white, others green,[2] some red, others purple, and some blue. Who are those, asked Panurge, and how do you call them? They are mongrels, quoth Ædituus.

We call them knight-hawks, and have a great number of rich commanderies[3] (fat livings) in your world. Good, your worship, said I, make them give us a song, an it please you, that we may know how they sing. They scorn your words, cried Ædituus, they are none of your singing birds; but, to make amends, they feed as much as the best two of them all. Pray, where are their hens? where are their females? said I. They have none, answered Ædituus. How comes it to pass, then, asked

[1] Pliny, 1. 21, ch. 7, speaking of the *polium*, which some, says he, call *teuthrion*, among other wonderful things which he relates of this herb, affirms the flower of it to be white in the morning, red at noon, and blueish in the evening.

[2] The Knights of St Lazere, who wore a green cross.

[3] Rabelais banteringly calls them the *gourmanderies*.

Panurge, that they are thus bescabbed, bescurfed, all embroidered over the phiz with carbuncles, pushes, and pock-royals, some of which undermine the handles of their faces. This same fashionable and illustrious disease, quoth Ædituus, is common among that kind of birds, because they are pretty apt to be tossed on the salt deep.

He then acquainted us with the occasion of their coming. This next to us, said he, looks so wistfully upon you, to see whether he may not find among your company a stately gaudy kind of huge dreadful birds of prey, which yet are so untoward, that they never could be brought to the lure, nor to perch on the glove.[4] They tell us that there are such in your world, and that some of them have goodly garters below the knee, with an inscription about them, which condemns him (*qui mal y pense*) who shall think ill of it, to be bewrayed and conskited. Others are said to wear the devil in a string before their paunches;[5] and others a ram's skin.[6] All that is true enough, good Master Ædituus, quoth Panurge; but we have not the honour to be acquainted with their knightships.

Come on, cried Ædituus in a merry mood, we have had chat enough of conscience! let's even go drink. And eat, quoth Panurge. Eat, replied Ædituus, and drink bravely, old boy; twist like plough-jobbers, and swill like tinkers; pull away and save tide, for nothing is so dear and precious as time, therefore we will be sure to put it to a good use.

He would fain have carried us first to bathe in the bagnios of the cardin-hawks, which are goodly delicious places, and have us licked over with

[4] Of the great falconer the Pope.
[5] Order of St Michael.
[6] Order of the Golden Fleece.

precious ointments by the *alyptes, alias* rubbers, as
soon as we should come out of the bath.   But
Pantagruel told him, that he could drink but too
much without that.   He then led us into a spacious
delicate refectory, or fratrie-room, and told us:
Braguibus, the hermit, made you fast four days
together; now contrariwise, I will make you eat and
drink of the best four days[7] through stitch, before
you budge from this place.   But hark ye me, cried
Panurge, may not we take a nap in the meantime?
Ay, ay, answered Ædituus, that is as you shall think
good,; for he that sleeps, drinks.   Good Lord! how
we lived! what good bub! what dainty cheer!   O
what an honest cod was this same Ædituus.

ON CHAP. V.—The dumb knight-hawks of the Ringing Island,
are the knights of Malta; the marks which they bear under
their left wing, is the cross of their order, which these knights
wear on their heart, of different colours, according to the pro-
vinces to which they belong.   They are said to be dumb, because
they do not say mass, nor officiate as priests and monks; and are
only obliged to read every day, or repeat some parts of their
breviary.   They have no females, says Ædituus, because there
are none of their order; yet they make themselves amends with
others out of every order: so that what is said of the pock-royals
that embroider their heads, and undermine the handle of their
faces, is true of many of them who are not always concerned in
holy wars.   They are all gentlemen, not shut up within monasteries; and though they sing not, feed, that is, spend and devour
as much as the best two that do.   Some of the livings or commanderies bring them in great sums yearly: and as they make a
vow never to marry, it is not strange they should meet with
such wounds, when they engage some other infidels than the
Turks.
      I have already spoken *en passant* of the Knights of the Garter,
of whom our author made mention in the same manner.   The

---

7 The author seems here to have an eye to what is practised
even now in the Trinity Hospital at Rome.   Such pilgrims as
come thither from any place in Italy, are lodged and fed for
three days; but the Ultramontanes are entertained a day longer.

knights who wear before their plumes *le trophée d'un calumniateur*, that is, the devil in a string before their paunches, are the knights of the Order of St Michael, pictured with the devil at his feet. It was the most honourable order in France in our author's time; for that of the Holy Ghost was instituted since, by Henry III. Those who wear a ram's skin, are the Knights of the Order of the Golden Fleece.—*M.*

CHAPTER VI

HOW THE BIRDS ARE CRAMMED IN THE RINGING ISLAND.

PANTAGRUEL looked I-do-not-know-howish, and seemed not very well pleased with the four days' junketing which Ædituus enjoined us. Ædituus, who soon found it out, said to him, You know, sir, that seven days before winter, and seven days after,[1] there is no storm at sea: for then the elements are still, out of respect for the halcyons, or king-fishers, birds sacred to Thetis, which then lay their eggs and hatch their young near the shore. Now here the sea makes itself amends for this long calm; and whenever any foreigners come hither it grows boisterous and stormy for four days together. We can give no other reason for it, but that it is a piece of its civility, that those who come among us may stay whether they will or no, and be copiously feasted all the while with the incomes of the ringing. Therefore pray do not think your time lost; for, willing, nilling, you will be forced to stay; unless you are resolved to encounter Juno, Neptune, Doris, Æolus, and his fluster-busters; and, in short, all the

[1] See Pliny, l. 10, ch. 12, and Plutarch, in the treatise where he examines who is wisest.

pack of ill-natured left-handed godlings and vejoves.
Do but resolve to be cheery, and fall to briskly.

After we had pretty well stayed our stomachs with
some tight snatches, Friar John said to Ædituus,
For aught I see, you have none but a parcel of
birds and cages in this island of yours, and the devil-
a-bit of one of them all that sets his hand to the
plough, or tills the land, whose fat he devours: their
whole business is to be frolic, to chirp it, to whistle
it, to warble it: tossing it, and roaring it merrily
night and day: pray then, if I may be so bold,
whence comes this plenty and overflowing of all
dainty bits and good things, which we see among
you? From all the other world, returned Ædituus,
if you except some part of the northern regions, who
of late years have stirred up the jakes.[2]   Mum!
they may chance ere long to rue the day they did
so; their cows shall have porridge, and their dogs
oats; there will be work made among them, that
there will: come! a fig for it, let us drink.——But
pray what countrymen are you? Tourain is our
country, answered Panurge.   Cod so! cried Ædituus,
you were not then hatched of an ill bird, I will say
that for you, since the blessed Tourain is your
mother: for from thence there comes hither every
year such a vast store of good things, that we were
told by some folks of the place, that happened to
touch at this island, that your Duke of Tourain's
income will not afford him to eat his bellyful of
beans and bacon (a good dish spoiled between
Moses and Pythagoras), because his predecessors
have been more than liberal to these most holy
birds of ours, that we might here munch it, twist
it, cram it, gorge it, craw it, riot it, junket it, and
tickle it off; stuffing our puddings with dainty

2 *Movere camerinam.*   See Cambridge Dictionary.

pheasants, partridges, pullets with eggs, fat capons of Loudunois, and all sorts of venison and wild fowl. Come, box it about, tope on, my friends : pray do you see yon jolly birds that are perched together, how fat, how plump, and in good case they look, with the income that Touraine yields us ! And in faith they sing rarely for their good founders, that is the truth on it. You never saw any Arcadian birds mumble more fairly than they do over a dish, when they see these two gilt batons,[3] or when I ring for them those great bells that you see above their cages. Drink on, sirs, whip it away : verily, friends, it is very fine drinking to-day, and so it is every day of the week; then drink on, toss it about, here is to you with all my soul; you are most heartily wel- come : never spare it, I pray you; fear not we should ever want good bub, and belly timber; for, look here, though the sky were of brass, and the earth of iron, we should not want wherewithal to stuff the gut, though they were to continue so seven or eight years longer than the famine in Egypt. Let us then, with brotherly love and charity, re- fresh ourselves here with the creature.

Woons, man ! cried Panurge, what a rare time you have of it in this world ! Pshaw ! returned Ædituus, this is nothing to what we shall have in the other : the Elysian fields will be the least that can fall to our lot. Come, in the meantime let us drink here; come, here is to thee, old fuddlecap.

Your first Siticines, said I, were superlatively wise, in devising thus a means for you to compass what- ever all men naturally covet so much; and so few, or, to speak more properly, none can enjoy together : I mean, a paradise in this life, and another in the next. Sure you were born wrapped in your mother's

[3] *Festes à bastons.*   A solemn festival.

32

smickets! O happy creatures! O more than men! Would I had the luck to fare like you!

ON CHAP. VI.—The author describes how the birds of the Ringing Island are crammed, and how, though not one of them sets his hand to the plough, or tills the land, whose fat he devours, they wallow in plenty, and do nothing but chirp it, whistle it, and warble it merrily night and day. All this chapter is a cutting satire, in which Rabelais ingeniously exposes the foolish bigotry of the great vulgar and the small, who have undone, and still ruin themselves daily, to maintain those lazy, hypocritical birds of prey, in idle ease, and luxurious pleasure ; though the ravenous tribe have nothing to give in return, but insignificant siticin prayers, and a doubtful hereafter for a certain now.—*M.*

CHAPTER VII

HOW PANURGE RELATED TO MASTER ÆDITUUS THE FABLE OF THE HORSE AND THE ASS

WHEN we had crammed and crammed again, Ædituus took us into a chamber that was well furnished, hung with tapestry, and finely gilt. Thither he caused to be brought store of mirobolans, cashou, green ginger preserved with plenty of Hippocras, and delicious wine. With those antidotes, that were like a sweet Lethe, he invited us to forget the hardships of our voyage; and at the same time he sent plenty of provisions on board our ship that rid in the harbour. After this, we then jogged to bed for that night; but the devil a bit poor Pilgarlic could sleep one wink: the everlasting jingle-jangle of the bells kept me awake whether I would or no.

About midnight Ædituus came to wake us, that we might drink. He himself showed us the way, saying: You men of the other world say that ignorance is the mother of all evil, and so far you are right; yet for all that, you do not take the least care to get rid of it, but still plod on, and live in it, with it, and by it; for which a plaguey deal of mischief lights on you every day, and you are right enough served: you are perpetually ailing somewhat, making a moan and never right. It is what I was ruminating upon just now. And, indeed, ignorance keeps you here fastened in bed, just as that bully-rook Mars was detained by Vulcan's art: for all the while you do not mind that you ought to spare some of your rest, and be as lavish as you can of the goods of this famous island. Come, come, you should have eaten three breakfasts already: and take this from me for a certain truth, That if you would consume the mouth-ammunition of this island, you must rise betimes: eat them, they multiply; spare them, they diminish.

For example: mow a field in due season, and the grass will grow thicker and better; do not mow it, and in a short time it will be floored with moss. Let us drink, and drink again, my friends: come let us all carouse it. The leanest [1] of our birds are now singing to us all; we will drink to them, if you please. Let us take off one, two, three, nine [2] bumpers. *Non zelus, sed charitas.*

At the break of day, he waked us again to take a dish of monastical brewess.[3] From that time we made but one meal, that only lasted the whole day: so that I cannot well tell how I may call it, whether

[1] The mendicant friars, who sing their matins at midnight.

[2] Referring to the number of the Graces and Muses. *Aut ter bibendum aut novies :* a proverb of the ancients, who, in point of drinking, were nothing to compare with this Ædituus, who here unites all the lessons of the different sorts of claustral matins.

[3] *Soupe de Prime.* So called from its being eaten at the hour of prime, which is the first of the canonical hours.

dinner, supper, nunchion, or after-supper; only to get a stomach, we took a turn or two in the island, to see and hear the blessed singing birds.

At night Panurge said to Ædituus, Give me leave, sweet sir, to tell you a merry story of something that happened some three-and-twenty moons ago, in the country of Chastelleraud.

One day in April,[4] a certain gentleman's groom, Roger by name, was walking his master's horses in some fallow ground: there it was his good fortune to find a pretty shepherdess, feeding her bleating sheep and harmless lambkins, on the brow of a neighbouring mountain, in the shade of an adjacent grove: near her, some frisking kids tripped it over a green carpet of nature's own spreading; and to complete the landscape, there stood an ass. Roger, who was a wag, had a dish of chat with her; and after some ifs, ands, and buts, hems and heighs on her side, got her in the mind to get up behind him, to go and see his stable, and there take a bit by-the-bye in a civil way. While they were holding a parley, the horse, directing his discourse to the ass (for all brute beasts spoke that year in divers places), whispered these words in his ear: Poor ass, how I pity thee! thou slavest like any hack, I read it on thy crupper: thou dost well, however, since God has created thee to serve mankind; thou art a very honest ass: but not to be better rubbed down, curricombed, trapped, and fed, than thou art, seems to me indeed to be too hard a lot. Alas! thou art all rough-coated,[5] in ill plight; jaded, foundered, crestfallen, and drooping,

[4] April is an amorous month. And the country of Chastelleraud abounds with these Arcadian nightingales (asses).

[5] It is *lanterné* in Rabelais, and means, thy whole body is transparent as a lantern, and the skin of thy sides depilated, *i.e.*, as free from hair as the smoothest parchment.

like a moulting duck, and feedest here on nothing
but coarse grass, or briars and thistles : therefore do
but pace it along with me, and thou shalt see how
we noble steeds, made by nature for war, are treated.
Come, thou wilt lose nothing by coming ; I will get
thee a taste of my fare.   In troth, sir, I can but
love you and thank you, returned the ass ; I will
wait on you, good Mr Steed.   Methinks, gaffer ass,
you might as well have said Sir Grandpaw Steed.
O ! cry mercy, good Sir Grandpaw ! returned the
ass ! we country clowns are somewhat gross, and apt
to knock words out of joint.   However, if it please
you, I will come after your worship at some distance,
lest for taking this run, my side should chance to be
firked and curried with a vengeance, as it is but too
often, the more is my sorrow.

The shepherdess being got behind Roger, the ass
followed, fully resolved to bait like a prince with
Roger's steed; but when they got to the stable, the
groom, who spied the grave animal, ordered one of
his underlings to welcome him with a pitchfork,
and curricomb him with a cudgel.   The ass, who
heard this, recommended himself mentally to the
god·Neptune,[6] and was packing off, thinking, and
syllogising within himself thus: Had not I been
an ass, I had not come here among great lords
when I must needs be sensible that I was only
made for the use of the small vulgar. Æsop had
given me a fair warning of this in one of his fables.
Well, I must e'en scamper, or·take what follows.[7]

[6] The ass saw the pitchfork held up to him.   In this danger
he addresses his prayer to Neptune, whose trident is a kind of
fork.

[7] It is in the original, I must even scamper as quick as a bundle
of asparagus is in boiling: a proverbial expression often used by
the Emperor Augustus.   See it both in Latin and Greek among
the adagia in most schoolbooks.

With this he fell a-trotting, and wincing, and yerk-
ing, and calcitrating, *alias* kicking, and farting, and
funking, and curveting, and bounding, and spring-
ing, and galloping full drive, as if the devil had
come for him *in propriâ personâ*.

The shepherdess, who saw her ass scour off, told
Roger that it was her cattle, and desired he might
be kindly used, or else she would not stir her foot
over the threshold.   Friend Roger no sooner knew
this, but he ordered him to be fetched in, and that
my master's horses should rather chop straw for a
week together, than my mistress' beast should want
his bellyful of corn.

The most difficult point was to get him back ; for
in vain the youngsters complimented and coaxed
him to come.   I dare not, said the ass, I am
bashful.   And the more they strove by fair means
to bring him with them, the more the stubborn
thing was untoward, and flew out at heels; insomuch that they might have been there to this hour
had not his mistress advised them to toss oats in a
sieve, or in a blanket, and call him; which was
done, and made him wheel about, and say, Oats by
mackins ! oats shall go to pot.   *Adveniat;* [8] oats will
do, there is evidence in the case: but none of the
rubbing down, none of the firking.   Thus melodiously singing (for, as you know, that Arcadian bird's
note is very harmonious) he came to the young
gentleman of the horse, *alias* black guard, who
brought him to the stable.

When he was there, they placed him next to the
great horse, his friend, rubbed him down, curricombed him, laid clean straw under him up to the
chin, and there he lay at rack and manger; the

[8] The pun is upon the word *avoine*, oats, and *adveniat*, let 'em
come.

first stuffed with sweet hay, the latter with oats: which when the horse's *valet-de-chambre* sifted, he clapped down his lugs, to tell them by signs that he could eat it but too well without sifting, and that he did not deserve so great an honour.

When they had well fed, quoth the horse to the ass: Well, poor ass, how is it with thee now? How dost thou like this fare? Thou wert so nice at first, a body had much ado to get thee hither. By the fig, answered the ass, which one of our ancestors eating, Philemon died laughing! this is all sheer ambrosia, good Sir Grandpaw; but what would you have an ass say? Methinks all this is yet but half cheer. Do not your worships here now and then use to take a leap? What leaping dost thou mean? asked the horse, the devil leap thee; dost thou take me for an ass? In troth, Sir Grandpaw, quoth the ass, I am somewhat a blockhead, you know, and cannot, for the heart's blood of me, learn so fast the court way of speaking of you gentlemen horses; I mean, don't you stallionise it sometimes here among your mettled fillies? Tush, whispered the horse, speak lower; for, by Bucephalus! if the grooms but hear thee, they will maul and belam thee thrice and threefold; so that thou wilt have but little stomach to a leaping bout. Cod so, man! we dare not so much as grow stiff at the tip of the lower-most snout, though it were but to leak or so, for fear of being jirked and paid out of our lechery. As for any thing else, we are as happy as our master, and perhaps more. By this pack-saddle! my old acquaintance, quoth the ass, I have done with you; a fart for thy litter and hay, and a fart for thy oats; give me the thistles of our fields, since there we leap when we list: eat less, and leap more, I say: it is meat, drink, and cloth to us. Ah! friend

Grandpaw, it would do thy heart good to see us at a fair, when we hold our provincial chapter! Oh! how we leap it, while our mistresses are selling their goslings and other poultry! With this they parted. *Dixi:* I have done.

Panurge then held his peace. Pantagruel would have had him to have gone on to the end of the chapter: but Ædituus said, A word to the wise is enough; I can pick out the meaning of that fable, and know who is that ass, and who the horse; but you are a bashful youth, I perceive. Well, know that there is nothing for you here; scatter no words. Yet, returned Panurge, I saw but even now a pretty kind of a cooing abbess-kite as white as a dove, and her I had rather ride than lead. May I never stir if she is not a dainty bit, and very well worth a sin or two. Heaven forgive me! I meant no more harm in it than you; may the harm I meant in it befall me presently.

ON CHAP. VII.—It is observable, that about midnight, which is the time that many monks are to rise to go to prayers, Ædituus wakes his guests, that they might drink; telling them they should have eaten three breakfasts already, and that if they would consume the mouth-ammunition of that country, they must rise betimes: Eat them, says he, they multiply; spare them, they diminish. The lean birds, who are singing to them while they are to drink, are the novices and sorry monklings, who chant at church matins or vespers, while the great ones snore or tope.

Panurge, who likes all this well enough, is yet for something else, and would mix the sports of love with those of Bacchus; and considering, that those ecclesiastics enjoy the latter at their ease, yet they dare not taste of the first without danger, he brings in the fable of the ass, who slighted the delicious food of the high-mettled prancers, because they were not allowed to be familiar with the mares. Our author ingeniously makes Panurge, who was for copulating in a lawful way, relate this to the priest; by which he would insinuate, that it were much better for them to have a liberty to marry.—*M.*

CHAPTER VIII

HOW WITH MUCH ADO WE GOT A SIGHT OF THE POPE-HAWK

Our junketing and banqueting held on at the same rate the third day, as the two former. Pantagruel then earnestly desired to see the pope-hawk: but Ædituus told him it was not such an easy matter to get a sight of him. How, asked Pantagruel, has he Plato's helmet[1] on his crown, Gyges' ring on his pounces, or a chameleon on his breast, to make him invisible when he pleases? No, sir, returned Ædituus; but he is naturally of pretty difficult access: however, I will see and take care that you may see him, if possible. With this he left us piddling: then within a quarter of an hour came back, and told us the pope-hawk is now to be seen: so he led us, without the least noise, directly to the cage wherein he sat, drooping with his feathers staring about him, attended by a brace of little cardin-hawks, and six lusty fusty bish-hawks.

Panurge stared at him like a dead pig, examining exactly his figure, size, and motions. Then with a loud voice he said, A curse light on the hatcher of the ill bird! on my word this is a filthy whoop-hooper. Hush, speak softly, said Ædituus; by God! he has a pair of ears, as formerly Michael de Matiscome remarked. What then, returned Panurge, so hath a whoopcat. Whist, said Ædituus, if he but hear you speak such another blasphemous

[1] Plato, l. x. of his Republic, uses indeed this proverb. But it should be Pluto's helmet. See Erasmus' Adages, at the words *orci galea.*

word, you had as good be damned; do you see that
bason[2] yonder in his cage? Out of it shall sally
thunderbolts and lightnings, storms, bulls, and the
devil and all, that will sink you down to Peg
Trantum's, an hundred fathom underground. It
were better to drink and be merry, quoth Friar
John.

Panurge was still feeding his eyes with the sight
of the pope-hawk and his attendants, when some-
where under his cage he perceived a madgehowlet.
With this he cried out, By the devil's maker!
master, there is roguery in the case; they put tricks
upon travellers here more than anywhere else, and
would make us believe that a turd is a sugar-loaf.
What damned cozening, gulling, and cony-catching
have we here! Do you see this madgehowlet?
By Minerva, we are all beshit. Odsoons! said
Ædituus, speak softly, I tell you: it is no madgehowlet, no she-thing on my honest word; but a
male, and a noble bird.

May we not hear the pope-hawk sing, asked
Pantagruel? I dare not promise that, returned
Ædituus; for he only sings and eats at his own
hours.[3] So do not I, quoth Panurge; poor Pilgarlic
is fain to make everybody's time his own: come,
then, let us go drink if you will. Now this is something like a tansy, said Ædituus, you begin to talk
somewhat like; still speak in that fashion,[4] and I
will secure you from being thought a heretic. Come
on, I am of your mind.

[2] A bell which is rung when any one is excommunicated.
[3] On the most solemn days in the year.
[4] That is, speak of drinking and guttling as much as you will,
and practise both to the full, in a country where there is the
inquisition; but speak not a word of religion, or the Pope's
authority.

As we went back to have the other fuddling bout, we spied an old green-headed bish-hawk,[5] who sat moping with his mate and three jolly bittern attendants, all snoring under an arbour. Near the old cuff stood a buxom abbess-kite, that sung like any linnet; and we were so mightily tickled with her singing, that I vow and swear we could have wished all our members but one turned into ears, to have had more of the melody. Quoth Panurge, this pretty cherubim of cherubims is here breaking her head with chaunting to this huge, fat, ugly face, who lies grunting all the while like a hog as he is. I will make him change his note presently in the devil's name. With this he rang a bell that hung over the bish-hawk's head; but though he rang and rang again, the devil a bit bish-hawk would hear; the louder the sound, the louder his snoring. There was no making him sing. By God! quoth Panurge, you old buzzard, if you will not sing by fair means, you shall by foul. Having said this, he took up one of St Stephen's loaves, *alias* a stone, and was going to hit him with it about the middle. But Ædituus cried to him, Hold, hold, honest friend! strike, wound, poison, kill, and murder all the kings and princes in the world, by treachery or how thou wilt, and as soon as thou wouldest, unnestle the angels from their cockloft; pope-hawk will pardon thee all this: but never be so mad as to meddle with these sacred birds, as much as thou lovest the profit, welfare, and life not only of thyself, and thy friends and relations alive or dead, but also of those that may be born hereafter to the thousandth generation; for so long thou wouldest entail misery upon them. Do but look upon that bason. Catso! let us rather

[5] Their arms are surmounted with a green hat, as a token of their being in hopes to be one day made cardinals.

drink, then, quoth Panurge. He that spoke last,
spoke well, Mr Antitus, quoth Friar John : while we
are looking on these devilish birds, we do nothing
but blaspheme ; and while we are taking a cup, we
do nothing but praise God. Come on, then, let us
go drink ; how well that word sounds !

The third day (after we had drank, as you must
understand) Ædituus dismissed us.[6] We made him
a present of a pretty little Pergois knife, which he
took more kindly than Artaxerxes did the cup of
cold water that was given him by a clown. He
most courteously thanked us, and sent all sorts of
provisions aboard our ships, wished us a prosperous
voyage, and success in our undertakings, and made
us promise and swear by Jupiter of stone[7] to come
back by his territories.   Finally he said to us, Friends,
pray note, that there are many more stones in the
world than men ;[8] take care you do not forget it.

On Chap. VIII.—With much ado our travellers get a sight of
the pope-hawk (it is Pope Julius III.) who sat drooping with his
feathers staring about him, attended by a brace of little cardin-
hawks, and six lusty fusty bish-hawks. Panurge seeing him, cries,
A curse light on the hatcher of the ill bird! on my word this is
a filthy whoophooper. A whoophooper, or a hooper, upupa, ἔποψ,
is a bird whose cop or tuft of feathers on its head is not altogether
unlike the Papal tiara, adorned with a triple crown: the whole
delight of that filthy fowl is to nestle in man's ordure; which
admirably denotes the inclinations of many of the holy fathers,
and particularly of Julius III., as I will immediately show.

The madgehowlet which was perceived under the pope-hawk's
cage, implies either a Pope of the female kind, as Pope Joan (if

---

[6] The custom is to treat and entertain pilgrims, in the hospitals
of Italy, for three days, but no longer; they must then depart.

[7] The Pope; inasmuch as by his thunder he makes himself be
feared by the present Romans, as much as Jupiter Lapis was by
the old ones.

[8] Men's stones: here we have a priest advancing, that it is to
be less than men to endure for so long a time together the
tyranny and vices of the monks and clergy.

there ever was any such), or rather a *donzella*, or concubine: unless some critic will offer to say, that this madgehowlet, which Ædituus swears is no she-thing, but a male and a noble bird, certainly was the Cardinal Innocent, with whom Pope Julius III. had been passionately in love while he was Legate at Bologna, and to whom, as a reward for his kind services, he had bestowed a cardinal's cap, when he was advanced to the Papal chair. Since that, this noble cardinal was so very intimate with that Pope, that Pasquin could not forbear to say, he believed nothing of all this, and that Innocent was not handsome enough to be Jupiter's Ganymede.

The brace of little cardin-hawks seem to mean either some such young sparks, or rather some of that Pope's bastards, or at least his predecessor's. Paul III. made two of his bastard daughter's sons cardinals; and Rabelais, in his fifteenth letter to the Bishop of Maillezais, calls them the little cardinals *de santa fiore*. That Pope himself, who had kept a Roman lady, Della Casa Rufina, and had a bastard son by another, had a sister once kept by Pope Alexander VI., who had her drawn like the Virgin Mary. She was married afterwards to a gentleman, who having noticed that the Pope lay with her in his absence, on his return stabbed her: so to make her brother amends, Alexander made him a cardinal while he was yet very young, and afterwards he was chosen Pope. Rabelais seems maliciously to pun upon one of those diminutive cardinals in his letters, calling him a cardinacule.

The old green-headed bish-hawk, snoring with his mate and three jolly bittern attendants under an arbour, so that he could not be waked by the buxom abbess-kite, that sung by them like any linnet, is John della Casa, Archbishop of Benevento, and Legate of the Holy See at Venice. His indifference for the fair is happily expressed by his snoring near the pretty abbess-kite, that so kindly invites him with her syren's voice; which yet proves too weak an allurement, and cannot wake him into a natural love.—*M.*

———

CHAPTER IX

HOW WE ARRIVED AT THE ISLAND OF TOOLS

HAVING well ballasted the holds of our human vessels, we weighed anchor, hoisted up sail, stowed

the boats, set the land, and stood for the offing with
a fair loom gale, and for more haste unparalleled the
mizzen-yard, and launched it and the sail over the
lee-quarter, and fitted gyves to keep it steady, and
boomed it out : so in three days we made the Island
of Tools, that is altogether uninhabited. We saw
there a great number of trees which bore mattocks,
pickaxes,   crows,   weeding-hooks,   scythes,   sickles,
spades, trowels, hatchets, hedging-bills, saws, adzes,
bills, axes, shears, pincers, bolts, piercers, augers,
and wimbles.

Others bore dags, daggers, poniards, bayonets,
square-bladed tucks, stilettoes, poinadoes, skenes,
penknives,   puncheons,   bodkins,   swords,   rapiers,
back-swords, cutlasses, scimitars, hangers, falchions,
glaives, raillons, whittles, and whinyards.

Whoever would have any of these, needed but
to shake the tree, and immediately they dropped
down as thick as hops, like so many ripe plums ; nay,
what is more, they fell on a kind of grass called
scabbard, and sheathed themselves in it cleverly.
But when they came down, there was need of
taking care lest they happened to touch the head,
feet, or other parts of the body. For they fell with
the point downwards, and in they stuck, or slit the
continuum of some member, or lopped it off like a
twig ; either of which generally was enough to have
killed a man, though he were a hundred years old,
and worth as many thousand spankers, spur-royals,
and rose-nobles.

Under some other trees, whose names I cannot
justly tell you, I saw some certain sorts of weeds
that grew and sprouted like pikes, lances, javelins,
javelots, darts, dartlets, halberts, boar-spears, eel-
spears, partizans, tridents, prongs, trout-staves, spears,
half-pikes, and hunting-staffs. As they sprouted up

45

and chanced to touch the tree, straight they met with their heads, points, and blades, each suitable to its kind, made ready for them by the trees over them, as soon as every individual weed was grown up, fit for its steel: even like the children's coats, that are made for them as soon as they wear them, and you wean them of their swaddling clothes. Nor do you mutter, I pray you, at what Plato, Anaxagoras, and Democritus have said: Od's fish! they were none of your lower-form gimcracks, were they?

Those trees seemed to us terrestrial animals, in no wise so different from brute beasts as not to have skin, fat, flesh, veins, arteries, ligaments, nerves, cartilages, kernels, bones, marrow, humours, matrices, brains, and articulations; for they certainly have some, since Theophrastus will have it so: but in this point they differed from other animals, that their heads, that is, the part of their trunks next to the root, are downwards; their hair, that is their roots, in the earth; and their feet, that is their branches, upside down: as if a man should stand on his head with outstretched legs. And as you, battered sinners, on whom Venus has bestowed something to remember her, feel the approach of rains, winds, cold, and every change of weather, at your ischiatic legs, and your omoplates, by means of the perpetual almanack which she has fixed there: so these trees have notice given them, by certain sensations which they have at their roots, stocks, gums, paps, or marrow, of the growth of the staffs under them; and accordingly they prepare suitable points and blades for them beforehand. Yet as all things, except God, are sometimes subject to error, nature itself is not free from it, when it produceth monstrous things; likewise I observed something amiss in these trees. For a half-pike, that grew up high enough to reach the branches of one of these

instrumentiferous trees, happened no sooner to touch
them, but instead of being joined to an iron head, it
impaled a stub broom at the fundament.   Well, no
matter, it will serve to sweep the chimney.   Thus a
partisan met with a pair of garden shears, Come, all
is good for something, it will serve to nip off little
twigs, and destroy caterpillars.   The staff of a halbert
got the blade of a scythe, which made it look like a
hermaphrodite.   Happy-be-lucky! it is all a case, it
will serve for some mower.   Oh, it is a great blessing
to put our trust in the Lord !   As we went back to
our ships, I spied behind I do not know what bush,
I do not know what folks, doing I do not know what
business, in I do not know what posture, scouring I
do not know what tools, in I do not know what
manner, and I do not know what place.

ON CHAP. IX.—The Island of Tools treats of things which
are not much less odious than the cages of the pope-hawk and
bish-hawk.   There is a catch in the prologue to the fourth book,
which is in a manner a key to this chapter : It is that which
follows :—

'Since tools without their hafts are useless lumber,
    And hatchets without helves are of that number ;
    That one may go in the other and may match it,
    I'll be the helve, and thou shalt be the hatchet.'

This chapter requires a larger comment ; but its subject being
none of the most modest, it is better to leave that to be done by
those who love to dive to the bottom of such matters.—*M*.

CHAPTER X

HOW PANTAGRUEL ARRIVED AT THE ISLAND OF SHARPING (OR GAMING)

WE left the Island of Tools to pursue our voyage,
and the next day stood in for the Island of Sharping,

the true image of Fontainebleau : for the land is so
very lean, that the bones, that is, the rocks, shoot
through its skin.   Besides, it is sandy, barren, un-
healthy, and unpleasant.'   Our pilot showed us there
two little square rocks, which had eight equal points
in the shape of a cube.   They were so white, that
I might have mistaken them for alabaster or snow,
had he not assured us they were made of bone.

He told us that twenty-one chance devils, very
much feared in our country, dwelt there in six
different storeys, and that the biggest twins or braces
of them were called sixes, and the smallest amb's-
ace ; the rest cinques, quatres, treys, and deuces.
When they were conjured up, otherwise coupled,
they were called either sice cinque, sice quatre, sice
trey, sice deuce, and sice ace ; or cinque quatre, cinque
trey, and so forth.   I made there a shrewd observation : would you know what it is, gamesters ?   It is
that there are very few of you in the world, but what
call upon and invoke the devils.   For the dice are no
sooner thrown on the board, and the greedy gazing
sparks have hardly said, Two sixes, Frank ; but Six
devils damn it ! cry as many of them.   If amb's-ace,
then, A brace of devils broil me, will they say.
Quarter deuce, Tom, The deuce take it, cries another.
And so on to the end of the chapter.   Nay, they do
not forget sometimes to call the black cloven-footed
gentlemen by their Christian names and surnames :
and what is stranger yet, they use them as the
greatest cronies, and make them so often the ex-
ecutors of their wills, not only giving themselves,
but every body, and every thing, to the devil, that
there is no doubt but he takes care to seize, soon or
late, what is so zealously bequeathed him.   Indeed,

---

¹ A description of the inconveniences and vexations that
attend gaming.

it is true, Lucifer does not always immediately appear by his lawful attorneys; but alas! it is not for want of good-will: he is really to be excused for his delay; for what the devil would you have a devil do? He and his blackguards are then at some other places, according to the priority of the persons that call on them: therefore, pray let none be so venturesome as to think that the devils are deaf and blind.

He then told us that more wrecks had happened about those square rocks, and a greater loss of body and goods, than about all the Syrtes, Scyllas and Charybdes, Sirens, Strophades, and gulfs in the universe. I had not much ado to believe it, remembering that formerly, among the wise Egyptians, Neptune was described in hieroglyphics for the first cube, Apollo by an ace, Diana by a deuce, Minerva by seven, and so forth.

He also told us that there was a phial of Sanc-Greal,[2] a most divine thing, and known to a few. Panurge did so sweeten up the syndics of the place, that they blessed us with a sight of it: but it was with three times more pother and ado, with more formalities and antic-tricks, than they show the pandects[3] of Justinian at Florence, or the holy Veronica at Rome. I never saw such a sight of flambeaux, torches, and hagios,[4] and sanctified tapers,

[2] The same as sang-real, *i.e.* royal blood, a pretended relic of Christ's blood preserved by Joseph of Arimathea, when he washed our Saviour's body before he embalmed it. The Saint Graal, another relic, is the precious dish in which the paschal lamb was served up which our Saviour ate with his disciples the eve of his death.

[3] Menage, and before him Politian, observe they never show this manuscript but by torchlight. There is not such a pother made about it now, because of its being printed since 1553, in a most beautiful and grand manner.

[4] A Greek word: it means holy. Here it means superstitious ceremonies. It comes from the *hagios ho theos* of Good Friday:

in my whole life.   After all, that which was shown us was only the ill-faced countenance of a roasted coney.

All that we saw there worth speaking of, was a good face set upon an ill game, and the shells of the two eggs formerly laid and hatched by Leda, out of which came Castor and Pollux, fair Helen's brothers.   These same syndics sold us a piece of them for a song, I mean, for a morsel of bread. Before we went, we bought a parcel of hats[5] and caps of the manufacture of the place; which, I fear, will turn to no very good account : nor are those who shall take them off our hands, more likely to commend their wearing.

ON CHAP. X.—After the venereal games, in the Island of Tools, we have those of chance in the Sharping Island.   It is said to be lean, sandy, barren, and unpleasant: because, in the main, seldom anything is to be got by games of hazard honestly. What is got at one time is generally lost at another, and goes as easily as it comes : for most gamesters, often prodigal of what they have got, seldom consider, that should their profits at the year's end balance their losses, they still will be found to have lost their time, and squandered away part of what should have made the scales even between profit and loss; and so, though they have won much, they are poorer many times than they would have been had they not played at all.   It is obvious that the two little white square rocks, with eight equal points in the shape of a cube, are the dice; the six different storeys are their six different sides and numbers, that ascend from 1, 2, 3, 4, 5, to 6.   Of which twenty-one points Rabelais makes so many devils, because they tempt and bewitch men so much; though, as he observes, the land is barren and unpleasant; for, after all, gaming is a tedious repetition of the same thing, and a continual gazing upon the dice or cards, without any pleasing discourse; not to speak of the fear and agony of gamesters; their toil when they

---

words which are then pronounced at the lifting up the cross, with that air of admiration and astonishment which strikes a religious awe into the beholders.

[5] He alludes to the promise of a cardinal's hat, a promise often paid very dear for and never performed.

pass whole nights at play, and break their rest and not their fast; their despair and curses when they have lost ; the mean actions by which they debase themselves to borrow or pawn; and the quarrels, and their sad consequences, among the greatest friends, on the account of play.   So that Pantagruel's pilot was in the right, when he told him that more wrecks had happened about those square rocks, than about all the others in the universe.

After the games of hazard, comes another, that is as deceitful at least: I mean the trick of relics.   The author places them in the Island of Sharping, because the Church of Rome sharps the superstitious laity out of great sums of money by the doubtful remains of as doubtful saints, much more than by the real relics of the true.   Accordingly our travellers, with a world of pother and ado, formalities, and antic tricks, were blessed at last with a sight of a phial of sanc-greal; that is, as I have observed on the forty-third chapter of the fourth book, what they impudently pretend to be our Saviour's blood; but, after all, it was only the scurvy face of a roasted coney.   Mr Emiliane, in his book of the frauds of the Romish priests, tells us, that such a kind of relic is in Italy to this day.   That pretended blood is shown with great ceremonies, and store of flambeaux, torches, and sanctified tapers, etc.   Our author says, that they saw nothing worth speaking of in that island, but a good face set upon an ill game; which suits well with the carriage of those who show such sham relics: accordingly, he says, they also saw the shells of the two eggs, formerly laid and hatched by Leda ; which indeed are most worthy of being placed among such relics.

The hats and caps of the manufactory of the place (*chapeaux de cassade*) may be mentioned to banter some prelates, who had a mind to be cardinals, and perhaps were fooled out of the money which they gave to the Pope's favourites to that intent.   *Avoir des cassades* is a burlesque expression ; such as, when we say, to be gulled, or swallow a gudgeon.   Yet, as Rabelais says that some of the company bought a piece of Leda's egg shells for a morsel of bread ; and then immediately adds, that they bought those hats and caps, which, he feared would turn to no very good account ; he may either mean that they were cheated there, or bought some sham *Agnus Dei's*, and such holy trumpery.   Whatever it be, we find that in the next chapter they went through the wicket ; and, for offering to sell them again, were clapped into lob's pound, by order of Gripe-men-all, Arch-duke of the Furred Law-cats.

CHAPTER XI

HOW WE PASSED THROUGH THE WICKET, INHABITED BY GRIPE-MEN-ALL, ARCH-DUKE OF THE FURRED LAW-CATS

FROM thence Condemnation was passed by us. It is another damned barren island, whereat none for the world cared to touch. Then we went through the wicket : but Pantagruel had no mind to bear us company ; and it was well he did not, for we were nabbed there, and clapped into lob's pound by order of Gripe-men-all, Arch-duke of the Furred Law-cats, because one of our company would have put upon a serjeant some hats of the Sharping Island.

The Furred Law-cats are most terrible and dreadful monsters, that devour little children, and trample [1] over marble stones. Pray tell me, noble topers, do they not deserve to have their snouts slit ? The hair of their hides does not lie outwards ; and every mother's son of them for his device wears a gaping pouch, but not all in the same manner: for some wear it tied to their neck scarf-wise, others upon the breech, some on the paunch, others on the side, and all for a cause, with reason and mystery. They have claws so very strong, long, and sharp, that nothing can get from them what is once fast between their clutches. Sometimes they cover

---

[1] The new editions of Rabelais have indeed *passent sur*, etc., but the true reading is *paissent*. They feed, they guttle, in a room paved with marble ; such as is, and always was, that called *la grande chambre*, belonging to the courts of judicature at Paris; where the lawyers play as good a knife as any inns of court gentlemen here with us.

their heads with mortar-like caps, at other times with mortified[2] caparisons.

As we entered their den, said a common mumper, to whom we had given half a teston, Worshipful culprits, God send you a good deliverance. Examine well, said he, the countenance of these stout props and pillars of this catch-coin law and iniquity; and pray observe, that if you still live but six olympiads, and the age of two dogs[3] more, you will see these Furred Law-cats lords of all Europe, and in peaceful possession of all the estates and dominions belonging to it: unless, by divine providence, what is got over the devil's back, is spent under his belly; or the goods which they unjustly get, perish with their prodigal heirs. Take this from an honest beggar.

Among them reigns the sixth essence; by the means of which they gripe all, devour all, conskite all, burn all, draw all, hang all, quarter all, behead all, murder all, imprison all, waste all, and ruin all, without the least notice of right or wrong: for among them vice is called virtue; wickedness, piety; treason, loyalty; robbery, justice. Plunder is their motto, and when acted by them, is approved by all men, except the heretics:[4] and all this they do, because they dare; their authority is sovereign and irrefragable. For a sign of the truth of what I tell you, you will find, that there the mangers are above the racks. Remember hereafter, that a fool told you this; and if ever plague, famine, war, fire, earthquakes, inundations, or other judgments befal the world, do not attribute them to the aspects and

---

[2] He puns upon the word *mortier;* a sort of cap (with brims turned up) worn in France by the lord chancellor, and presidents of sovereign courts on high days.

[3] Twenty years, more or less.

[4] At that time the parliament caused them to be burnt.

conjunctions of the malevolent planets, to the abuses of the court of Romania, or the tyranny of secular kings and princes: to the impostures of the false zealots of the cowl, heretical bigots, false prophets, and broachers of sects; to the villainy of griping usurers, clippers, and coiners; nor to the ignorance, impudence, and imprudence of physicians, surgeons, and apothecaries; nor to the lewdness of adultresses, and destroyers of by-blows; but charge them all, wholly and solely, to the inexpressible, incredible, and inestimable wickedness and ruin which is continually hatched, brewed, and practised in the den or shop of those Furred Law-cats. Yet it is no more known in the world than the cabala of the Jews; the more is the pity; and, therefore, it is not detested, chastised, and punished, as it is fit it should be. But should all their villainy be once displayed in its true colours, and exposed to the people; there never was, is, nor will be any spokesman so sweet-mouthed, whose fine colloguing tongue could save them; nor any law so rigorous and draconic, that could punish them as they deserve; nor yet any magistrate so powerful, as to hinder their being burnt alive in their coney-burrows without mercy. Even their own furred kittlings, friends, and relations would abominate them.

For this reason, as Hannibal was solemnly sworn by his father Amilcar to pursue the Romans with the utmost hatred, as long as ever he lived: so, my late father has enjoined me to remain here without, till God Almighty's thunder reduce them there within to ashes, like other presumptuous Titans, profane wretches, and opposers of God: since mankind is so inured to their oppressions, that they either do not remember, foresee, or have a sense of the woes and miseries which they have caused;

or if they have, either will not, dare not, or cannot
root them out.

How! said Pannrge, say you so? Catch me there
and hang me! Damme! let us march off? This
noble beggar has scared me worse than thunder in
autumn. Upon this we were filing off; but alas!
we found ourselves trapped: the door was double-
locked and barricadoed. Some messengers of ill
news told us, it was full as easy to get in there as
into hell, and no less hard to get out. Aye! there
indeed lay the difficulty, for there is no getting loose
without a pass and discharge in due course from the
bench. This for no other reason than because folks
go easier out of a church than out of a spunging-
house,[5] and because they could not have our company[6] when they would. The worst of it was when
we got through the wicket: for we were carried,
to get out our pass or discharge, before a more dreadful monster than ever was read of in the legends
of knight errantry. They called him Gripe-men-
all. I cannot tell what to compare it to, better
than to a chimera, a Sphynx, a Cerberus; or to the
image of Osiris, as the Egyptians represented him,

[5] It is in the original, because folks go easier out of a market
than out of a fair; a French proverb, the ground whereof is,
that your pedlars and petty chapmen are forced to pay ready
money in a fair, whereas in a market they may and often do go
upon tick. In this place, by the word fair (*foire*) the author
means the courts of judicature, forum, and what he intends by it
is this; that different from what is practised at the châtelet (or
ordinary sessions-house) here the fees of parliament (*i.e.* supreme
judges) are deposited beforehand, lest the country people should
make up matters before the decree is taken out.

[6] The original has it because we were *piedz pouldreux*, or dusty-
footed, *i.e.*, foreign dealers; who in fairs have their particular
jurisdiction, which holds no longer than the fair. Such were
Pantagruel and his people, in the furred cats' opinion; and they
were resolved not to part with such pigeons without plucking.

with three heads, one of a roaring lion, the other
of a fawning cur, and the last of a howling, prowling
wolf, twisted about with a dragon biting his tail,
surrounded with fiery rays.   His hands were full
of gore, his talons like those of the harpies, his snout
like a hawk's bill, his fangs or tusks like those of
an overgrown brindled wild boar; his eyes were
flaming, like the jaws of hell, all covered with
mortars interlaced with pestles, and nothing of his
arms was to be seen, but his clutches.   His hutch,
and that of the warren-cats, his collaterals, was a
long, spick-and-span new rack, a-top of which (as
the mumper told us) some large, stately mangers[7]
were fixed in the reverse.   Over the chief seat
was the picture of an old woman, holding the case[8]
or scabbard of a sickle in her right hand, a pair of
scales in her left, with spectacles on her nose : the
cups or scales of the balance were a pair of velvet
pouches : the one full of bullion, which overpoised
the other, empty and long, hoisted higher than the
middle of the beam.   I am of opinion it was the
true effigies of Justice Gripe-men-all; far different
from the institution of the ancient Thebans, who
set up the statues of their Dicasts[9] without hands,
in marble, silver, or gold, according to their merit,
even after their death.

When we made our personal appearance before
him, a sort of I do not know what men, all clothed
with I do not know what bags and pouches, with

[7] Here we find the mangers above the rack, and indeed it
could not possibly be otherwise ; for the forms or benches on
which the furred cats sat are the rack, and the mangers were the
furred cats themselves, or rather resided in them ; the word
mangerie, from the French verb *manger* (to eat), signifying both a
manger and extortion.

[8] The picture of injustice.

[9] Judges.   See Plutarch in his Isis and Osiris.

long scrolls in their clutches, made us sit down upon
a cricket [such as criminals sit on when tried in
France]. Quoth Panurge to them, Good my lords,
I am very well as I am; I would as lieve stand, if it
please you. Besides, this same stool is somewhat of
the lowest for a man that has new breeches and a
short doublet.[10] Sit you down, said Gripe-men-all
again, and look that you do not make the court bid
you twice. Now, continued he, the earth shall
immediately open its jaws, and swallow you up to
quick damnation, if you do not answer as you should.

ON CHAP. XI.—Pantagruel prudently passed by Condemnation
with his fleet; but some of his companions, more unfortunate
or less wise, were stopped at the wicket, and obliged to take
their trial. That wicket is the Inquisition in general; and, in
particular, the court established in 1548, at Paris, against the
Lutherans: for we find that the Furred Law-cats (which mean
the judges, *presidents à mortier*, i.e., *en parlement*) have mortar-like
caps and furred gowns. A common mumper gives an admirable
account of the place. He speaks of it as a hellish court, where,
without the least regard to right or wrong, they imprison, behead,
hang, and burn those who fall into their clutches; where vice
passes for virtue, wickedness for piety, treason for loyalty, and
robbery for justice: yet whatever is acted by them, is approved
by all men except the heretics; and he charges on its members
all the woes that infest the world. One would almost think
that Rabelais meant some of the nobility in the Netherlands by
this noble *gueux*, noble beggar; for so he styles him, after he
had called him *gueux de l'hostiere, ostiarius mendicus,* a common
mumper; which he probably did to hide his thought, or turn
that of the reader from the subject, at the same time that he
speaks to him about it; a method which he has followed almost
throughout this work. It is known that the Protestant nobility,
and others in the Netherlands, got the name of *gueux*, i.e.,
beggars, it is said for opposing themselves to the setting up the
Inquisition; and though some trace the original of that nickname
no higher than the time of Margaret of Parma's government,
others pretend it was given them long before, by the Spaniards,

10 New breeches are generally not very supple, which, together
with a short doublet, might make the judges laugh at the expense
of a poor wretch sitting upon a stool so low as a cricket.

on that account. If this be not meant of those noble assertors
of their liberties in the Netherlands, as being written some years
before that name of *gueux* was universally spread, it must yet be
owned, that it refers to the persecuting courts of judicature in
those times, chiefly to the Inquisition, or at least to the tournelle;
that is, that part of the Courts of Parliament in France that tries
criminals; for in France men have not the privilege of being tried
by their juries, or their peers, which Englishmen enjoy.   Gripe-
men-all is the head of the Inquisition, or perhaps the president
of that court which used the Protestants so severely in France
in 1548.   The picture over the chief seat is that of injustice.

CHAPTER XII

HOW GRIPE-MEN-ALL PROPOUNDED A RIDDLE TO US

WHEN we were sate, Gripe-men-all, in the middle of
his furred cats, called to us in a hoarse dreadful voice,
Well! come on, give me presently—an answer.
Well! come on, muttered Panurge between his
teeth, give, give me presently—a comforting dram.
Hearken to the court, continued Gripe-men-all.

AN ENIGMA.

A young tight thing, as fair as may be,
Without a dad conceived a baby;
And brought him forth without the pother
In labour made by teeming mother.
Yet the cursed brat feared not to gripe her,
But gnawed, for haste, her sides like viper.
Then the black upstart boldly sallies,
And walks and flies o'er hills and valleys.
Many fantastic sons of wisdom,
Amazed, foresaw their own in his doom;
And thought, like an old Grecian noddy,
A human spirit moved his body.

Give, give me out of hand—an answer to this
riddle, quoth Gripe-men-all. Give, give me—leave
to tell you, good, good, my lord, answered Panurge,
that if I had but a sphynx at home,[1] as Verres, one
of your precursors, had, I might then solve your
enigma presently: but verily, good my lord, I was
not there; and, as I hope to be saved, am as innocent
in the matter as the child unborn. Foh! give me—
a better answer, cried Gripe-men-all; or, by gold! this
shall not serve your turn: I will not be paid in such
coin: if you have nothing better to offer, I will let
your rascalship know, that it had been better for you
to have fallen into Lucifer's own clutches, than into
ours. Dost thou see them here, sirrah? ha! and
dost thou prate here of thy being innocent, as if
thou couldest be delivered from our racks and tortures
for being so! Give me—Patience! thou widgeon.
Our laws are like cobwebs: your silly little flies are
stopped, caught, and destroyed therein; but your
stronger ones break them, and force and carry them
which way they please. Likewise, do not think we
are so mad as to set up your nets to snap up your
great robbers and tyrants: no, they are somewhat too
hard for us, there is no meddling with them; for
they would make no more of us than we make of the
little ones: but you paltry, silly, innocent wretches,
must make us amends; and, by gold! we will
innocentise[2] your fopship with a wannion; you never

---

[1] Alluding to the fable of the sphynx, inasmuch as that fable
gave Tully an occasion to say a very good thing by way of
repartee to the orator Hortensius, to whom Verres had made
a present of a large and rich figure of that monster, to engage
him to undertake his defence against Tully. See Plutarch's
Apophthegms.

[2] Allusion to a custom which Cotgrave says the Papists have
in France on Childermas or Innocents' Day, to jerk, or slap with
the palm of the hand, the backsides of all such young persons as

were so innocentised in your days; the devil shall
sing mass among ye.[3]

Friar John, hearing him run on at that mad rate,
had no longer the power to remain silent, but cried
to him, Heigh-dey! Prythee, Mr Devil in a coif,
wouldest thou have a man tell thee more than he
knows? Has not the fellow told you he does not
know a word of the business? His name is Twyford.
A plague rot you, will not truth serve your turns?
Why! how now, Mr Prate-apace? cried Gripe-men-
all, taking him short, Marry come up! who made
you so saucy as to open your lips before you were
spoken to? Give me—Patience! By gold! this is
the first time, since I have reigned, that any one has
had the impudence to speak before he was bidden.
How came this mad fellow to break loose? (Villain!
thou liest, said Friar John, without stirring his lips.)

they can find in bed, or others, whose breech they may otherwise
easily come at; nor is that whipping always the *ne plus ultra* of
this merry custom, adds M. Duchat (who does not confine it to
the Papists alone, as Cotgrave does). Marot, in his epigram on
Innocents' Day:

> Knew I but where my charmer meant to lay
> Her pretty person, on the approaching day
> Of Innocents, O how exceeding early
> Would I go visit her I love so dearly!
> Yes, gentle conqueror of my heart, I'd fly
> With wings of love——not at your feet to sigh,
> But to touch, handle, feel thy velvet skin:
> And should some spoil-sport chance to enter in
> To interrupt our bliss, why let it be,
> I would make show of Innocensing thee?
> Who could disprove so plausible a plea?

[3] M. Duchat says, that Grippeminaud (Gripe-men-all) by way
of opposition to what is customary at mass, where nobody is
forced to act the part of a responder (*i.e.*, make responses), here
calls by the name of the devil's mass, the interrogatory which
one that is accused is obliged to answer to, whether he is willing
or no.

Sirrah, sirrah, continued Gripe-men-all, I doubt thou
wilt have business enough on thy hands, when it
comes to thy turn to answer. (Damme! thou
liest, said Friar John, silently.) Dost thou think,
continued my lord, thou art in the wilderness
of your foolish university, wrangling and bawling
among the idle, wandering searchers and hunters
after truth? By gold! we have here other fish to
fry; we go anothergates way to work, that we do.
By gold! people here must give categorical answers
to what they do know. By gold! they must confess
they have done those things which they have not
nor ought to have done. By gold! they must protest
that they know what they never knew in their lives;
and, after all, patience, *per force*, must be their only
remedy, as well as a mad dog's. Here, silly geese
are plucked, yet cackle not. Sirrah! give me—an
account, whether you had a letter of attorney, or
whether you were fee'd or no, that you offered to
bawl in another man's cause? I see you had no
authority to speak, and I may chance to have you
wed to something you will not like. Oh, you devils!
cried Friar John, proto-devils! panto-devils! you
would wed a monk, would you? Ho hu! ho hu!
A heretic! a heretic! I will give thee out for a rank
heretic.

———

CHAPTER XIII

HOW PANURGE SOLVED GRIPE-MEN-ALL'S RIDDLE

GRIPE-MEN-ALL, as if he had not heard what Friar
John said, directed his discourse to Panurge, saying
to him, Well, what have you to say for yourself, Mr
Rogue-enough, hah? Give, give me out of hand—

an answer.   Say? quoth Panurge, why, what would
you have me say? I say, that we are damnably
beshit, since you give no heed at all to the equity
of the plea, and the devil sings among you: let this
serve for all, I beseech you, and let us go out about
our business; I am no longer able to hold out, as gad
shall judge me!

Go to, go to, cried Gripe-men-all; when did you
ever hear that for these three hundred years last past,
anybody ever got out of this weal without leaving
something of his behind him? No, no, get out of
the trap if you can without losing leather, life, or at
least some hair, and you will have done more than
ever was done yet. For why, this would bring the
wisdom of the court into question, as if we had took
you up for nothing, and dealt wrongfully by you.
Well, by hook or by crook, we must have something
out of you. Look ye! it is a folly to make a rout
for a fart and ado; one word is as good as twenty;
I have no more to say to thee, but that as thou likest
thy former entertainment, thou wilt tell me more of
the next; for it will go ten times worse with thee,
unless, by gold! you give me—a solution to the
riddle I propounded. Give, give—it, without any
more ado.

By gold! quoth Panurge, it is a black mite or
weevil, which is born of a white bean, and sallies
out at the hole which he makes, gnawing it: the
mite, being turned into a kind of fly, sometimes
walks and sometimes flies, over hills and dales.
Now, Pythagoras, the Greek sage, and his sect,
besides many others, wondering at its birth in such
a place (which makes some argue for equivocal
generation), thought that, by a metempsychosis, the
body of that insect was the lodging of a human soul.
Now, were you men here, after your welcome death,

according to his opinion, your souls would most
certainly enter into the body of mites or weevils;
for, as in your present state of life, you are good for
nothing in the world, but to gnaw, bite, eat, and
devour all things; so in the next you will even gnaw
and devour your mother's very sides, as the vipers
do.   Now, by gold! I think I have fairly solved and
resolved your riddle.

May my bauble be turned into a nut-cracker,
quoth Friar John, if I could not almost find in my
heart to wish that what comes out at my bung-hole
were beans, that these evil weevils might feed as
they deserve.

Panurge then, without any more ado, threw a
large leathern purse, stuffed with gold crowns (*escus
au soleil*) among them.

The Furred Law-cats no sooner heard the jingling
of the chink, but they all began to bestir their claws,
like a parcel of fiddlers running a division: and then
fell to it, squimble, squamble, catch that catch can.
They all said aloud, These are the fees, these are
the gloves; now, this is somewhat like a tansy.
Oh! it was a pretty trial, a sweet trial, a dainty
trial.   On my word, they did not starve the cause:
these are none of your snivelling *forma pauperis'*;
no, they are noble clients, gentlemen every inch of
them.   By gold! it is gold, quoth Panurge, good old
gold, I'll assure you.

Saith Gripe-men-all, The court, upon a full hearing (Of the gold, quoth Panurge), and weighty reasons
given, finds the prisoners not guilty, and accordingly
orders them to be discharged out of custody, paying
their fees.   Now, gentlemen, proceed, go forwards,
said he to us: we have not so much of the devil in
us as we have of his hue; though we are stout,
we are merciful.

As we came out at the wicket, we were conducted to the port by a detatchment of certain highland griffins, who advised us, before we came to our ships, not to offer to leave the place until we had made the usual presents, first to the Lady Gripe-men-all, then to all the furred law-pusses; otherwise we must return to the place from whence we came. Well, well, said Friar John, we will fumble in our fobs, examine every one of us his concern, and even give the women their due; we will never boggle nor stick out on that account; as we tickled the men in the palm, we will tickle the women in the right place. Pray, gentlemen, added they, do not forget to leave somewhat behind you for us poor devils to drink your healths. O lawd! never fear, answered Friar John, I do not remember that I ever went anywhere yet, where the poor devils are not remembered and encouraged.

CHAPTER XIV

HOW THE FURRED LAW-CATS LIVE ON CORRUPTION

FRIAR JOHN had hardly said these words ere he perceived seventy-eight galleys and frigates just arriving at the port. So he hied him thither to learn some news; and as he asked what goods they had on board, he soon found that their whole cargo was venison, hares, capons, turkeys, pigs, swine, bacon, kids, calves, hens, ducks, teals, geese, and other poultry and wildfowl.

He also spied among these some pieces of velvet, satin, and damask. This made him ask the new-

comers, Whither, and to whom, they were going to
carry those dainty goods? They answered, that
they were for Gripe-men-all and the Furred Law-
cats.

Pray, asked he, what is the true name of all these
things in your country language? Corruption, they
replied. If they live on corruption, said the Friar,
they will perish with their generation. May the
devil be damned! I have it now: their fathers
devoured the good gentlemen, who, according to
their state of life, used to go much a-hunting and
hawking, to be the better inured to toil in time of
war; for hunting is an image of a martial life; and
Xenophon was much in the right of it, when he
affirmed that hunting had yielded a great number of
excellent warriors, as well as the Trojan horse. For
my part, I am no scholar, I have it but by hearsay,
yet I believe it. Now, the souls of those brave
fellows, according to Gripe-men-all's riddle, after
their decease, enter into wild boars, stags, roebucks,
herons, and such other creatures, which they loved,
and in quest of which they went while they were
men; and these Furred Law-cats, having first destroyed
and devoured their castles, lands, demesnes, posses-
sions, rents, and revenues, are still seeking to have
their blood and soul in another life. What an
honest fellow was that same mumper, who had fore-
warned us of all these things, and bid us take notice
of the mangers above the racks!

But, said Panurge to the new-comers, how do you
come by all this venison? Methinks the great king
has issued out a proclamation, strictly inhibiting the
destroying of stags, does, wild boars, roebucks, or
other royal game, on pain of death. All this is true
enough, answered one for the rest, but the great
king is so good and gracious, you must know, and

these Furred Law-cats so cursed and cruel, so mad, and thirsting after Christian blood, that we have less cause to fear in trespassing against that mighty sovereign's commands, than reason to hope to live, if we do not continually stop the mouths of these Furred Law-cats with such bribes and corruption. Besides, added he, to-morrow Gripe-men-all marries a Furred Law-puss of his to a high and mighty Double-furred Law-tybert. Formerly we used to call them chop-hay; but, alas! they are not such clean creatures now as to eat any, or chew the cud. We call them chop-hares, chop-partridges, chop-woodcocks, chop-pheasants, chop-pullets, chop-venison, chop-conies, chop-pigs, for they scorn to feed on coarser meat. A turd for their chops, cried Friar John, next year we will have them called chop-dung, chop-stront, chop-filth.

Would you take my advice? added he to the company. What is it? answered we. Let us do two things, returned he. First, let us secure all this venison and wild fowl,—I mean paying well for them; for my part, I am but too much tired already with our salt meat, it heats my flanks so horribly. In the next place, let us go back to the wicket, and destroy all these devilish Furred Law-cats. For my part, quoth Panurge, I know better things: catch me there, and hang me: no, I am somewhat more inclined to be fearful than bold; I love to sleep in a whole skin.

CHAPTER XV

HOW FRIAR JOHN TALKS OF ROOTING OUT THE FURRED LAW-CATS

VIRTUE of the frock, quoth Friar John, what kind of voyage are we making? A shitten one, on my word: the devil of anything we do, but fizzling, farting, funking, squattering, dozing, raving, and doing nothing. Odd's belly! it is not in my nature to lie idle; I mortally hate it: unless I am doing some heroic feat every foot, I cannot sleep one wink at nights. Damn it! did you then take me along with you for your chaplain, to sing mass and shrive you? By Maunday Thursday! the first of ye all that comes to me on such an account shall be fitted; for the only penance I will enjoin shall be, that he immediately throw himself headlong over-board into the sea, like a base cow-hearted son of ten fathers. This in deduction of the pains of purgatory.

What made Hercules such a famous fellow, do you think? Nothing, but that while he travelled, he still made it his business to rid the world of tyrannies, errors, dangers, and drudgeries; he still put to death all robbers, all monsters, all venomous serpents, and hurtful creatures. Why then do we not follow his example, doing as he did in the countries through which we pass? He destroyed the Stymphalides, the Lernæan Hydra, Cacus, Antheus, the Centaurs, and what not; I am no *clericus*, those that are such tell me so.

In imitation of that noble by-blow, let us destroy and root out these wicked Furred Law-cats, that are a kind of ravenous devils; thus we shall remove all manner of tyranny out of the land. Mahomet's

tutor swallow me body and soul, tripes and guts! if
I would stay to ask your help or advice in the matter,
were I but as strong as he was. Come, he that
would be thought a gentleman, let him storm a
town; well, then, shall we go? I dare swear we
will do their business for them with a wet finger;
they will bear it, never fear: since they could swallow
down more foul language that came from us, than
ten sows and their babies could swill hogwash. Damn
them! they do not value all the ill words or dis-
honour in the world at a rush, so they but get the
coin into their purses, though they were to have it
in a shitten clout. Come, we may chance to kill
them all, as Hercules would have done, had they
lived in his time. We only want to be set to work
by another Eurystheus, and nothing else for the
present, unless it be what I heartily wish them, that
Jupiter may give them a short visit, only some two
or three hours long, and walk among their lordships
in the same equipage[1] that attended him when
he came last to his Miss Semele, jolly Bacchus'
mother.

It is a very great mercy, quoth Panurge, that you
have got out of their clutches: for my part, I have no
stomach to go there again; I am hardly come to
myself yet, so scared and appalled I was; my hair
still stands up on end when I think on it; and
most damnably troubled I was there, for three
very weighty reasons. First, because I was *troubled*.
Secondly, because I *was* troubled. Thirdly and
lastly, *because* I was troubled. Hearken to me a
little on the right side, Friar John, my left cod,
since thou wilt not hear at the other; whenever
the maggot bites thee to take a trip down to
hell, and visit the tribunal of Minos, Æacus,

[1] Armed with thunder and lightning.

Rhadamanthus, and Dis, do but tell me, and I
will be sure to bear thee company, and never
leave thee, as long as my name is Panurge, but
will wade over Acheron, Styx, and Cocytus, drink
whole bumpers of Lethe's water,—though I mortally
hate that element,—and even pay thy passage to
that bawling, cross-grained ferryman, Charon. But
as for the damned wicket, if thou art so weary of
thy life as to go thither again, thou mayest even
look for somebody else to bear thee company, for
I will not move one step that way: even rest
satisfied with this positive answer. By my good
will! I will not stir a foot to go thither as long
as I live, any more than Calpe [2] will come over to
Abyla. Was Ulysses so mad as to go back into
the Cyclops' cave to fetch his sword? No, marry
was he not! Now I have left nothing behind
me at the wicket through forgetfulness; why then
should I think of going thither?

Well, quoth Friar John, as good sit still as rise up
and fall; what cannot be cured must be endured.
But prythee, let us hear one another speak in turn.
Come, wert thou not a wise doctor to fling away a
whole purse of gold on those mangy scoundrels?
Ha! A squinzy choke thee! we were too rich,
were we? Had it not been enough to have thrown
the hell-hounds a few cropped pieces of white cash?

How could I help it? returned Panurge? Did
you not see how Gripe-men-all held his gaping
velvet pouch, and every moment roared and
bellowed, By gold! give me out of hand! by
gold! give, give, give me presently? Now,
thought I to myself, we shall never come off
scot-free; I will even stop their mouths with

[2] Calpe is a mountain in Spain, that faces another, called
Abyla, in Mauritania, both said to have been severed by Hercules.

gold, that the wicket may be opened, and we may get out; the sooner the better. And I judged that lousy silver would not do the business; for, do you see, velvet pouches do not use to gape for little paltry clipped silver and small cash; no, they are made for gold, my friend John, that they are, my dainty cod. Ah! when thou hast been larded, basted, and roasted, as I was, thou wilt hardly talk at this rate, I doubt. But now what is to be done ?—We are enjoined by them to go forwards.

The scabby slabberdegullions still waited for us at the port, expecting to be greased in the fist as well as their masters. Now, when they perceived that we were ready to put to sea, they came to Friar John, and begged that we would not forget to gratify the apparitors before we went off, according to the assessment for the fees at our discharge. Hell and damnation ! cried Friar John, are ye here still, ye bloodhounds, ye citing, scribbling imps of Satan ? Rot you, am I not vexed enough already, but you must have the impudence to come and plague me, ye scurvy fly-catchers you? By cob's-body! I will gratify your ruffianships as you deserve; I will apparatorize you presently, with a wannion, that I will! With this he lugged out his slashing cutlass, and, in a mighty heat, came out of the ship, to cut the cozening varlets into steaks, but they scampered away and got out of sight in a trice.

However, there was somewhat more to do, for some of our sailors, having got leave of Pantagruel to go ashore, while we were had before Gripe-men-all, had been at a tavern near the haven, to make much of themselves, and roar it, as seamen will do when they come into some port. Now I do not know

whether they had paid their reckoning to the full or
no, but, however it was, an old fat hostess, meeting
Friar John on the quay, was making a woeful com-
plaint before a serjeant, son-in-law to one of the
Furred Law-cats, and a brace of bums, his assistants.

The Friar, who did not much care to be tired
with their impertinent prating, said to them, Harkee
me! ye lubberly gnat-snappers, do ye presume to
say, that our seamen are not honest men? I will
maintain they are, ye dotterels, and will prove it to
your brazen faces, by justice: I mean this trusty
piece of cold iron by my side. With this he lugged
it out and flourished with it. The forlorn lobcocks
soon showed him their backs, betaking themselves to
their heels; but the old fusty landlady kept her
ground, swearing like any butter-whore, that the
tarpaulins were very honest cods, but that they
only forgot to pay for the bed on which they had
lain after dinner, and she asked fivepence French
money, for the said bed. May I never sup! said
the Friar, if it be not dog-cheap; they are sorry
guests, and unkind customers, that they are; they
do not know when they have a pennyworth, and
will not always meet with such bargains; come,
I myself will pay you the money, but I would
willingly see it first.

The hostess immediately took him home with her,
and showed him the bed, and having praised it for
its good qualifications, said, that she thought, as
times went, she was not out of the way in asking
fivepence for it. Friar John then gave her the
fivepence; and she no sooner turned her back,
but he presently began to rip up the ticking
of the feather-bed and bolster, and threw all
the feathers out at the window. In the mean
time the old hag came down, and roared out for

71

help, crying out murder, to set all the neighbourhood in an uproar. Yet she also fell to gathering
the feathers that flew up and down in the air,
being scattered by the wind. Friar John let her
bawl on, and, without any further ado, marched
off with the blanket, quilt, and both the sheets,
which he brought aboard undiscovered, for the
air was darkened with the feathers, as it uses
sometimes to be with snow. He gave them away
to the sailors, then said to Pantagruel, that beds
were much cheaper at that place than in Chinnonois, though we have there the famous geese of
Pautilé; for the old beldam had asked him but
fivepence for a bed, which, in Chinnonois, had
been worth about twelve francs. As soon as
Friar John and the rest of the company were
embarked, Pantagruel set sail. But there arose
a south-east wind, which blew so vehemently they
lost their way, and in a manner going back to
the country of the Furred Law-cats, they entered
into a huge gulf, where the sea ran so high and
terrible, that the ship-boy on the top of the mast
cried out, he again saw the habitation of Gripe-
men-all; upon which Panurge, frightened almost
out of his wits, roared out, Dear master, in spite
of the wind and waves, change your course, and
turn the ship's head about: O my friend, let us
come no more into that cursed country, where I
left my purse. So the wind carried them near an
island, where, however, they did not dare at first
to land, but entered about a mile off.

On Chap. XII., etc.—Panurge being brought to the bar,
Gripe-men-all propounds to him a riddle, and tells him, that the
earth shall immediately open its jaws, and swallow him to quick
damnation, if he do not solve it. This is exactly the practice of
the Inquisition: the party that is accused is obliged to guess his

crime, and the name of his accusers; and if he guesses amiss, he is certainly undone ; but if he has the wit or good fortune to discover them, he generally comes off better; and a round fine, with St Benet's cap, save him from being burned.

Panurge vainly insists on his innocence; for Gripe-men-all replies, That if he hath nothing better to offer, he will let him know, that it had been better for him to have fallen into Lucifer's clutches; that their laws are like cobwebs, in which little flies are caught and destroyed, but which are too weak to stop great ones. This may have been spoke on the account of Pantagruel, who would not pass through the wicket, that is to say, who would not submit to the Inquisition.

Gripe-men-all says, When did you hear that for these three hundred years last past, anybody ever got out of this weal without leaving something of his behind him ? This is true enough, if spoken of the Inquisition; and about three hundred years before Rabelais wrote, a Court of Inquisition was set up at Toulouse, against the Albigenses, by Lewis the Ninth, called the saint.

CHAPTER XVI

HOW PANTAGRUEL CAME TO THE ISLAND OF THE APE-DEFTS,[1] OR IGNORAMUSES, WITH LONG CLAWS AND CROOKED PAWS, AND OF TERRIBLE ADVENTURES AND MONSTERS THERE

As soon as we had cast anchor, and had moored the ship, the pinnace was put over the ship's side, and manned by the cockswain's crew. When the good Pantagruel had prayed publicly, and given thanks to the Lord, that had delivered him from so great a danger, he stepped into the pinnace with his whole company, to go on shore, which was no ways diffi-

[1] 'Απαίδευτοι, uneducated. The gentlemen of one branch of the exchequer (*chambre des comptes*) are called Apedefts, by the author, because, as he says lower, there was no occasion to be graduated (any great scholars) to exercise those offices.

cult to do, for, as the sea was calm, and the winds laid, they soon got to the cliffs. When they were set on shore, Epistemon, who was admiring the situation of the place, and the strange shape of the rocks, discovered some of the natives. The first he met had on a short purple gown, a doublet cut in panes, like a Spanish leather jerkin, half sleeves of satin, and the upper part of them leather, a coif like a black pot tipped with tin. He was a good likely sort of a body, and his name, as we heard afterwards, was Double-fee. Epistemon asked him, How they called those strange craggy rocks and deep valleys? He told them it was a colony, brought out of Attorneyland, and called Process; and that if we forded the river somewhat further beyond the rocks, we should come into the island of the Apedefts. By the sacred memory of the decretals! said Friar John, tell us, I pray you, what you honest men here live on? Could not a man take a chirping bottle with you, to taste your wine? I can see nothing among you but parchment, ink-horns, and pens. We live on nothing else, returned Double-fee; and all who live in this place must come through my hands. How, quoth Panurge, are you a shaver, then? Do you fleece them? Ay, ay, their purse, answered Double-fee, nothing else. By the foot of Pharaoh! cried Panurge, the devil a sou will you get of me. However, sweet sir, be so kind as to show an honest man the way to those Apedefts, or ignorant people, for I come from the land of the learned, where I did not learn over much.

Still talking on, they got to the island of the Apedefts, for they were soon got over the ford. Pantagruel was not a little taken up with admiring the structure and habitation of the people of the

place.   For they live in a swingeing winepress, fifty
steps up to it.   You must know there are some of
all sorts, little, great, private, middle-sized, and so
forth.   You go through a large peristyle, *alias* a long
entry set about with pillars, in which you see, in a
kind of landscape, the ruins of almost the whole
world; besides so many gibbets for great robbers,[2]
so many gallows and racks, that it is enough to
fright you out of your seven senses.   Double-fee
perceiving that Pantagruel was taken up with contemplating those things, Let us go further, sir, said
he to him, all this is nothing yet.   Nothing, quotha !
cried Friar John ; by the soul of my overheated cod-
piece, friend Panurge and I here shake and quiver
for mere hunger !   I had rather be drinking, than
staring on these ruins.   Pray come along, sir, said
Double-fee.   He then led us into a little wine-
press, that lay backwards in a blind corner, and was
called Pithies in the language of the country.   You
need not ask whether Master John and Panurge
made much of their sweet selves there ; it is enough
that I tell you there was no want of Bolonia sausages,[3]
turkey-poults, capons, bustards, malmsey-wine, and
all other sorts of good belly-timber, very well
dressed.
    A pimping son of ten fathers, who, for want of
a better, did the office of a butler, seeing that Friar
John had cast a sheep's eye at a choice bottle that
stood near a cupboard by itself, at some distance
from the rest of the bottelic magazine, like a jack-

    [2] *Potences de grands larrons.*   The author distinguishes be-
tween gallows and gibbets: these last he calls *potences ;* to hang
the *potentes,* the great robbers upon.   It is a good pun enough
upon the word *potence,* the common word for a gallows, derived,
I suppose, from *poteau,* a post, though Rabelais ludicrously derives
it *a potentibus.*
    [3] Milan sausages in the original.

in-an-office, said to Pantagruel, Sir, I perceive that one of your men here is making love to this bottle: he ogles it, and would fain caress it; but I beg that none offer to meddle with it; for it is reserved for their worships. How! cried Panurge, there are some grandees here then, I see. It is vintage time with you, I perceive.

Then Double-fee led up to a private staircase, and showed us into a room, whence, without being seen, out at a loophole, we could see their worships in the great wine-press, where none could be admitted without their leave. Their worships, as he called them, were about a score of fusty crack-ropes and gallows-clappers, or rather more, all posted before a bar,[4] and staring at each other like so many dead pigs; their paws or hands were as long as a crane's leg, and their claws or nails four-and-twenty inches long at least; for you must know, they are enjoined never to pare off the least chip of them, so that they grow as crooked as a Welch hook, or a hedging-bill.[5]

We saw a swingeing bunch of grapes, that are gathered and squeezed in that country, brought in by them. As soon as it was laid down, they clapped it into the press, and there was not a bit of it out of which each of them did not squeeze some oil of gold. Insomuch that the poor grape was tried with a witness, and brought off so drained and picked, and so dry, that there was not the least moisture, juice, or substance left in it; for they had pressed out its very quintessence.

Double-fee told us, they had not often such huge

---

[4] It should be round a great green-covered table (not a bar); *bureau*, nor *barreau*: Rabelais, in his merry way, spells *bureau*, *bourreau*, which signifies the common hangman, alluding to what he called them just before, crack-ropes, etc.

[5] In the original, *rivereau*, a boat-hook; not a hedging-bill.

bunches; but, let the worst come to the worst, they
were sure never to be without others in their press.
But hark you me, master of mine! asked Panurge,
have they not some of different growth? Ay! marry
have they, quoth Double-fee. Do you see here this
little bunch, to which they are going to give the
other wrench? It is of tythe-growth, you must
know; they crushed, wrung, squeezed, and strained
out the very heart's blood of it but the other day:
but it did not bleed freely; the oil came hard, and
smelt of the priest's chest;[6] so that they found there
was not much good to be got out of it. Why then,
said Pantagruel, do they put it again into the press?
Only, answered Double-fee, for fear there should
still lurk some juice among the husks and hullings,
in the mother of the grape. The devil be damned!
cried Friar John, do you call these same folks
illiterate lobcocks, and dunsical doddipoles? May
I be broiled like a red herring, if I do not think they
are wise enough to skin a flint, and draw oil out of a
brick wall. So they are, said Double-fee; for they
sometimes put castles, parks, and forests into the
press, and out of them all extract *aurum potabile*.
You mean *portabile*, I suppose, cried Epistemon,
such as may be borne. I mean as I said, replied
Double-fee, *potabile*, such as may be drunk; for it
makes them drink many a good bottle more than
otherwise they should.

But I cannot better satisfy you as to the growth
of the vine-tree syrup that is here squeezed out of
grapes, than in desiring you to look yonder in that
backyard, where you will see above a thousand
different growths that lie waiting to be squeezed
every moment. Here are some of the public and

[6] Musty, because a priest keeps things as long as ever he can,
and gives away as little as possible.

77

some of the private growth; some of the fortifica-
tions, loans, gifts, and gratuities, escheats, forfeitures,
fines and recoveries, penal statutes, crown lands
and demesnes, privy purse, post-offices, offerings,
lordships of manors, and a world of other growths,
for which we want names. Pray, quoth Epistemon,
tell me of what growth is that great one, with all
those little grapelings about it. Oh, oh! returned
Double-fee, that plump one is of the treasury, the
very best growth in the whole country. Whenever
any one of that growth is squeezed, there is not one
of their worships but gets juice enough of it to soak
his nose six months together. When their worships
were up, Pantagruel desired Double-fee to take us
into that great wine-press, which he readily did.
As soon as we were in, Epistemon, who understood
all sorts of tongues, began to show us many devices
on the press, which was large and fine, and made of
the wood[7] of the cross—at least Double-fee told us
so. On each part of it were names of everything in
the language of the country. The spindle of the
press was called *receipt;* the trough, *costs and
damages;* the hole for the vice-pin, *state;* the
side-boards, *money paid into the office;* the great
beam, *respite of homage;* the branches, *radietur;*
the side-beams, *recuperetur;*[8] the fats,[9] *ignoramus;*

[7] The effects of such as had been hanged. *Crux* signifying a
gallows as well as a cross.

[8] In the chamber of accounts this is a term for annulling any
gift the king should make of an excessive sum, without just
cause, or having been first examined into by the chamber. See
Bodin. Repub. et Juv. des Ursins, Hist. cha. VII. on the year
1389.

[9] So M. Motteux wittily translates it; for he professes he
knew not what the original *plusvaleur* meant. Nor indeed can
I find out by any books what it should mean. Cotgrave translates it : *An overvalue, surplusage*, etc., but the true term here is
surcharge, a law term like recuperetur, etc.

the two-handled basket, *the rolls;* the treading-place, *acquittance;* the dossers, *validation;* the panniers, *authentic decrees;* the pailes, *potentials;* the funnels, *quietus est.*

By the Queen of the Chitterlings,[10] quoth Panurge, all the hieroglyphics of Egypt are mine arse to this jargon. Why! here are a parcel of words full as analogous as chalk and cheese, or a cat and a cart wheel! But why, prythee, dear Double-fee, do they call these worshipful dons of yours ignorant fellows? Only, said Double-fee, because they neither are, nor ought to be, clerks, and all must be ignorant as to what they transact here; nor is there to be any other reason given, but, The court hath said it; The court will have it so; The court has decreed it. Cop's body! quoth Pantagruel, they might full as well have called them necessity; for necessity has no law.

From thence, as he was leading us to see a thousand little puny presses, we spied another paltry bar, about which sat four or five ignorant waspish churls, of so testy, fuming a temper, like an ass with squibs and crackers tied to its tail, and so ready to take pepper in the nose for yea and nay, that a dog would not have lived with them. They were hard at it with the lees and dregs of the grapes, which they griped over and over again, might and main, with their clenched fists. They were called contractors, in the language of the country. These are the ugliest, misshapen, grim-looking scrubs, said Friar John, that ever were beheld, with or without spectacles. Then we passed by an infinite number of little pimping wine-presses, all full of vintage-mongers, who were picking, examining, and raking

[10] The idol Niphleseth, by whose name the author calls the Queen of Chitterlings, was herself an hieroglyphic.

the grapes with some instruments, called bills of charge.

Finally we came into a hall down stairs, where we saw an overgrown cursed mangy cur, with a pair of heads, a wolf's belly, and claws like the devil of hell. This son of a bitch was fed with costs, for he lived on a multiplicity of fine amonds[11] and amerciaments by order of their worships, to each of whom the monster was worth more than the best farm in the land. In their tongue of ignorance they called him Twofold. His dam lay by him, and her hair and shape was like her whelp's, only she had four heads, two male and two female, and her name was Fourfold. She was certainly the most cursed and dangerous creature of the place, except her grandam, which we saw, and had been kept locked up in a dungeon, time out of mind, and her name was Refusing-of-fees.

Friar John (who had always twenty yards of gut ready empty, to swallow a gallimaufry of lawyers) began to be somewhat out of humour, and desired Pantagruel to remember he had not dined, and bring Double-fee along with him. So away we went, and as we marched out at the back-gate, whom should we meet but an old piece of mortality in chains? He was half ignorant and half learned, like an hermaphrodite of Satan.[12] The fellow was all caparisoned with spectacles,[13] as a tortoise is with shells, and lived on nothing but a sort of food which, in their gibberish, was called *appeals*. Pantagruel asked Double-fee of what breed was that prothonotary, and what name

[11] A quibble upon the word *amende* (a mulct or fine in French) and almonds to eat.

[12] In matter of law-suits a very devil; in other things a very dunce in name and nature.

[13] The functions of his office consisted entirely in revising the process.

they gave him ?   Double-fee told us that time out of
mind, he had been kept there in chains,[14] to the grief
of their worships, who starved him, and his name was
Review.   By the Pope's sanctified two-pounders !
cried Friar John, I do not much wonder at the
meagre cheer which this old chuff finds among their
worships.   Do but look a little on the weather-beaten
scratch-toby, friend Panurge; by the sacred tip of
my cowl ! I will lay five pounds to a hazel-nut, the
foul thief has the very looks of Gripe-men-all.
These same fellows here, ignorant as they be, are
as sharp and knowing as other folks.   But were it
my case, I would send him packing with a squib in
his breech, like a rogue as he is.   By my oriental
barnacles ![15] quoth Panurge, honest Friar, thou art
in the right, for if we but examine that treacherous
Review's ill-favoured phiz, we find that the filthy
smudge is yet more mischievous and ignorant than
these ignorant wretches here, since they (honest
dunces) grapple and glean with as little harm and
pother as they can, without any long fiddle-cum-farts
or tantalising in the case; nor do they dally and
demur in your suit, but, in two or three words, wnip-
stitch, in a trice, they finish the vintage of the close,
bating you all these damned tedious interlocutories,
examinations, and appointments, which fret to the
heart's blood your Furred Law-cats.

On Chap. XVI.—The island of the Apedefts is a satire on

[14] It should be, to his great grief by their worships, who had
taken from him great part of the fines, which he claimed as his
dues, to subsist on.

[15] Oriental spectacles ; *lunettes* is French for a pair of spectacles.   The Turks, who are orientals to us, have the moon
(*lune*) for the symbol of their empire.   Rabelais quibbles on the
words *lune* and *lunettes*, moon and spectacles ; a pun not capable
of being preserved in English, perhaps not worthy of it. [Bar-
nacles is a corruption of binocles, from *binoculi*, double eyes.]

some courts of judicature, whose members squeeze out the blood and substance not only of the wrangling part of the world, but of those peaceable persons whom some litigious adversaries compel to fall into their clutches. The little wine-press, called *pithies* in the language of the country, that lay backwards in a blind corner, signifies the *beuvettes*, drinking places, which are generally in the very buildings where are the courts of judicature in France, whither the lawyers go to refresh themselves at the expense of the clients. That word comes from the Greek πίθι, drink. The ancients had also a festival sacred to Bacchus, which was called πιθοιγία, which comes from πίθος, a wine hogshead. It used to be celebrated at the time of the year when tuns and hogsheads used to be new hooped and fitted up, and, while it lasted, all comers and goers drank wine gratis, just as they do in France on St Martin's eve. The Athenians kept that festival in the month which they call Anthesteron, which is our month of November, as Gaza proves it, Lib. de Mensibus Atheniensium. By which it appears, that the custom used on St Martin's day in France, on which the parliaments as well as others make merry, succeeded to the *pithægia* of the ancients.

All this chapter may be easily understood, by those who are acquainted with the customs of France ; and, as it may be applicable also to other countries, it cannot seem very dark to others.—*M.*

———

CHAPTER XVII

HOW WE WENT FORWARDS, AND HOW PANURGE HAD LIKE TO HAVE BEEN KILLED

WE put to sea that very moment, steering our course forwards, and gave Pantagruel a full account of our adventures, which so deeply struck him with compassion, that he wrote some elegies on that subject, to divert himself during the voyage. When we were safe in the port we took some refresh-

ment, and took in fresh water and wood.   The
people of the place, who had the countenance of
jolly fellows, and boon companions, were all of them
forward folks, bloated and puffed up with fat; and
we saw some who slashed and pinked their skins, to
open a passage to the fat, that it might swell out at
the slits and gashes which they made; neither more
nor less than the shit-breech fellows in our country
bepink and cut open their breeches, that the taffety
on the inside may stand out and be puffed up.   They
said, that what they did was not out of pride or
ostentation, but because otherwise their skins would
not hold them without much pain.   Having thus
slashed their skin, they used to grow much bigger,
like the young trees, on whose barks the gardeners
make incisions, that they may grow the better.

Near the haven there was a tavern, which forwards
seemed very fine and stately.   We repaired thither,
and found it filled with people of the forward
nation, of all ages, sexes, and conditions; so that we
thought some notable feast or other was getting
ready, but we were told that all that throng were
invited to the bursting of mine host, which caused
all his friends and relations to hasten thither.

We did not understand that jargon, and, therefore,
thought in that country, by that bursting they meant
some merry meeting or other, as we do in ours by
betrothing, wedding, groaning, christening, church-
ing (of women), shearing (of sheep), reaping (of
corn, or harvest-home), and many other junketing
bouts that end in 'ing.'   But we soon heard that
there was no such matter in hand.

The master of the house, you must know, had
been a good fellow in his time, loved heartily to
wind up his bottom, to bang the pitcher, and lick
his dish: he used to be a very fair swallower of gravy

soup, a notable accountant in matter of hours,[1] and his whole life was one continual dinner, like mine host at Rouillac [in Perigord].   But now, having farted out much fat for ten years together, according to the custom of the country, he was drawing towards the bursting hour; for neither the inner thin caul wherewith the entrails are covered, nor his skin that had been jagged and mangled so many years, were able to hold and enclose his guts any longer, or hinder them from forcing their way out.   Pray, quoth Panurge, is there no remedy, no help for the poor man, good people?   Why do you not swaddle him round with good tight girths, or secure his natural tub with a strong sorb-apple-tree hoop? Nay, why do not you iron-bind him, if needs be? This would keep the man from flying out and bursting.   The word was not yet out of his mouth, when we heard something give a loud report, as if a huge sturdy oak had been split in two.   Then some of the neighbours told us, that the bursting was over, and that the clap or crack, which we heard, was the last fart, and so there was an end of mine host.

This made me call to mind a saying of the venerable abbot of Castilliers,[2] the very same who never cared to humph his chambermaids, but when he was *in pontificalibus*.   That pious person, being much dunned, teased, and importuned by his re-

---

[1] So they call in Poictou any great talker, who, when he has no more tales to tell, will count the hours, when the clock strikes, and that aloud, though others hear the clock as well as he.   But in this place it also means a smell-feast, a gormandizing hanger-on, a guttling spunger, who that he may not slip the critical minute when people use to dine, counts the hours, nay, the quarters 'of every clock that strikes, and that with the utmost exactness.

[2] See for this Vigneul-Maurville, in his Miscellanies, vol. 3, p. 247.   Rotterdam edition.

lations to resign his abbey in his old age, said and professed, That he would not strip till he was ready to go to bed, and that the last fart which his reverend paternity was to utter, should be the fart of an abbot.

On Chap. XVII.—The forward nation *is* easily known to be those boon companions, who, as the author says, love heartily to wind up their bottom, bang the pitcher, and lick the dish; men who have been fair swallowers of gravy soup, notable accountants in matter of hours, whose whole lives are one continual dinner, and who at last die of too much fat, of diseases got by eating or drinking to excess. This also reflects upon those who prodigally spend their estates, and at last crack their credits, and are forced to abscond, and thus may, in a manner, be said to be dead. This chapter, which now ends with the pleasant story of the abbot of Castilliers, who never used to be familiar with his maids but when he was dressed *in pontificalibus*, is imperfect; or there is a mistake in the account of its contents, which promise a relation of the danger which Panurge was in, though not one word of it is mentioned in the whole book.—*M.*

CHAPTER XVIII

HOW OUR SHIPS WERE STRANDED, AND WE WERE RELIEVED BY SOME PEOPLE THAT WERE SUBJECT TO QUEEN WHIMS (QUI TENOIENT DE LA QUINTE)

WE weighed and set sail with a merry westerly gale, when about seven leagues off (twenty-two miles) some gusts or scuds of wind suddenly arose, and the wind veering and shifting from point to point, was, as they say, like an old woman's breech, at no certainty; so we first got our starboard tacks aboard, and hauled off our lee-sheets. Then the gusts increased, and by fits blowed all at once from several quarters, yet we neither settled nor braded up close our sails, but only let fly the sheets, not to go against the master of the ship's direction; and thus having let go amain, lest we should spend our topsails, or the ship's quick-side should lie in the water, and she be over-set, we lay by and run adrift; that is, in a landloper's phrase, we temporised it. For he assured us that, as these gusts and whirlwinds would not do us much good, so they could not do us much harm, consider-ing their easiness and pleasant strife, as also the clearness of the sky and calmness of the current. So that we were to observe the philosopher's rule, bear and forbear; that is, trim, or go according to·the time.

However, these whirlwinds and gusts lasted so long, that we persuaded the master to let us go and lie at try with our main course : that is, to haul the tack aboard, the sheet close aft, the bowline set up, and the helm tied close aboard; so, after a stormy gale of wind, we broke through the whirlwind. But it was like falling into Scylla to avoid Charybdis. For we had not sailed a league, ere our ships were stranded upon some sands, such as are the flats of St Maixant.

All our company seemed mightily disturbed, ex-cept Friar John, who was not a jot daunted, and with sweet sugar-plum words, comforted now one and then another, giving them hopes of speedy assistance from above, and telling them that he had seen Castor at the main-yard arm. Oh! that I were but now ashore, cried Panurge, that is all I wish for myself at present, and that you, who like the sea so well, had each man of you two hundred thousand crowns; I would fairly let you set up shop on these sands,[1]

---

[1] Rabelais' words will by no means bear this construction; ' Je vous mettrois ung veau en meuë, et refraicherois ung cent de fagots pour votre retour.' On which M. Duchat observes that though Panurge seems to say, I would prepare a fat calf for you, it was not by any means his intention so to do; for as people do not use to put up calves to fat in a hen-coop (*meuë*), any more than they cool or throw water on faggots they would have burn

86

and would get a fat calf dressed, and a hundred of
faggots cooled for you against you come ashore. I
freely consent never to mount a wife, so you but set
me ashore, and mount me on a horse, that I may go
home; no matter for a servant, I will be contented
to serve myself; I am never better treated than when
I am without a man. Faith! old Plautus was in
the right of it when he said, the more servants the
more crosses; for such they are, even supposing they
could want what they all have but too much of, a
tongue, that most busy, dangerous, and pernicious
member of servants: accordingly, it was for their
sakes alone that the racks and tortures for confession
were invented, though some foreign civilians in our
time have drawn alogical and unreasonable consequences from it.

That very moment we spied a sail that made towards us. When it was close by us, we soon knew
what was the lading of the ship, and who was aboard
of her. She was full freighted with drums: I was
acquainted with many of the passengers that came
in her, who were most of them of good families;
among the rest Harry Cotiral, the chemist, an old
toast, who had got a swingeing ass's touch-tripe
fastened to his waist, as the good women's beads
are to their girdle. In his left hand he held an old
overgrown greasy foul cap, such as your scald-pated
fellows wear, and in the right a huge cabbage stump.

As soon as he saw me he was overjoyed, and
bawled out to me, What cheer, ho? How dost like
me now? Behold the true Algamana (this, he said,
showing me the ass's tickle-gizzard). This doctor's cap
is my true elixo; and this (continued he, shaking the

easily; so, instead of engaging himself here to any thing, he only
laughs at those who, together with himself, had too easily com-
mitted their persons to the dangers of the sea.

cabbage stump in his fist) is *lunaria major;* [3] I have it, old boy, I have it; we will blow the coal when thou art come back. But pray, father, said I, whence come you? Whither go you? What is your lading? Have you smelt the sea? To these four questions he answered, From Queen Whims; for Touraine; alchymy; to the very bottom.[4]

Whom have you got on board? said I. Said he, Astrologers, fortune - tellers, alchymists, rhymers, poets, painters, projectors, mathematicians, watch-makers, sing-songs, musicianers, and the devil and all of others that are subject to Queen Whims.[5] They have very fair legible patents to show for it, as anybody may see. Panurge had no sooner heard this, but he was upon the high-rope, and began to rail at them like mad. What the devil do you mean, cried he, to sit idly here, like a pack of loitering sneaksbies, and see us stranded, while you may help us, and tow us off into the current! A plague on your whims! you can make all things whatsoever, they say, so much as good weather and little children; yet will not make haste to fasten some hawsers and cables, and get us off. I was just coming to set you afloat, quoth Harry Cotiral: by Trismegistus! I will

[3] Because the leaves of it are like those of the sea-cabbage, which bears a great reputation, and is in mighty vogue with the alchymists.

[4] Not unlike this is a story of Henry IV. of France, who being overtaken upon the road by a clergyman that was posting to court; the King, putting his head out of his coach, asked the man in his hasty way, Whence come ye? Whither go ye? What want ye? The clergymen, without any ceremony or hesitation, made answer: From Blois; to Paris; a benefice. With which the King was so well pleased, he instantly granted his request.

[5] *La quinte.* This means a fantastic humour: maggots or a foolish giddiness of brain; and also a fifth, or the proportion of five in music, etc.

clear you in a trice. With this he caused 7,532,810 huge drums to be unheaded on one side, and set that open side so that it faced the end of the streamers and pendants; and having fastened them to good tacklings, and our ship's head to the stern of theirs, with cables fastened to the bits abaft the manger in the ship's loof, they towed us off ground at one pull, so easily and pleasantly, that you would have wondered at it, had you been there. For the dub-a-dub rattling of the drums, with the soft noise of the gravel, which murmuring disputed us our way, and the merry cheers and huzzas of the sailors, made an harmony almost as good as that of the heavenly bodies, when they roll and are whirled round their spheres, which rattling of the celestial wheels Plato said he heard some nights in his sleep.

We scorned to be behind-hand with them in civility, and gratefully gave them store of our sausages and chitterlings, with which we filled their drums ; and we were just a-hoisting two-and-sixty hogsheads of wine out of the hold, when two huge whirlpools (physeters) with great fury made towards their ship ; spouting more water than is in the river Vienne (Vigenne), from Chinon to Saumur : to make short, all their drums, all their sails, their concerns, and themselves, were soused, and their very hose were watered by the collar.

Panurge was so overjoyed, seeing this, and laughed so heartily, that he was forced to hold his sides, and it set him into a fit of the cholic for two hours and more. I had a mind, quoth he, to make the dogs drink, and those honest whirlpools, egad ! have saved me that labour and that cost. There's sauce for them; ἄριστον μὲν ὕδωρ. Water is good, saith a poet; let them Pindarise upon it: they never cared for fresh water, but to wash their hands or their glasses.

This good salt water will stand them in good stead, for want of sal ammoniac and nitre in Geber's kitchen.[6]

We could not hold any further discourse with them, for the former whirlwind hindered our ship from feeling the helm. The pilot advised us henceforwards to let her run adrift, and follow the stream, not busying ourselves with anything, but making much of our carcasses. For our only way to arrive safe at the Queendom of Whims, was to trust to the whirlwind, and be led by the current.

On Chap. XVIII.—To attain to the knowledge of truth, it is necessary to take a survey of everything : so our travellers, steering their course to its oracle, sail towards the Queendom of Whims; by which, in general, may be understood all sorts of strange whimsical notions, and alchymy in particular.

Accordingly, as they come near that country, that is, imitate the fantastic wavering people that fill their heads with all the strange imaginations which we call whimsies, some sudden gusts or scuds of wind arise, and the wind shifting from point to point is at no certainty. They tack about, the gusts increase, and by fits blow at once from several quarters. This very well represents an unfixed mind, that unmethodically applies itself to many things at once; then leaves them to think on others, which soon resign the working brain to a crowd of succeeding raw and undigested notions.

The master of the ship orders the sheets to be let fly, for fear of oversetting the ship, and is for running adrift, or temporising, as the author calls. it ; those gusts not being dangerous. This may mean, that it is not always proper to oppose altogether the inclinations of some men, even while it leads them to studies and attempts that seem insignificant; since time soon weans them of their darling follies; and thus they know the better how to distinguish between the useful and the unprofitable.

After all, this may refer to some of those doubtful points, about which the learned were as idly busy in that age, as nowadays many are about them and others; placing religion more in notions than in actions, and neglecting the practice to talk of the theory. Such questions are those of free-will, predestination, justification, etc., by which the people reap as little benefit as the

---

[6] An ancient Arabian alchymist, whose works are extant.

teachers gain glory, when they display their learned ignorance about them. Pantagruel's ship that is stranded, or run aground, endeavouring to weather-coil and break through the whirlwind, after it has been tossed by it, is an image of those, who thinking to ease their fluctuating minds, at last venture on some new notion, which at first seems plausible to some; but they are soon gravelled, and do not know how to get off. The empty drums, which were on board the ship that came from Queen Whims, which towed the Pantagruelists off ground, put me in mind of the help which school-divinity affords in such doubts: an empty noise, mere wind, and that is all; just as harmonious as the sound made by the gravel, and the seamen's cheers. Even that fantastic relief proves real to some, who are whimsically drawn by it, and by that means are in a fair way to proceed, and, being led by the current, like our travellers, arrive at the Queendom of Whims.—*M.*

CHAPTER XIX

HOW WE ARRIVED AT THE (QUEENDOM OF WHIMS), OR KINGDOM OF QUINTESSENCE, CALLED EN-TELECHY

WE did as he directed us for about twelve hours, and on the third day the sky seemed to us somewhat clearer, and we happily arrived at the port of Mateotechny,[1] not far distant from the palace of Quintessence.

We met full-butt on the quay a great number of guards, and other military men that garrisoned the arsenal; and we were somewhat frighted at first, because they made us all lay down our arms, and, in a haughty manner, asked us whence we came?

[1] There is no pains more foolishly employed about any one thing than in the search of the philosopher's stone; but there are likewise other vain sciences, and the author means to say, that such as confine themselves thereto are arrived at the port of Mateotechny. Μάταιος, *vanus*; Τέχνη, *ars*.

Cousin, quoth Panurge to him that asked the question, we are of Touraine, and come from France, being ambitious of paying our respects to the Lady Quintessence, and visit this famous realm of Entelechy.

What do you say? cried they: do you call it Entelechy, or Endelechy? Truly, truly, sweet cousins, quoth Panurge, we are a silly sort of grout-headed lobcocks, an it please you; be so kind as to forgive us if we chance to knock words out of joint; as for anything else, we are downright honest fellows, and true hearts.

We have not asked you this question without a cause, said they: for a great number of others, who have passed this way from your country of Touraine, seemed as mere joltheaded doddipoles as ever were scored over the coxcomb, yet spoke as correct as other folks. But there has been here from other countries a pack of I know not what overweening self-conceited prigs, as moody as so many mules, and as stout as any Scotch lairds, and nothing would serve these, forsooth, but they must wilfully wrangle and stand out against us at their coming; and much they got by it after all. Troth, we even fitted them, and clawed them off with a vengeance, for all they looked so big and so grum.

Pray tell me, does your time lie so heavy upon you in your world, that you do not know how to bestow it better than in thus impudently talking, disputing, and writing of our sovereign lady? There was much need that your Tully, the consul, should go and leave the care of his commonwealth to busy himself idly about her; and after him, your Diogenes Laertius, the biographer, and your Theodorus Gaza, the philosopher, and your Argiropilus, the emperor, and your Bessario, the cardinal, and your Politian, the pedant, and your Budæus, the judge, and your

Lascaris, the ambassador, and the devil and all of those you call lovers of wisdom; whose number, it seems, was not thought great enough already, but likely your Scaliger, Bigot, Chambrier, Francis Fleury, and I cannot tell how many such other junior sneaking fly-blows, must take upon them to increase it.

A squincy gripe the cod's-headed changelings at the swallow, and eke at the cover-weesel! we shall make them—But the deuce take them! (They flatter the devil here, and smoothify his name, quoth Panurge, between their teeth); you do not come here, continued the captain, to uphold them in their folly, you have no commission from them to this effect; well then, we will talk no more of it.

Aristotle, that first of men, and peerless pattern of all philosophy, was our sovereign lady's godfather: and wisely and properly gave her the name of Entelechy. Her true name then is Entelechy, and may he be in tail beshit, and entail a shit-a-bed faculty, and nothing else, on his family, who dares call her by any other name: for whoever he is, he does her wrong, and is a very impudent person. You are heartily welcome, gentlemen. With this they colled and clipped us about the neck, which was no small comfort to us, I will assure you.

Panurge then whispered me, Fellow-traveller, quoth he, hast thou not been somewhat afraid this bout? A little, said I. To tell you the trnth of it, quoth he, never were the Ephraimites in a greater fear and quandary, when the Gileadites killed and drowned them for saying Sibboleth instead of Shibboleth; and among friends, let me tell you, that perhaps there is not a man in the whole country of Beauce, but might easily have stopped my bung-hole with a cart-load of hay.

93

The captain afterwards took us to the Queen's palace, leading us silently with great formality. Pantagruel would have said something to him; but the other, not being able to come up to his height, wished for a ladder, or a very long pair of stilts; then said, Patience, if it were our sovereign lady's will, we would be as tall as you; well, we shall, when she pleases.

In the first galleries, we saw great numbers of sick persons, differently placed according to their maladies. The leprous were apart; those that were poisoned on one side; those that had got the plague, *alias* the pox,[2] in the first rank, accordingly.

On CHAP. XIX.—That place, which is also called Entelechy, and its ruler Queen Whims, or Quintessence, is alchymy, the pretended philosophical stone; as also quacks, and those beggarly projectors, who, if you will believe them, can make you rich, and promise mountains of gold, whereas they sometimes want brass to buy bread: and more generally, this refers to all addle-headed students and contrivers. All know how infatuated many of the chemists are with the *lapis, aurum potabile,* and a thousand medicines, at whose very sight, they will tell you, diseases disappear. The leprosy, the plague, poisons, though never so corrosive, the venereal disease, the gout, palsies; in short, all obstinate and dangerous evils are cured by them in an unaccountable manner, if you will believe them. Now Rabelais, who, as Thuanus says, was a most learned and experienced physician, gives us freely to understand that all those pretenders are so many cheats, who sometimes deceive themselves, but generally others. For this reason, the first port of that island, whereat he makes his fleet touch, is Mateotechny, Ματαιοτεχνία; that is the study of foolish unprofitable arts: yet he makes those who profess them give their country the name of Entelechy, from Ἐντελεχεία, *actus et perfectio;* as it is rendered in Aristotle's second Book *De Anima.* Tully, *Tuscul.,* lib. 1, would have it to signify a perpetual motion. Now, as several learned men in former ages have almost as largely descanted upon the word, as some in this have lost time about the thing, Rabelais reflects upon them for it in this chapter;

---

[2] It is on their account principally that the chemical medicines are in vogue.

and at the same time those grammarians who dispute so hotly about words and neglect things may be aimed at, as deserving to be placed among those who apply themselves to unprofitable studies.—*M.*

CHAPTER XX

HOW THE QUINTESSENCE CURED THE SICK WITH A SONG

THE captain showed us the Queen, attended with her ladies and gentlemen in the second gallery. She looked young, though she was at least eighteen hundred years old ; [1] and was handsome, slender, and as fine as a queen, that is as hands could make her. He then said to us, It is not yet a fit time to speak to the Queen ; be you but mindful of her doings in the meanwhile.

You have kings in your world that fantastically pretend to cure some certain diseases; as for example, scrofula or wens, swelled throats, nicknamed the king's evil, and quartan agues, only with a touch : now our Queen cures all manner of diseases without so much as touching the sick, but barely with a song, according to the nature of the distemper. He then showed us a set of organs, and said, that when it was touched by her, those miraculous cures were performed. The organ was indeed the strangest that ever eyes beheld : for the pipes were of cassia fistula in the cod ; the top and cornice of guiacum; the bellows of rhubarb ; the pedals of turbith; and the clavier (or keys) of scammony.

[1] With respect to the time when Aristotle flourished, who was the first coiner of the word entelechy.

95

While we were examining this wonderful new make of an organ, the leprous were brought in by her abstractors, spodizators, masticators, pregustics, tabachins, chachanins, neemanins, rabrebans, nercins, rozuins, nebidins, tearins, segamions, perarons, chasinins, sarins, soteins, aboth, enilins, archasdarpenins, mebins, chabourins, and other officers, for whom I want names ; so she played them I do not know what sort of a tune, or song, and they were all immediately cured.

Then those who were poisoned were had in, and she had no sooner given them a song, but they began to find a use for their legs, and up they got. Then came on the deaf, the blind, and the dumb, and they too were restored to their lost faculties and senses with the same remedy ; which did so strangely amaze us (and not without reason, I think), that down we fell on our faces, remaining prostrate, like men ravished in ecstasy, and were not able to utter one word through the excess of our admiration, till she came, and having touched Pantagruel with a fine fragrant nosegay of red roses, which she held in her hand, thus made us recover our senses and get up. Then she made us the following speech in Byssin words, such as Parisatis desired should be spoken to her son Cyrus, or at least of crimson alamode.

The probity that scintillises in the superficies of your persons, informs my ratiocinating faculty, in a most stupendous manner, of the radiant virtues latent within the precious caskets and ventricles of your minds. For, contemplating the mellifluous suavity of your thrice discreet reverences, it is impossible not to be persuaded with facility, that neither your affections nor your intellects are vitiated with any defect, or privation of liberal and exalted sciences : far from it, all must judge

that in you are lodged a cornucopia, and encyclo-
pedia, an unmeasureable profundity of knowledge
in the most peregrine and sublime disciplines, so
frequently the admiration, and so rarely the con-
comitants of the imperite vulgar. This gently
compels me, who in preceding times indefatigably
kept my private affections absolutely subjugated, to
condescend to make my application to you in the
trivial phrase of the plebeian world ; and assure
you, that you are well, more than most heartily
welcome.

I have no hand at making of speeches, quoth
Panurge to me privately : prythee, man, make
answer to her for us, if thou canst. This would not
work with me, however, neither did Pantagruel
return a word : so that Queen Whims, or Queen
Quintessence (which you please), perceiving that we
stood as mute as fishes, said : Your taciturnity speaks
you not only disciples of Pythagoras, from whom the
venerable antiquity of my progenitors, in successive
propagation was emaned, and derives its original ;
but also discovers, that through the revolution of
many retrograde moons, you have in Egypt pressed
the extremities of your fingers, with the hard tenants
of your mouths, and scalptized your heads with
frequent applications of your unguicules.[2] In the
school of Pythagoras, taciturnity was the symbol of
abstracted and superlative knowledge ; and the
silence of the Egyptians was agnized as an expres-
sive manner of divine adoration : this caused the
pontiffs of Hierapolis to sacrifice to the great deity
in silence, impercussively, without any vociferous
or obstreperous sound. My design is not to enter

---

[2] It is in the original, with one finger; a sign of effeminacy
and indolence, with which Pompey was formerly reproached, as
Seneca, Plutarch, and others have observed.

into a privation of gratitude towards you; but by a vivacious formality, though matter were to abstract itself from me, excentricate to you my cogitations.

Having spoken this, she only said to her officers, Tabachins, a panacea;[3] and straight they desired us not to take it amiss, if the Queen did not invite us to dine with her; for she never ate anything at dinner but some categories, jecabots, emnins, dimions, abstractions, harborins, chelemins, second intentions, carradoths, antitheses, metempsychoses, transcendent prolepsies, and such other light food.

Then they took us into a little closet, lined through with alarums, where we were treated God knows how. It is said that Jupiter writes whatever is transacted in the world, on the dipthera or skin of the Amalthæan goat that suckled him in Crete, which pelt served him instead of a shield against the Titans, whence he was nicknamed Ægiochos. Now as I hate to drink water, brother topers, I protest it would be impossible to make eighteen goat-skins hold the description of all the good meat they brought before us; though it were written in characters as small as those in which were penned Homer's Iliads, which Tully tells us he saw enclosed in a nutshell.

For my part, had I one hundred mouths, as many tongues, a voice of iron, a heart of oak, and lungs of leather, together with the mellifluous abundance of Plato; yet I never could give you a full account of a third part of a second of the whole.

Pantagruel was telling me, that he believed the

[3] Cotgrave says it is a call to meat (à pan) like à manger. It is likewise an herb called in English all-heal, for it cures all distempers (credat quicunque vult). Pliny and Dioscorides speak of this wonderful vegetable, which Erasmus in his Encomium Moriæ, says must grow, if anywhere, in the Fortunate Islands, which produce every thing at a wish.

Queen had given the symbolic word used among her subjects, to denote sovereign good cheer, when she said to her tabachins, a panacea ; just as Lucullus used to say, In Apollo, when he designed to give his friends a singular treat ; though sometimes they took him at unawares, as, among the rest, Cicero and Hortensius sometimes used to do.

On Chap. XX.—Rabelais ridicules here those empirics whose chief talent is impudence and lies, while they pretend to the cure of incurable diseases; and also those who seek an universal remedy, Rosicrucians, disciples of Trismegistus, Raimond Lullius, Arnold of Villeneuve, and such as are said to have understood the great work, or *arcanum philosophicum*, and—if you will believe them—the only true sons of wisdom. This makes him say, that Queen Whims cured all manner of diseases with a song, full as effectually as some kings rid men of the evil, that takes its name from their dignity: by which he meant, that all those pretended cures are just as solid as a song, and are nothing but vain talk.

The Queen's affected pedantic speech mimics the way of talk of some of our demi-virtuosos, who cannot think any one speaks well, unless he express himself with far-fetched metaphors, long tropes, uncommon words, *per ambages*, tedious circumlocutions, and such fulsome stuff. Accordingly we find that Panurge could not tell how to answer her in the same cant; neither did Pantagruel return a word. However they dined never the worse after it, while the Queen fed on nothing but categories, abstractions, second intentions, metempsychoses, transcendent prolepsies, expressions, deceptions, dreams, etc., in Greek and Hebrew.—*M*.

CHAPTER XXI

HOW THE QUEEN PASSED HER TIME AFTER DINNER

When we had dined, a chachanin led us into the Queen's hall, and there we saw how, after dinner, with the ladies and princes of her court, she used to sift, searse, boult, range, and pass away time with a fine large white and blue silk sieve. We also perceived how they revived ancient sports, diverting themselves together at

1. Cordax.[1] 6. Phrygia.   9. Molossia, 12. Terminalia.
2. Emmelia. 7. Thracia. 10. Cerno-   13. Floralia.
3. Sicinnia. 8. Cala-   phorum. 14. Pyrrhice.
4. Jambics.   brisme. 11. Monogas. 15. Nicatism.[2]
5. Persica.

And a thousand other dances.

Afterwards she gave orders that they should show us the apartments and curiosities in her palace; accordingly we saw there such new, strange, and wonderful things, that I am still ravished in admiration every time I think on it. However, nothing surprised us more than what was done by the gentlemen of her household, abstractors, parazons, nebidins, spodizators, and others, who freely, and without the least dissembling, told us, that the Queen, their mistress, did all impossible things, and cured men of incurable diseases; and they, her officers, used to do the rest.

I saw there a young parazon cure many of the new consumption, I mean the pox, though they were never so peppered: had it been the rankest Roan

[1] 1. A sort of country dance. 2. A still tragic dance. 3. Dancing and singing used at funerals. 4. Cutting sarcasms and lampoons. 5. The Persian dance. 6. Tunes, whose measure inspired men with a kind of divine fury. 7. The Thracian movement. 8. Smutty verses. 9. A measure to which the Molossi of Epirus danced a certain morrice. 10. A dance with bowls or pots in their hands. 11. A song where one sings alone. 12. Sports at the holidays of the god of bounds. 13. Dancing naked at Flora's holidays. 14. The Trojan-dance in armour. Le Duchat differs a little in the order of these names.

[2] Athenæus, lib. xiv., cap. 7, makes mention of all these dances of the ancients, even nicatism, which Sir T. U. and all the new editions have omitted.

ague,[3] it was all one with him; touching only their dentiform vertebræ thrice with a piece of a wooden shoe, he made them as wholesome as so many sucking pigs.

Another did thoroughly cure folks of dropsies, tympanies, ascites, and hyposarcides, striking them on the belly nine times with a Tenedian hatchet,[4] without any solution of the continuum.

Another cured all manner of fevers and agues on the spot, only with hanging a fox tail [5] on the left side of tho patient's girdle.

One removed the toothache only with washing thrice the root of the aching tooth with elder-vinegar, and letting it dry half-an-hour in the sun.[6]

Another the gout, whether hot or cold, natural or accidental, by barely making the gouty person shut his mouth, and open his eyes.

I saw another ease nine gentlemen of St Francis' distemper,[7] in a very short space of time, having clapped a rope about their necks, at the end of which hung a box with ten thousand gold crowns in it.

One with a wonderful engine, threw the houses

---

[3] It should be Rouen, not Roan; they are two different towns in France, at a vast distance from each other.   Why the pox is denoimated from Rouen, is either because it first appeared there, or because such as have it in a violent degree are *enrouez*, made hoarse by it.

[4] It is the tenedia bipennis (a twy-bill, or two-edged axe of Tenedos: see Cambridge Dict.).   It was, as M. Duchat observes, a symbol of extreme severity.   This axe or bipennis gave rise to the French word *besaguë*, from *bisacuta*, because of its double edge.

[5] To drive away the flies which pestered the patient.

[6] No shorter nor better way to cure the toothache, than to pull out the tooth that causes it.

[7] A consumption in the pocket, or want of money : for those of St Francis' order must carry none about them.

out at the windows, by which means they were purged of all pestilential air.

Another cured all the three kinds of hectics, the tabid, atrophied, and emaciated, without bathing, without Tabian milk, dropax, *alias* depilatory, or other such medicaments; only turning the consumptive for three months into monks: and he assured me that if they did not grow fat and plump in a monastic way of living, they never would be fattened in this world, either by nature, or by art.

I saw another surrounded with a crowd of two sorts of women. Some were young, quaint, clever, neat, pretty, juicy, tight, brisk, buxom, proper, kind-hearted, and as right as my leg, to any man's thinking. The rest were old, weather-beaten, over-ridden, toothless, blear-eyed, tough, wrinkled, shrivelled, tawny, mouldy, phthysicky, decrepit hags, beldams, and walking carcasses. We were told that this office was to cast anew those she-pieces of antiquity, and make them such as the pretty creatures whom we saw, who had been made young again that day, recovering at once the beauty, shape, size, and disposition, which they enjoyed at sixteen; except their heels, that were now much shorter than in their former youth.

This made them yet more apt to fall backwards, whenever any man happened to touch them, than they had been before. As for their counterparts, the old mother-scratch-tobies, they most devoutly waited for the blessed hour, when the batch that was in the oven was to be drawn, that they might have their turns, and in a mighty haste they were pulling and hauling the man like mad, telling him, that it is the most grievous and intolerable thing in nature for the tail to be on fire, and the head to scare away those who should quench it.

The officer had his hands full, never wanting patients; neither did his place bring him in little, you may swear. Pantagruel asked him whether he could also make old men young again? He said he could not. But the way to make them new men, was to get them to cohabit with a new-cast female: for thus they caught that fifth kind of crinckams, which some call pellade, in Greek, ὀφίασις, that makes them cast off their old hair and skin, just as the serpents do; and thus their youth is renewed like the Arabian phœnix's. This is the true fountain of youth, for there the old and decrepit become young, active, and lusty.

Just so, as Euripides tells us, Iolaus was transmogrified; and thus Phaon, for whom kind-hearted Sappho ran wild, grew young again for Venus' use: so Tithon by Aurora's means; so Æson by Medæa, and Jason also, who, if you will believe Pherecides and Simonides, was new-vamped and dyed by that witch: and so were the nurses of jolly Bacchus, and their husbands, as Æschylus relates.

On Chap. XXI.—Our travellers see the Queen, and some of her subjects, who sift, searse, boult, range, and pass away time, and revive ancient sports. This reflects on those who wholly apply themselves to the study of the customs of the ancients, while many times they are ignorant in those of the moderns ; a sort of book-worms, some of which, conversing with none but the dead, are hardly qualified for the company of the living. Our author, who seldom forgets the monks, says, that one of the Queen's officers cured the consumptive by turning them into monks, by which means they grew fat and plump. What he says of the nine gentlemen who were rid of their poverty, having a rope put about their necks, at the end of which hung a box with ten thousand crowns in it, may refer to some in those times who either had, or fancied they were to have, the collar of the order of St Michael, or some other, bestowed on them with a pension.—M.

CHAPTER XXII

HOW QUEEN WHIMS' OFFICERS WERE EMPLOYED: AND
HOW THE SAID LADY RETAINED US AMONG HER
ABSTRACTORS

I then saw a great number of the Queen's officers,
who made black-a-moors white, as fast as hops, just
rubbing their bellies with the bottom of a pannier.

Others, with three couples of foxes in one yoke,
ploughed a sandy shore, and did not lose their seed.

Others washed burnt tiles, and made them lose
their colour.

Others extracted water out of pumice-stones;
braying them a good while in a mortar, and changed
their substance.

Others sheared asses, and thus got long fleece
wool.

Others gathered off of thorns grapes, and figs off
of thistles.

Others stroked he-goats by the dugs, and saved
their milk in a sieve; and much they got by it.

Others washed asses' heads, without losing their
soap.

Others taught cows to dance, and did not lose
their fiddling.

Others pitched nets to catch the wind, and took
cock lobsters in them.

I saw a spodizator, who very artificially got farts
out of a dead ass, and sold them for fivepence
an ell.

Another did putrefy beetles. O the dainty food !

Poor Panurge fairly cast up his accounts, and
gave up his halfpenny [*i.e.*, vomited], seeing an
archasdarpenin, who laid a huge plenty of chamberlye

to putrefy in horse-dung, mis-mashed with abundance of Christian sir-reverence. Pugh! fie upon him, nasty dog! However, he told us, that with this sacred distillation he watered kings and princes, and made their sweet lives a fathom or two the longer.

'Others built churches to jump over the steeples.[1]

Others set carts before the horses,' and began to flay eels at the tail; neither did the eels cry before they were hurt, like those of Melun.

Others out of nothing made great things, and made great things return to nothing.

Others cut fire into steaks, with a knife, and drew water with a fish net.

'Others made chalk of cheese,'[2] and honey of a dog's turd.

We saw a knot of others, about a baker's dozen in number, tippling under an arbour. They toped out of jolly bottomless cups, four sorts of cool, sparkling, pure, delicious, vine-tree syrup, which went down like mother's milk; and healths and bumpers flew about like lightning. We were told, that these true philosophers were fairly multiplying the stars by drinking till the seven were fourteen, as brawny Hercules did with Atlas.

Others made a virtue of necessity, and the best of a bad market, which seemed to me a very good piece of work.

Others made alchymy with their teeth, and clapping their hind retort to the recipient, made scurvy faces, and then squeezed.

Others, in a large grass-plat, exactly measured how

---

[1] This, and the other article with turned commas, are not in Rabelais, who says here, Others broke (*andouilles*) chitterlings against their knees.

[2] The original says, Lanterns of bladders, and brass shovels of clouds.

far the fleas could go at a hop, a step, and a jump;
and told us, that this was exceedingly useful for the
ruling of kingdoms, the conduct of armies, and the
administration of commonwealths; and that Socrates,
who first got philosophy out of heaven, and from
idle and trifling, made it profitable and of moment,
used to spend half his philosophising time in measur-
ing the leaps of fleas, as Aristophanes, the quintes-
sential, affirms.

I saw two giborins by themselves, keeping watch
on the top of a tower, and we were told, they
guarded the moon from the wolves.

In a blind corner, I met four more very hot at it,
and ready to go to loggerheads. I asked what was
the cause of the stir and ado, the mighty coil and
pother they made? And I heard that for four or
five livelong days, those overwise roisters had been
at it ding-dong, disputing on three high, more than
metaphysical propositions, promising themselves
mountains of gold by solving them; the first was
concerning a he-ass' shadow; the second, of the
smoke of a lantern; and the third, of goat's hair,
whether it were wool or no? We heard that they
did not think it a bit strange, that two contradictions
in mode, form, figure, and time, should be true.
Though I will warrant the sophists of Paris had
rather be unchristened than own so much.

While we were admiring all those men's wonderful doings, the evening star already twinkling; the
Queen (God bless her) appeared attended with her
court, and again amazed and dazzled us. She perceived it and said to us:

What occasions the aberrations of human cogitations through the perplexing labyrinths and abysses
of admiration, is not the source of the effects, which
sagacious mortals visibly experience to be the conse-

quential result of natural causes: it is the novelty of
the experiment which makes impressions on their
conceptive, cogitative faculties; that do not previse
the facility of the operation adequately, with a subact
and sedate intellection, associated with diligent and
congruous study.   Consequently let all manner of
perturbation abdicate the ventricles of your brains,
if any one has invaded them while they were contemplating what is transacted by my domestic
ministers.   Be spectators and auditors of every
particular phenomenon, and every individual pro-
position, within the extent of my mansion; satiate
yourselves with all that can fall here under the consideration of your visual or ascultating powers, and
thus emancipate yourselves from the servitude of
crassous ignorance.   And that you may be induced
to apprehend how sincerely I desire this in consideration of the studious cupidity that so demonstratively
emicates at your external organs, from this present
particle of time, I retain you as my abstractors:
Geber, my principal tabachin, shall register and
initiate you at your departing.

We humbly thanked her queenship, without saying a word, accepting of the noble office she conferred
on us.

On Chap. XXII.—This chapter ridicules those who attempt
impossibilities: accordingly, our author says they made black-a-
moors white, rubbing their bellies with the bottom of a pannier;
ploughed a sandy shore with three couples of foxes in one yoke,
and did not lose their seed: which undertakings have given
occasion to several proverbs among the ancients, to denote labour
in vain, as ' Æthiopem dealbare; arenas arare; laterem lavare;
pumice aridius; ex asino lanam;' and others, which our author
has purposely mentioned.   Some mathematicians, dialecticians,
naturalists, and metaphysicians, are ingeniously satirised in this
chapter.—M.

CHAPTER XXIII

HOW THE QUEEN WAS SERVED AT DINNER, AND OF HER WAY OF EATING

Queen Whims, after this, said to her gentlemen: The orifice of the ventricle, that ordinary embassador for the alimentation of all members, whether superior or inferior, importunes us to restore, by the apposition of idoneous sustenance, what was dissipated by the internal calidity's action on the radical humidity. Therefore spodizators, gesinins, memains, and parazons, be not culpable of dilatory protractions in the apposition of every re-roborating species, but rather let them pullulate and superabound on the tables. As for you, noblissime prægustators, and my gentilissime masticators, your frequently experimented industry, internected with perdiligent sedulity, and sedulous perdiligence, continually adjuvates you to perficiate all things in so expeditious a manner, that there is a necessity of exciting in you a cupidity to consummate them. Therefore I can only suggest to you still to operate, as you are assuefacted indefatigably to operate.

Having made this fine speech, she retired for a while with part of her women, and we were told, that it was to bathe, as the ancients did more commonly than we use nowadays to wash our hands before we eat. The tables were soon placed, the cloth spread, and then the Queen sat down. She ate nothing but celestial ambrosia, and drank nothing but divine nectar. As for the lords and ladies that were there, they as well as we fared on as rare, costly, and dainty dishes, as ever Apicius wot or dreamed of in his life.

When we were as round as hoops, and as full as eggs, with stuffing the gut, an olla podrida[1] was set before us, to force hunger to come to terms with us, in case it had not granted us a truce; and such a huge vast thing it was, that the golden platter which Pythius Althius gave King Darius, would hardly have covered it. The olla consisted of several sorts of pottages, salads, fricassees, saugrénées, cabirotadoes, roast and boiled meat, carbonadoes, swingeing pieces of powdered beef, good old hams, dainty deifical somates, cakes, tarts, a world of curds after the Moorish way, fresh cheese, jellies, and fruit of all sorts. All this seemed to me good and dainty: however the sight of it made me sigh; for alas, I could not taste a bit of it; so full I had filled my puddings before, and a bellyful *is* a bellyful you know. Yet I must tell you what I saw, that seemed to me odd enough of conscience: it was some pasties in paste ; and what should those pasties in paste be, do you think, but pasties in pots? At the bottom I perceived store of dice, cards, tarots, luettes, chess-men and chequers, besides full bowls of gold crowns, for those who have a mind to have a game or two, and try their chance. Under this I saw a jolly company of mules in stately trappings, with velvet foot-cloths, and a troop of ambling nags, some for men and some for women; besides I do not know how many litters all lined with velvet, and some coaches of Ferrara make: all this for those who had a mind to take the air.

This did not seem strange to me: but if anything did, it was certainly the Queen's way of eating; and truly it was very new, and very odd: for she chewed nothing, the good lady; not but that she had good sound teeth, and her meat required to be masticated;

---

[1] Rabelais, *pot-poxrry*.

but such was her highness' custom. When her *pragustators* had tasted the meat, her *masticators* took it and chewed it most nobly: for their dainty chops and gullets were lined through with crimson satin, with little welts, and gold purls, and their teeth were of delicate white ivory. Thus, when they had chewed the meat ready for her highness' maw, they poured it down her throat through a funnel of fine gold, and so on to her craw. For that reason, they told us, she never visited a close-stool but by proxy.

ON CHAP. XXIII.—Queen Whims' or Quintessence's supper is not more substantial than her dinner: for she eats nothing but ambrosia; drinks nothing but nectar; and the lords and ladies that were there fared on such dishes as Apicius dreamed of. All this is dream and poetical food, and consequently of easy digestion. An olla or hodgepodge follows, which may represent a mixture of confused notions jumbled together. The cards, dice, chequers, and bowls full of gold (for those who would play), the mules in stately trappings, velvet litters and coaches, are the vain hopes of those who are subject to whims, and dream of finding the philosopher's stone.

The Queen tastes and chews nothing : her *pragustators* and *masticators* (her tasters and chewers) do that for her; and she never visits a close-stool but by proxy. This signifies, that those who employ those cheats, who pretend to make gold, swallow every thing that comes from them without examining the sense of it, or chewing the cud upon the matter: all goes down glibly with them, so greedy they are of possessing such a mighty secret. But the alchymists, whom they trust, bestir their grinders lustily, in the meantime, and do not feed altogether on smoke, as do their patrons, who are here said never to go to stool but by proxy, because they are only fed with words and promises: all vanishes in smoke. The word *spodizator* signifies one who fairly gets soot from brass, by trying and melting it down.—*M.*

CHAPTER XXIV

HOW THERE WAS A BALL IN THE MANNER OF A TOURNAMENT, AT WHICH QUEEN WHIMS WAS PRESENT

AFTER supper there was a ball in the form of a tilt or a tournament, not only worth seeing, but also never to be forgotten. First, the floor of the hall was covered with a large piece of velveted white and yellow chequered tapestry, each chequer exactly square, and three full spans in breadth.

Then thirty-two young persons came into the hall; sixteen of them arrayed in cloth of gold; and of these, eight were young nymphs, such as the ancients described Diana's attendants : the other eight were a king, a queen, two wardens of the castle, two knights, and two archers. Those of the other band were clad in cloth of silver.

They posted themselves on the tapestry in the following manner : the kings on the last line of the fourth square ; so that the golden king was on a white square, and the silvered king on a yellow square, and each queen by her king ; the golden queen on a yellow square, and the silvered queen on a white one : and on each side stood the archers to guide their kings and queens ; by the archers the knights, and the wardens by them. In the next row before them stood the eight nymphs ; and between the two bands of nymphs four rows of squares stood empty.

Each band had its musicians, eight on each side, dressed in its livery ; the one with orange-coloured damask, the other with white ; and all played on different instruments most melodiously and harmoniously, still varying in time and measure as the figure

of the dance required. This seemed to me an admirable thing, considering the numerous diversity of
steps, back-steps, bounds, rebounds, jerks, paces,
leaps, skips, turns, coupés, hops, leadings, risings,
meetings, flights, ambuscadoes, moves, and removes.

I was also at a loss, when I strove to comprehend
how the dancers could so suddenly know what every
different note meant: for they no sooner heard this
or that sound, but they placed themselves in the
place which was denoted by the music, though their
motions were all different. For the nymphs that
stood in the first file, as if they designed to begin
the fight, marched straight forwards to their enemies
from square to square, unless it were the first step,
at which they were free to move over the two steps
at once. They alone never fall back (which is not
very natural to other nymphs) and if any of them
is so lucky as to advance to the opposite king's row,
she is immediately crowned queen of her king, and
after that, moves with the same state, and in the
same manner as the queen; but till that happens,
they never strike their enemies but forwards, and
obliquely in a diagonal line. However, they make
it not their chief business to take their foes; for if
they did, they would leave their queen exposed to
the adverse parties, who then might take her.

The kings move and take their enemies on all
sides squareways, and only step from a white square
into a yellow one, and vice versa, except at their
first step the rank should want other officers than the
wardens; for then they can set them in their place,
and retire by him.

The queens take a greater liberty than any of the
rest; for they move backwards and forwards all
manner of ways, in a straight line, as far as they
please, provided the place be not filled with one of

their own party, and diagonally also, keeping to the colour on which they stand.

The archers move backwards or forwards, far and near, never changing the colour on which they stand. The knights move, and take in a lineal manner, stepping over one square, though a friend or foe stand upon it, posting themselves on the second square to the right or left, from one colour to another, which is very unwelcome to the adverse party, and ought to be carefully observed, for they take at unawares.

The wardens move, and take to the right or left, before or behind them, like the kings, and can advance as far as they find places empty; which liberty the kings take not.

The law which both sides observe, is, at the end of the fight, to besiege and enclose the king of either party, so that he may not be able to move; and being reduced to that extremity, the battle is over, and he loses the day.

Now, to avoid this, there is none of either sex of each party, but is willing to sacrifice his or her life, and they begin to take one another on all sides in time, as soon as the music strikes up. When any one takes a prisoner, he makes his honours, and striking him gently in the hand, puts him out of the field and combat, and encamps where he stood.

If one of the kings chance to stand where he might be taken, it is not lawful for any of his adversaries that had discovered him, to lay hold on him : far from it, they are strictly enjoined humbly to pay him their respects, and give him notice, saying, God preserve you, sir ! that his officers may relieve and cover him, or he may remove, if unhappily he could not be relieved. However, he is not to be taken, but greeted with a Good-morrow !

the others bending the knee : and thus the tournament uses to end.

CHAPTER XXV

HOW THE THIRTY-TWO PERSONS AT THE BALL FOUGHT

THE two companies having taken their stations, the
music struck up, and, with a martial sound, which
had something of horrid in it, like a point of war,
roused and alarmed both parties, who now began to
shiver, and then soon were warmed with warlike rage ;
and having got in readiness to fight desperately,
impatient of delay, stood waiting for the charge.

Then the music of the silvered band ceased playing, and the instruments of the golden side alone
were heard, which denoted that the golden party at-
tacked.   Accordingly, a new movement was played
for the onset, and we saw the nymph, who stood
before the queen, turn to the left towards her king,
as it were to ask leave to fight : and thus saluting her
company at the same time, she moved two squares
forwards, and saluted the adverse party.

Now the music of the golden brigade ceased
playing, and their antagonists began again.   I ought
to have told you that the nymph, who began by
saluting her company, had by that formality also
given them to understand that they were to fall on.
She was saluted by them, in the same manner, with
a full turn to the left, except the queen, who went
aside towards her king to the right ; and the same
manner of salutation was observed on both sides
during the whole ball.

The silvered nymph that stood before her queen
likewise moved, as soon as the music of her party
sounded a charge: her salutations, and those of her
side, were to the right, and her queen's to the left.
She moved in the second square forwards, and
saluted her antagonists, facing the first golden
nymph: so that there was not any distance between
them, and you would have thought they two had
been going to fight: but they only strike sideways.

Their comrades, whether silvered or golden,
followed them in an intercalary figure, and seemed
to skirmish a while, till the golden nymph, who had
first entered the lists, striking a silvered nymph in
the hand on the right, put her out of the field, and
set herself in her place. But soon the music playing
a new measure, she was struck by a silvered archer,
who after that was obliged himself to retire. A
silvered knight then sallied out, and the golden
queen posted herself before her king.

Then the silvered king, dreading the golden
queen's fury, removed to the right, to the place
where his warden stood, which seemed to him strong
and well guarded.

The two knights on the left, whether golden or
silvered, marched up, and on either side, took up
many nymphs, who could not retreat; principally
the golden knight, who made this his whole business;
but the silvered knight had greater designs, dissembling all along, and even sometimes not taking a
nymph when he could have done it, still moving on
till he was come up to the main body of the enemies,
in such a manner, that he saluted their king with a
God save you, sir!

The whole golden brigade quaked for fear and
anger, those words giving notice of their king's
danger; not but that they could soon relieve him,

but because their king being thus saluted, they were to lose their warden on the right wing, without any hopes of a recovery. Then the golden king retired to the left, and the silver knight took the golden warden, which was a mighty loss to that party. However, they resolved to be revenged, and surrounded the knight that he might not escape. He tried to get off, behaving himself with a great deal of gallantry, and his friends did what they could to save him; but at last he fell into the golden queen's hands, and was carried off.

Her forces, not yet satisfied, having lost one of her best men, with more fury than conduct, moved about, and did much mischief among their enemies. The silvered party warily dissembled, watching their opportunity to be even with them, and presented one of their nymphs to the golden queen, having laid an ambuscado; so that the nymph being taken, a golden archer had like to have seized the silvered queen. Then the golden knight undertakes to take the silvered king and queen, and says, Goodmorrow! Then the silvered archer salutes them, and was taken by a golden nymph, and she herself by a silvered one.

The fight was obstinate and sharp. The wardens left their posts, and advanced to relieve their friends. The battle was doubtful, and victory hovered over both armies. Now the silvered host charge and break through their enemy's ranks, as far as the golden king's tent, and now they are beaten back: the golden queen distinguishes herself from the rest by her mighty achievements, still more than by her garb and dignity; for at once she takes an archer, and going sideways seizes a silvered warden. Which thing the silvered queen perceiving, she came forwards, and rushing on with equal bravery, takes the last golden warden, and some nymphs. The two queens fought a long while hand to hand; now striving to take each other by surprise, then to save themselves, and sometimes to guard their kings. Finally, the golden queen took the silvered queen; but presently after she herself was taken by the silvered archer.

Then the silvered king had only three nymphs, an archer, and a warden left, and the golden only three nymphs and the right knight, which made them fight more slowly and warily than before. The two kings seemed to mourn for the loss of their loving queens, and only studied and endeavoured to get new ones out of all their nymphs, to be raised to that dignity, and thus be married to them. This made them excite those brave nymphs to strive to reach the farthest rank, where stood the king of the contrary party, promising them certainly to have them crowned if they could do this. The golden nymphs were beforehand with the others, and out of their number was created a queen, who was dressed in royal robes, and had a crown set on her head. You need not doubt the silvered nymphs made also what haste they could to be queens: one of them was within a step of the coronation place; but there the golden knight lay ready to intercept her, so that she could go no further.

The new golden queen, resolved to show herself valiant, and worthy of her advancement to the crown, achieved great feats of arms. But, in the meantime, the silvered knight takes the golden warden who guarded the camp: and thus there was a new silvered queen, who, like the other, strove to excel in heroic deeds at the beginning of her reign. Thus the fight grew hotter than before. A thousand stratagems, charges, rallyings, retreats, and attacks, were tried on both sides; till at last the silvered queen, having by stealth advanced as far as the golden king's tent, cried, God save you, sir! Now none but his new queen could relieve him: so she bravely came and exposed herself to the utmost extremity to deliver him out of it. Then the silvered warden, with his queen, reduced the golden king to such a stress, that, to save himself, he was forced to lose his queen: but the golden king took him at last. However, the rest of the golden party were soon taken; and that king being left alone, the silvered party made him a low bow, crying, Good-morrow, sir! which denoted that the silvered king had got the day.

This being heard, the music of both parties loudly proclaimed the victory. And thus the first battle ended to the unspeakable joy of all the spectators.

After this the two brigades took their former stations, and began to tilt a second time, much as they had done before, only the music played somewhat faster than at the first battle, and the motions were altogether different. I saw the golden queen sally out one of the first, with an archer and a knight, as it were angry at the former defeat, and she had like to have fallen upon the silvered king in his tent among his officers; but having been baulked in her attempt, she skirmished briskly, and overthrew so many silvered nymphs and officers, that it was a most amazing sight. You would have sworn she had been another Penthesilea; for she behaved herself with as much bravery as that Amazonian queen did at Troy.

But this havoc did not last long; for the silvered party, exasperated by their loss, resolved to perish, or stop her progress; and having posted an archer in

ambuscado, on a distant angle, together with a
knight-errant, her highness fell into their hands,
and was carried out of the field. The rest were
soon routed after the taking of their queen, who,
without doubt, from that time resolved to be more
wary, and keep near her king, without venturing so
far amidst her enemies, unless with more force to
defend her. Thus the silver brigade once more got
the victory.

This did not dishearten or deject the golden
party: far from it, they soon appeared again in the
field to face their enemies; and being posted as
before, both the armies seemed more resolute and
cheerful than ever. Now the martial concert began,
and the music was above a hemiole the quicker,
according to the warlike Phrygian mode, such as
was invented by Marsyas.

Then our combatants began to wheel about, and
charge with such a swiftness, that in an instant they
made four moves, besides the usual salutations. So
that they were continually in action, flying, hovering,
jumping, vaulting, curveting, with petauristical turns
and motions, and often intermingled.

Seeing them then turn about on one foot after
they had made their honours, we compared them to
your tops or gigs, such as boys use to whip about;
making them turn round so swiftly, that they sleep,
as they call it, and motion cannot be perceived, but
resembles rest, its contrary: so that if you make a
point or mark on some part of one of those gigs, it
will be perceived not as a point, but a continual line
in a most divine manner, as Cusanus has wisely
observed.

While they were thus warmly engaged, we heard
continually the claps and episemapsies, which those
of the two bands reiterated at the taking of their

enemies; and this, joined to the variety of their motions and music, would have forced smiles out of the most severe Cato, the never-laughing Crassus, the Athenian man-hater, Timon: nay, even whining Heraclitus, though he abhorred laughing, the action that is most peculiar to man. For who could have forborne? seeing those young warriors, with their nymphs and queens, so briskly and gracefully advance, retire, jump, leap, skip, spring, fly, vault, caper, move to the right, to the left, every way still in time, so swiftly, and yet so dexterously, that they never touched one another but methodically.

As the number of the combatants lessened, the pleasure of the spectators increased; for the stratagems and motions of the remaining forces were more singular. I shall only add, that this pleasing entertainment charmed us to such a degree, that our minds were ravished with admiration and delight; and the martial harmony moved our souls so powerfully, that we easily believed what is said of Ismenias' having excited Alexander to rise from table and run to his arms, with such a warlike melody. At last the golden king remained master of the field: and while we were minding those dancers, Queen Whims vanished, so that we saw her no more from that day to this.

Then Geber's michelots conducted us, and we were set down among her abstractors, as her queenship had commanded. After that we returned to the port of Mateotechny, and thence straight aboard our ships: for the wind was fair, and had we not hoisted out of hand, we could hardly have got off in three quarters of a moon in the wane.

On Chaps. XXIV. and XXV.—The ball in the manner of a tournament, which was performed before the Queen, is a most lively and ingenious description of the game of chess. The floor of the hall, which is covered with a large piece of velveted white and yellow chequered tapestry, means the chequer board. The thirty-two young persons, one-half dressed in cloth of gold, and the other in cloth of silver, are the thirty-two chess-men; kings, queens, bishops, knights, rooks and pawns. They play three games ; the two first are won by the silvered king, and the last by his adversary.

Our author, who cannot be too much admired for his art in raising satirical reflections of great moment, most naturally, out of trifles where they are least expected, in the midst of this admirable allegory, seems to have reflected upon his King Francis' rashness, which made him to be taken prisoner at the battle of Pavia; for, speaking of the golden queen, who, in this latruncularian war (if I may use the expression) skirmished too boldly, and was taken, he says, the rest were soon routed after the taking of their queen; who, without doubt, from that time resolved to be more wary, and not to venture so far amidst her enemies, unless with more forces to defend her.

He also brought in very pleasantly Cardinal Cusa's boyish observation, in his simile on a top or gig ; and so he has done almost all over this work.

He is not less artful in bringing off his Pantagruelists, that they may no longer be hindered by whims from arriving at the Oracle of Truth: for he says, that while they minded this pleasing entertainment, and were charmed with the melody that played to the dancers, Queen Whims vanished; and they straight went on board their ships, the wind being fair: for had they not set sail immediately, they could hardly have got off in three quarters of a·moon in the wane. That is to say, by the means of music, ingenious games, dancing, and other innocent recreations, many ease their minds of perplexing thoughts, and leave those crabbed, whimsical, unprofitable studies, which wholly possessed them before; for those idle busy fancies vanish, like the evil spirit of Saul, at the harmonious sound of instruments: but should not the mind, after this, be immediately applied to some solid inquiries that may engross all its faculties, it would be in danger of being taken up again with unnecessary and uncertain businesses.

It is observable that Rabelais has made these chapters very clear, and almost sufficient to teach a man to play at chess; that his satirical allegories throughout the work, which are darker, might be thought of no greater moment than this ball and tournament.—*M.*

CHAPTER XXVI

HOW WE CAME TO THE ISLAND OF ODES, WHERE THE WAYS GO UP AND DOWN

WE sailed before the wind, between a pair of courses, and in two days made the Island of Odes, at which place we saw a very strange thing. The ways there are animals; so true is Aristotle's saying, that all self-moving things are animals. Now the ways walk there. Ergo, they are then animals. Some of them are strange unknown ways, like those of the planets; others are highways, crossways, and bye-ways. I perceived that the travellers and inhabitants of that country asked—Whither does this way go? Whither does that way go? Some answered, between Midy and Fevrolles, to the parish church, to the city, to the river, and so forth. Being thus in their right way, they used to reach their journey's end without any further trouble, just like those who go by water from Lyons to Avignon or Arles.

Now, as you know that nothing is perfect here below, we heard there was a sort of people whom they called highwaymen, way-beaters, and makers of inroads in roads; and that the poor ways were sadly afraid of them, and shunned them as you do robbers. For these used to waylay them, as people lay trains for wolves, and set gins for woodcocks. I saw one who was taken up with a lord chief justice's warrant, for having unjustly, and in spite of Pallas, taken the schoolway, which is the longest. Another boasted that he had fairly taken the shortest, and that doing so, he first compassed his design. Thus, Carpalim, meeting once Epistemon looking upon a wall with his fiddle-diddle, or live urinal, in his hand, to make a little maid's water, cried, that he did not wonder now how the other came to be still the first at Pantagruel's levee, since he held his shortest and least used.

I found Bourges highway among these. It went with the deliberation of an abbot, but was made to scamper at the approach of some waggoners, who threatened to have it trampled under their horses' feet, and make their waggons run over it, as Tullia's chariot did over her father's body.

I also espied there the old way between Peronne and St Quentin, which seemed to me a very good, honest, plain way, as smooth as a carpet, and as good as ever was trod upon by shoe of leather.

Among the rocks I knew again the good old way to La Ferrare, mounted on a huge bear. This at a distance would have put me in mind of St Jerome's picture, had but the bear been a lion; for the poor way was all mortified, and wore a long hoary beard uncombed and entangled, which looked like the picture of winter, or at least like a white-frosted bush.

On that way were store of beads or rosaries, coarsely made of wild pine-tree; and it seemed kneeling, not standing, nor lying flat; but its sides and middle were beaten with huge stones, insomuch that it proved to us at once an object of fear and pity.

While we were examining it, a runner, bachelor of the place, took us aside, and showing us a white smooth way, somewhat filled with straw, said, Henceforth, gentlemen, do not reject the opinion of Thales the Milesian, who said that water is the beginning of all things; nor that of Homer, who tells us that all things derive their original from the ocean: for this same way which you see here had its beginning from water, and is to return whence she came, before two months come to an end; now carts are driven here where boats used to be rowed.

Truly, said Pantagruel, you tell us no news; we see five hundred such changes, and more, every year, in our world. Then reflecting on the different manner of going of those moving ways, he told us he believed that Philolaus and Aristarchus had philosophised in this island, and that Seleucus, indeed, was of opinion, the earth turns round about its poles, and not the heavens, whatever we may think to the contrary: As, when we are on the river Loire, we think the trees and the shore move, though this is only an effect of our boat's motion.

As we went back to our ships, we saw three way-layers, who, having been taken in ambuscado, were going to be broken on the wheel; and a huge fornicator was burned with a lingering fire, for beating away and breaking one of its sides: we were told it was the way of the banks of the Nile in Egypt.

ON CHAP. XXVI.—The Island of Odes, where the ways go up and down, is the subject of this chapter. The author seems partly inclined to droll, by the means of an hypallagical expression, used by the English as well as by the French; while, speaking of a way or road, we ask, whither it goes? instead of asking, to what place men go by that way? He takes thence an opportunity to banter Aristotle's saying, that all self-moving things are animals.

By-the-bye, he gives a touch to the schoolmen, when he says, that he saw one taken up with a warrant, for having, in spite of Pallas (invitâ Minerva), taken the schoolway, which is the longest. What he says of Bourges highway, which went with the deliberation of an abbot, must be understood of that university, famous for the study of the civil law.

He calls it the Island of Odes, from 'Οδὸς, which signifies a way or road; a conveniency to forward us in a journey, as a waggon, boat, etc.; a way or rule of living; a method; and finally, an ambush on a road by robbers.—M.

CHAPTER XXVII

HOW WE CAME TO THE ISLAND OF SANDALS; AND OF THE ORDER OF SEMIQUAVER FRIARS

THENCE we went to the Island of Sandals, whose inhabitants live on nothing but ling-broth. However, we were very kindly received and entertained by Benius the Third, king of the island, who, after he had made us drink, took us with him to show us a spick-and-span new monastery, which he had contrived for the Semiquaver Friars: so he called the religious men whom he had there. For he said that, on the other side of the water lived friars who styled themselves her sweet ladyship's most humble servants. Item, the goodly Friar-minors, who are semibreves of bulls; the smoked-herring tribe of Minim Friars; then the Crotchet Friars. So that these diminutives could be no more than Semiquavers. By the statutes, bulls, and patents of Queen Whims, they were all dressed like so many house-burners, except that, as in Anjou your tilers used to quilt their knees when they tile houses, so these holy friars had usually quilted bellies, and thick quilted paunches were among them in much repute. Their codpieces were cut slipper-fashion, and every monk among them wore two—one sewed before and another behind—reporting that some certain dreadful mysteries were duly represented by this duplicity of codpieces.

They wore shoes as round as basons, in imitation of those who inhabit the sandy sea. Their chins were close-shaved, and their feet iron-shod; and to show they did not value fortune, Benius made them shave and poll the hind part of their polls, as bare as a bird's arse, from the crown to the shoulder-blades; but they had leave to let their hair grow before, from the two triangular bones in the upper part of the skull.

Thus did they not value Fortune a button, and cared no more for the goods of this world than you or I do for hanging. And to show how much they defied that blind jilt, all of them wore, not in their hands like her, but at their waist, instead of beads, sharp razors, which they used to new grind twice a day, and set thrice a night.

Each of them had a round ball on their feet, because Fortune is said to have one under hers.

The flap of their cowls hanged forward, and not backwards, like those of others; thus, none could see their noses, and they laughed without fear both at fortune and the fortunate; neither more nor less than our ladies laugh at bare-faced trulls, when they have those mufflers on, which they call masks, and which were formerly much more properly called charity, because they cover a multitude of sins.

The hind part of their heads was always uncovered, as are our faces, which made them either go with the belly or the arse foremost, which they pleased. When their hind face went forwards, you would have sworn this had been their natural gait, as well on account of their round shoes as of the double cod-piece, and their face behind, which was as bare as the back of my hand, and coarsely daubed over with two eyes and a mouth, such as you see on some Indian nuts. Now, if they offered to waddle along with their bellies forwards, you would have then thought they were playing at blindman's buff. May I never be hanged if it was not a comical sight.

Their way of living was thus. About owl-light they charitably began to boot and spur one another; this being done, the least thing they did was to sleep and snore; and thus sleeping, they had barnacles on the handles of their faces, or spectacles at most.

You may swear we did not a little wonder at this odd fancy: but they satisfied us presently, telling us that the day of judgment is to take mankind napping; therefore, to show they did not refuse to make their personal appearance, as Fortune's darlings used to do, they were always thus booted and spurred, ready to mount whenever the trumpet should sound.

At noon, as soon as the clock struck, they used to awake. You must know that their clock bell, church bells, and refectuary bells, were all made according to the pontial device, that is, quilted with the finest down, and their clappers of fox tails.

Having then make shift to get up at noon, they pulled off their boots, and those that wanted to speak with a maid, *alias* piss, pissed; those that wanted to scumber, scumbered; and those that wanted to sneeze, sneezed. But all, whether they would or no (poor gentlemen!), were obliged largely and plentifully to yawn; and this was their first breakfast (O rigorous statute!). Methought it was very comical to observe their transactions: for, having laid their boots and spurs on a rack, they went into the cloisters; there they curiously washed their hands and mouths, then sat them down on a long bench, and picked their teeth till the provost gave the signal, whistling through his fingers; then every he stretched out his jaws as much as he could, and they gaped and yawned for about half-an-hour, sometimes more, sometimes less, according as the prior judged the breakfast to be suitable to the day.

After that they went in procession, two banners being carried before them, in one of which was the picture of Virtue, and that of Fortune in the other. The last went before, carried by a semi-

quavering friar, at whose heels was another, with
the shadow or image of Virtue in one hand, and
an holy-water-sprinkle in the other; I mean of
that holy mercurial water, which Ovid describes
in his Fasti. And as the preceding Semiquaver
rang a hand-bell, this shaked the sprinkle with his
fist. With that, says Pantagruel, This order contradicts the rule which Tully and the academics
prescribed, that Virtue ought to go before, and
Fortune follow. But they told us they did as they
ought, seeing their design was to breech, lash, and
bethwack Fortune.

During the processions, they trilled and quavered
most melodiously betwixt their teeth, I do not know
what antiphonies, or chauntings, by turns; for my
part, it was all Hebrew-Greek to me, the devil
a word I could pick out of it; at last, pricking up
my ears, and intensely listening, I perceived they
only sang with the tip of theirs. Oh, what a rare
harmony it was! How well it was tuned to the
sound of their bells! You will never find those
to jar, that you will not. Pantagruel made a
notable observation upon the processions: For, says
he, have you seen and observed the policy of these
Semiquavers? To make an end of their procession,
they went out at one of their church doors and
came in at the other; they took a deal of care
not to come in at the place whereat they went out.
On my honour, these are a subtle sort of people,
quoth Panurge; they have as much wit as three
folks, two fools and a madman; they are as wise
as the calf that ran nine miles to suck a bull,
and when he came there it was a steer. This
subtilty and wisdom of theirs, cried Friar John,
is borrowed from the occult philosophy: may I
be gutted like an oyster if I can tell what to make

of it. Then the more it is to be feared, said
Pantagruel; for subtilty suspected, subtilty foreseen,
subtilty found out, loses the essence and very name
of subtilty, and only gains that of blockishness.
They are not such fools as you take them to be;
they have more tricks than are good, I doubt.

After the procession they went sluggingly into
the fratry-room, by the way of walk and healthful
exercise, and there kneeled under the tables, leaning
their breasts on lanterns. While they were in that
posture, in came a huge Sandal, with a pitchfork
in his hand, who used to baste, rib-roast, swaddle,
and swinge them well-favouredly, as they said,
and in truth treated them after a fashion. They
began their meal as you end yours—with cheese,
and ended it with mustard and lettuce, as Martial
tells us the ancients did. Afterwards, a platter full
of mustard was brought before every one of them,
and thus they made good the proverb—after meat
comes mustard.

Their diet was this :

On Sundays they stuffed their puddings with
puddings, chitterlings, links, Bologna sausages, forced-
meats, liverings, hogs'-haslets, young quails, and
teals : you must also always add cheese for the first
course, and mustard for the last.

On Mondays they were crammed with pease and
pork, cum commento, and interlineary glosses.

On Tuesdays they used to twist store of holy-
bread, cakes, buns, puffs, lenten loaves, jumbals,
and biscuits.

On Wednesdays my gentlemen had fine sheep's-
heads, calves'-heads, and brocks'-heads, of which
there is no want in that country.

On Thursdays they guzzled down seven sorts of
porridge, not forgetting mustard.

On Fridays they munched nothing but services or sorb-apples; neither were these full ripe, as I guessed by their complexion.

On Saturdays they gnawed bones; not that they were poor or needy, for every mother's son of them had a very good fat belly-benefice.

As for their drink, it was an antifortunal; thus they called I do not know what sort of a liquor of the place.

When they wanted to eat or drink, they turned down the back-points or flaps of their cowls forwards, below their chins, and that served them instead of gorgets or slabbering-bibs.

When they had well dined, they prayed rarely all in quavers and shakes; and the rest of the day, expecting the day of judgment, they were taken up with acts of charity, and particularly

On Sundays, rubbers at cuffs.

On Mondays, lending each other flirts and fillips on the nose.

On Tuesdays, clapperclawing one another.

On Wednesdays, sniting and fly-flapping.

On Thursdays, worming and pumping.

On Fridays, tickling.

On Saturdays, jerking and firking one another.

Such was their diet when they resided in the convent, and if the prior of the monk-house sent any of them abroad, then they were strictly enjoined neither to touch nor eat any manner of fish, as long as they were on sea or rivers, and to abstain from all manner of flesh whenever they were at land; that every one might be convinced that, while they enjoyed the object, they denied themselves the power, and even the desire, and were no more moved with it than the Marpesian rock.

All this was done with proper antiphones, still

sung and chaunted by ear, as we have already
observed.

When the sun went to bed, they fairly booted
and spurred each other as before, and having
clapped on their barnacles, even jogged to bed too.
At midnight the Sandal came to them, and up they
got, and having well whetted and set their razors,
and been a-processioning, they clapped the tables
over themselves, and like wire-drawers under their
work, fell to it as aforesaid.

Friar John des Entonneures, having shrewdly
observed these jolly Semiquaver friars, and had a
full account of their statutes, lost all patience, and
cried out aloud—Bounce tail! and God have mercy
guts! if every fool should wear a bauble, fuel would
be dear. A plague rot it! we must know how
many farts go to an ounce. Would Priapus were
here, as he used to be at the nocturnal festivals
in Crete, that I might see him play backwards, and
wriggle and shake to the purpose. Ay, ay! this
is the world, and that other is the country; may
I never piss if this be not an antichthonian land,
and our very antipodes. In Germany they pull
down monasteries and unfrockify the monks; here
they go quite kam, and act clean contrary to others,
setting new ones up, against the hair.

On Chap. XXVII.—The Island of the Sandals is the next
place which our travellers visit. Rabelais calls it *l'isle des
Esclots*. Esclot is a patten, sandal, or a wooden shoe in some
parts of France, particularly towards Toulouse; so because it
is the dwelling of friars, and many of them wear sandals or
clogs, I call it the Island of Sandals. Yet as the word *esclop*
was formerly used in France for *esclave*, a slave, I am persuaded
that our author gave that name of *esclot* to this island, chiefly
to disguise his intent, which was to tell us that its inhabitants
are *esclops*, slaves: for such all monks become to the will of
their superiors, by the vow of obedience which they are obliged
to make at their admission into their respective sodalities. All

this chapter is a most cutting satire on monachism in general, and seems to reflect particularly on the Jesuits; but the author has affected to be mystical all along, in what may be applied to them.

The Jesuits may well be called slaves, considering their rules; some of which are these, exhibited in *Exercita spiritualia Ign. Loyolæ*, printed at Antwerp, ' They must abandon all judgment of their own, be always ready to obey the Church of Rome, and believe that black is white, and white is black, if she says it: they ought to regard the command of their superior, as that of God himself, and submit to his government, as though they were mere machines, or an old man's staff, to be moved at his pleasure.'

It was upon this account that Pope Paul III. confirmed the establishment of their society, which was not to exceed sixty, in 1540, about ten years before Rabelais wrote this book.   The time of their institution agrees very well with what Rabelais says, that Benius III. showed a spick-and-span new monastery to our travellers, contrived by him for the Semiquaver friars.   What is added may refer to all monks and friars in general.

By the statutes, bulls, and patents of Queen Whims, they were all dressed like so many house-burners: this reflects first on the Pope and his bulls, as being whimsical, for setting up new monasteries against the hair, while many pull them down; and then implies that they burn the houses where they come; wasting the substance of families, and blowing up the fire of division everywhere.

Their quilted paunches show that they love to stuff their hides to the purpose.

Their double codpieces, one before and the other behind, show, that many a monk, and particularly a Jesuit, is *ad utrumque paratus; à parte post et à parte ante*; and may well say *hanc veniam petimusque damusque vicissim*. This abominable practice of theirs made the author say, that some dreadful mysteries were duly represented by this duplicity of codpieces; and as he speaks in the plural, they may also imply, that a monk does as much work as two others at the venereal exercise.

Their shoes are round; that they may move forward, backward, or sideways, as their interest guides them.

Their chins are close-shaven; to show there is no holding or fleecing a monk; or, to speak more plainly, nothing to be got by them.

Their feet are iron-shod; because there is no driving them out when once they get footing: for they stick close, and firmly keep their hold.

They shave the hind parts of their polls, from the crown to

the omoplata, or the muscles of the shoulder-blade; that none may take hold of them behind.

They wear sharp razors at their waist. This may mean a good stomach, or that they cut to the quick whatever lies in their way.

They grind them twice a day, and set them thrice a night; by the means of their matins, vigils, the office of the day, etc.

They have a round ball on their feet. This ball is the world, which they would gladly bring under their subjection: neither is it strange it should be said to be on their feet, in opposition to Fortune that has a ball under hers. For, it is said by Friar John, at the end of the chapter; Ay, ay, this is the world, and the other is the country: may I never piss, if this be not an antichthonian land; and our very antipodes. So that, according to the vulgar acceptation, supposing the earth to be here under our feet, it must be on or above our antipodes.

The flaps of their cowls hide their noses; so they laugh without fear both at Fortune and the fortunate: that is, within their monasteries, they laugh in their sleeves at those whose good fortune enables them, and whose foolishness inclines them, to help to maintain them in their idleness.

The hind-parts of their heads are always uncovered; as are our faces, and coarsely daubed over with eyes and a mouth: which denotes the grimaces and antic tricks with which they amuse the silly people, in a manner only showing their backside to them, while, as we have said, they really laugh to one another at the gulled mob's simplicity.

When their hind face went forward, you would have sworn this had been their natural gait: that is, by their vow of poverty they grow rich, rule by their vow of obedience, are the lewder for their vow of chastity, and get forward when they seem to lose ground.

If they offered to waddle along with their bellies forwards, you would have thought they were then playing at blind-man's-buff: because they are not used to walk fairly, or act like other people, and are to seek when they must leave their crooked ways, and go the right way to work.

They are booted and spurred, as it were, to take a journey to heaven; but instead of hastening thither on horseback, they sleep and snore as soon as it is owl-light.

They are obliged to yawn, and that is their breakfast. This implies their laziness, and perhaps the singing or bawling at matins.

They wash their hands and mouths. This may be the taking of holy water.

Then they sit down on a long bench, and pick their teeth, till the provost gives the signal; which heard, they stretch out their jaws as wide as they can, and gape and yawn for about half-an-hour, more or less, according to the day. This may mean their sitting down, while the office of the day is read, and then their singing and quavering.

After this, they went in procession, going out at another door than that through which they came into the church: whence Pantagruel concludes, that they are not such fools as his attendants take them to be, having more holes than one to creep out at.

> Cogitato mus pusillus quam sit sapiens bestia,
> Ætatem qui uni cubili nunquam committit suam;
> Quia si unum ostium obsideatur, aliud perfugium quærit.
>
> PLAUTUS, *Must*. act. 4.

At the procession, the idol of Fortune is carried in state, and the image of Virtue follows it, carried by a Semiquaver, who all the while besprinkles the idol with holy water: which shows that Fortune goes before Virtue among the monks, and that they are lavish of their incense to none but the fortunate.

After the procession, they went into the fratry-room, and there kneeled under the tables; because it is the heaven where reside the only gods they adore, placed in the dishes as on so many thrones. This way of explaining this dark passage, appears the more justifiable, considering what Pantagruel says, in the 34th chapter, to the illustrious lantern that guided him and his company through an arbour covered over with leaves and branches of vines, and loaded with clusters. 'Jupiter's priestess,' said he, 'would not, like us, have walked under this arbour.' 'There was a mystical reason,' answered the most conspicuous lantern, 'that would have hindered her ; for had she gone under it, the wine, or the grapes of which it is made, that is the same thing, had been over her head, and then she would have seemed over-topped and mastered by wine ; which signifies,' etc.

They had each of them a lantern below the breast and stomach, on which they leaned. The lantern should be an empty belly: for after their breakfast, which consisted only of yawning, chanting, and quavering, they had not so filled themselves as not to want to stuff the gut.

The huge Sandal, who, while they were in that posture, used to come in with a pitchfork in his hand, and treated them after a fashion, is the friar, who always comes in with a book, in which he reads while they are at table.

They begin their meal with cheese, and end it with mustard and lettuce. This shows, like most of this chapter, that these

Semiquavers affect a way of living quite contrary to other men's; and as cheese is esteemed heavy food, and hard to be digested, when much of it is eaten, principally by itself, and before we are filled with other things, whose digestion it might help; so by cheese may be meant the benedicite, or grace before meat, which is as heavy, tedious, and irksome to the gluttonous hungry fraternity, as a long-winded Presbyterian grace to a half-famished libertine, when dinner is upon the table.

The mustard and lettuce, with which they end the meal, is the agimus, or grace after meat, almost as unpleasant to the Semiquavers, who think it unseasonable, because they are in haste to go about the recreations mentioned in the next chapter.   Our author, according to his custom of hiding his touches of the satire in equivocal expressions, may mean, that this ceremony after dinner, *moult tarde, multum tardat,* is tedious, and *les tue,* is death to them; thus punning upon *moutarde* and *laitue.*

After dinner, they pass some time in praising those gods who blessed them with so sweet a life, and are taken up the rest of the day with acts of charity; as rubbers at cuffs, sniting and fly-flapping, worming and pumping, tickling, jerking, and firking one another; and such other pious deeds, as are contained in the twenty-eighth chapter.

Then at night they boot and spur each other (by which something very odious seems meant), and clap their barnacles on the handles of their faces; which may imply that they are obliged to look about them, for fear of being discovered.

At midnight they are called up by one of their brother Sandals, and do as in the daytime.

When they are on the sea and rivers, they are enjoined neither to touch nor eat any manner of fish; and to abstain from all manner of flesh when they are at land.   That is, monks use to seem kind to those who are near them, and who support them, and only bite the absent: yet even this is not always true; but it is more certain, that as they are dainty, they long for things that are not easily got; as for example, fresh meat at sea, and fresh fish at land, chiefly in such inland places as are very remote from seas or rivers.—*M.*

CHAPTER XXVIII

HOW PANURGE ASKED A SEMIQUAVER FRIAR MANY
QUESTIONS, AND WAS ONLY ANSWERED IN MONO-
SYLLABLES

PANURGE, who had since been wholly taken up with
staring at these royal Semiquavers, at last pulled one
of them by the sleeve, who was as lean as·a rake,[1]
and asked him,—

Harkee me, Friar Quaver, Semiquaver, Demi-
semiquavering quaver, where is the punk !

The Friar, pointing downwards, answered, There.

PAN. Pray, have you many ? FRI. Few.

PAN. How many scores have you ? FRI. One.

PAN. How many would you have ? FRI. Five.

PAN. Where do you hide them ? FRI. Here.

PAN. I suppose they are not all of one age ; but,
pray, how is their shape ? FRI. Straight.

PAN. Their complexion ? FRI. Clear.

PAN. Their hair ? FRI. Fair.

PAN. Their eyes ? FRI. Black.

PAN. Their features ? FRI. Good.

PAN. Their brows ? FRI. Soft.

PAN. Their graces ? FRI. Ripe.

PAN. Their looks ? FRI. Free.

PAN. Their feet ? FRI. Flat.

PAN. Their heels ? FRI. Short.

PAN. Their lower parts ? FRI. Rare.

PAN. And their arms ? FRI. Long.

PAN. What do they wear on their hands ? FRI.
Gloves.

[1] As a dried red-herring devil, in the original.

PAN. What sort of rings on their fingers ? FRI. Gold.

PAN. What rigging do you keep them in ? FRI. Cloth.

PAN. What sort of cloth is it ? FRI. New.

PAN. What colour ? FRI. Sky.

PAN. What kind of cloth is it ? FRI. Fine.

PAN. What caps do they wear ? FRI. Blue.

PAN. What is the colour of their stockings ? FRI. Red.

PAN. What wear they on their feet ? FRI. Pumps.

PAN. How do they use to be ? FRI. Foul.

PAN. How do they use to walk ? FRI. Fast.

PAN. Now let us talk of the kitchen, I mean that of the harlots, and without going hand over head, let us a little examine things by particulars. What is in their kitchens ? FRI. Fire.

PAN. What fuel feeds it ? FRI. Wood.

PAN. What sort of wood is it ? FRI. Dry.

PAN. And of what kind of trees ? FRI. Yew.

PAN. What are the faggots and brushes of ? FRI. Holme.

PAN. What wood do you burn in your chambers ? FRI. Pine.

PAN. And of what other trees ? FRI. Lime.

PAN. Harkee me ; as for the buttocks, I will go your halves : pray, how do you feed them ? FRI. Well.

PAN. First, what do they eat ? FRI. Bread.

PAN. Of what complexion ? FRI. White.

PAN. And what else ? FRI. Meat.

PAN. How do they love it dressed ? FRI. Roast.

PAN. What sort of porridge ? FRI. None.

PAN. Are they for pies and tarts ? FRI. Much.

PAN. Then I am their man. Will fish go down with them ? FRI. Well.

Pan. And what else? Fri. Eggs.
Pan. How do they like them? Fri. Boiled.
Pan. How must they be done? Fri. Hard.
Pan. Is this all they have? Fri. No.
Pan. What have they besides, then? Fri. Beef.
Pan. And what else? Fri. Pork.
Pan. And what more? Fri. Geese.
Pan. What then? Fri. Ducks.
Pan. And what besides? Fri. Cocks.
Pan. What do they season their meat with? Fri. Salt.
Pan. What sauce are they most dainty for? Fri. Must.
Pan. What is their last course? Fri. Rice.
Pan. And what else? Fri. Milk.
Pan. What besides? Fri. Peas.
Pan. What sort? Fri. Green.
Pan. What do they boil with them? Fri. Pork.
Pan. What food do they eat? Fri. Good.
Pan. How? Fri. Raw.
Pan. What do they end with? Fri. Nuts.
Pan. How do they drink? Fri. Neat.
Pan. What liquor? Fri. Wine.
Pan. What sort? Fri. White.
Pan. In winter? Fri. Strong.
Pan. In the spring? Fri. Brisk.
Pan. In summer? Fri. Cool.
Pan. In autumn. Fri. New.

Buttock of a monk! cried Friar John, how plump these plaguey trulls, these arch Semiquavering strumpets must be! That damned cattle are so high fed that they must needs be high-mettled, and ready to wince, and give two ups for one go-down, when any one offers to ride them below the crupper.

Prythee, Friar John! quoth Panurge, hold thy
prating tongue, stay till I have done.

Till what time do the doxies sit up? FRI.
Night.

PAN. When do they get up? FRI. Late.

PAN. May I ride on a horse that was foaled of an
acorn, if this be not as honest a cod as ever the
ground went upon, and as grave as an old gate-post
into the bargain. Would to the blessed St Semiquaver, and the blessed worthy virgin St Semi-
quavera, he were lord chief president (justice) of
Paris. Obsbodikins! how he would dispatch!
With what expedition would he bring disputes
to an upshot! What an abbreviator and clawer
of law-suits, reconciler of differences, examiner
and fumbler of bags, peruser of bills, scribbler of
rough drafts, and an engrosser of deeds, would he
not make! Well, Friar, spare your breath to
cool your porridge: come, let us now talk with
deliberation, fairly and softly, as lawyers go to
heaven. Let us know how you victual the venereal camp. How is the snatchblatch? FRI.
Rough.

PAN. How is the gateway? FRI. Free.

PAN. And how is it within? FRI. Deep.

PAN. I mean, what weather is it there? FRI.
Hot.

PAN. What shadows the brooks? FRI. Groves.

PAN. Of what is the colour of the twigs? FRI.
Red.

PAN. And that of the old? FRI. Grey.

PAN. How are you when you shake? FRI.
Brisk.

PAN. How is their motion? FRI. Quick.

PAN. Would you have them vault or wriggle
more? FRI. Less.

Pan. What kind of tools are yours? Fri. Big.

Pan. And in their helves? Fri. Round.

Pan. Of what colour is the tip? Fri. Red.

Pan. When they have been used, how are, they? Fri. Shrunk.

Pan. How much weighs each bag of tools? Fri. Pounds.

Pan. How hang your pouches? Fri. Tight.

Pan. How are they when you have done? Fri. Lank.

Pan. Now, by the oath you have taken, tell me, when you have a mind to cohabit, how you throw them. Fri. Down.

Pan. And what do they say then? Fri. Fie!

Pan. However, like maids, they say nay, and take it; and speak the less, but think the more; minding the work in hand : do they not? Fri. True.

Pan. Do they get you bairns? Fri. None.

Pan. How do you pig together? Fri. Bare.

Pan. Remember you are upon your oath, and tell me justly, and bonâ fide, how many times a day you monk it? Fri. Six.

Pan. How many bouts a-nights? Fri. Ten.

Catso! quoth Friar John, the poor fornicating brother is bashful, and sticks at sixteen, as if that were his stint. Right, quoth Panurge, but couldst thou keep pace with him, Friar John, my dainty cod? May the devil's dam suck my teat, if he does not look as if he had got a blow over the nose with a Naples cowl-staff.[1]

Pan. Pray, Friar Shakewell, does your whole fraternity quaver and shake at that rate? Fri. All.

Pan. Who of them is the best cock of the game? Fri. I.

[1] *Lux Venerea.*

PAN. Do you never commit dry-bobs or flashes in the pan ? FRI. None.

PAN. I blush like any black dog, and could be as testy as an old cook, when I think on all this ; it passes my understanding. But, pray, when you have been pumped dry one day, what have you got the next ? FRI. More.

PAN. By Priapus ! they have the Indian herb, of which Theophrastus spoke, or I am much out. But harkee me, thou man of brevity, should some impediment, honestly, or otherwise, impair your talents, and cause your benevolence to lessen, how would it fare with you, then ? FRI. Ill.

PAN. What would the wenches do ? FRI. Rail.

PAN. What if you skipped, and let them fast a whole day ? FRI. Worse.

PAN. What do you give them then ? FRI. Thwacks.

PAN. What say they to this ? FRI. Bawl.

PAN. And what else ? FRI. Curse.

PAN. How do you correct them ? FRI. Hard.

PAN. What do you get out of them then ? FRI. Blood.

PAN. How is their complexion then ? FRI. Odd.

PAN. What do they mend it with ? FRI. Paint.

PAN. Then, what do they do ? FRI. Fawn.

PAN. By the oath you have taken, tell me truly, what time of the year do you do it least in ? FRI. Now.[2]

PAN. What season do you do it best in ? FRI. March.

PAN. How is your performance the rest of the year ! FRI. Brisk.

Then, quoth Panurge, sneering, Of all, and of all, commend me to Ball ; this is the friar of the world

[2] August.

for my money : you have heard how short, concise, and compendious he is in his answers ? Nothing is to be got out of him but monosyllables ? By jingo ! I believe he would make three bites of a cherry.

Damn him ! cried Friar John, that is as true as I am his uncle : the dog yelps at anothergates rate when he is among his bitches ; there he is polysyllable enough, my life for yours. You talk of making three bites of a cherry ! God send fools more wit, and us more money ; may I be doomed to fast a whole day, if I do not verily believe he would not make above two bites of a shoulder of mutton, and one swoop of a whole pottle of wine ; zoons, do but see how down of the mouth the cur looks ! He is nothing but skin and bones, he has pissed his tallow.

Truly, truly, quoth Epistemon, this rascally monastical vermin all over the world mind nothing but their gut, and are as ravenous as any kites, and then, forsooth, they tell us they have nothing but food and raiment in this world : 'sdeath, what more have kings and princes ?

On Chap. XXVIII.—Panurge asks a Semiquaver friar many questions concerning the private customs of the monastic tribe, particularly their chastity and sobriety: to which the good friar, in more than laconic terms, gives serious and most pertinent answers: and though nothing but monosyllables can be got from him, he speaks so fully, clearly, and to the purpose, that all the twenty-eighth chapter needs no commentary. By this affected brevity, Rabelais ridicules that of some of the hypocritical monks, when they come among the laity; which makes Friar John say, the dog yelps at another-guess rate when he is among his bitches; there he is polysyllable enough, my life for yours.—M.

CHAPTER XXIX

HOW EPISTEMON DISLIKED THE INSTITUTION OF LENT

PRAY did you observe, continued Epistemon, how this damned ill-favoured Semiquaver mentioned March as the best month for caterwauling. True, said Pantagruel, yet Lent and March always go together, and the first was instituted to macerate and bring down our pampered flesh, to weaken and subdue its lusts, and to curb and assuage the venereal rage.

By this, said Epistemon, you may guess what kind of a Pope it was who first enjoined it to be kept, since this filthy wooden-shoed Semiquaver owns that his spoon is never oftener nor deeper in the porringer of lechery than in Lent. Add to this, the evident reasons given by all good and learned physicians, affirming, that throughout the whole year no food is eaten, that can prompt mankind to lascivious acts, more than at that time.

As for example, beans, peas, phasels, or long-peason, ciches, onions, nuts, oysters, herrings, salt-meats, garum (a kind of anchovy), and salads, wholly made up of venereous herbs and fruits, as,

Rocket,	Parsley,	Hop-buds,
Nose-smart,	Rampions,	Figs,
Taragon,	Poppy,	Rice,
Cresses,	Celery,	Raisins, and others.

It would not a little surprise you, said Pantagruel, should a man tell you, that the good Pope, who first ordered the keeping of Lent, perceiving that at that time of the year the natural heat (from the centre of the body, whither it was retired during the winter's cold) diffuses itself, as the sap does in trees, through

the circumference of the members, did therefore in
a manner prescribe that sort of diet to forward the
propagation of mankind. What makes me think so,
is, that by the registers of christenings at Tours, it
appears that more children are born in October and
November than in the other ten months of the year,
and, reckoning backwards, it will be easily found
that they were all made, conceived, and begotten in
Lent.

I listen to you with both my ears, quoth Friar
John, and that with no small pleasure, I assure you.
But I must tell you, that the vicar of Jambert
ascribed this copious prolification of the women,
not to that sort of food that we chiefly eat in Lent,
but to the little licensed stooping members, your
little-booted Lent-preachers, your little draggle-
tailed father confessors, who, during all that time
of their reign, damn all husbands that run astray,
three fathoms and a half below the very lowest pit
of hell. So the silly cod's-headed brothers of the
noose dare not then stumble any more at the truckle-
bed, to the no small discomfort of their maids, and
are even forced, poor souls, to take up with their
own bodily wives. *Dixi*, I have done.

You may descant on the institution of Lent as
much as you please, cried Epistemon ; so many men
so many minds ; but certainly all the physicians
will be against its being suppressed, though I think
that time is at hand : I know they will, and have
heard them say, were it not for Lent, their art
would soon fall into contempt, and they would get
nothing, for hardly anybody would be sick.

All distempers are sowed in Lent ; it is the true
seminary and native bed of all diseases ; nor does it
only weaken and putrefy bodies, but also makes
souls mad and uneasy. For then the devils do their

best, and drive a subtle trade, and the tribe of canting dissemblers come out of their holes. It is then term-time with your cucullated pieces of formality, that have one face to God and the other to the devil; and a wretched clutter they make with their sessions, stations, pardons, syntereses, confessions, whippings, anathematisations, and much prayer, with as little devotion. However, I will not offer to infer from this that the Arimaspians are better than we are in that point; yet I speak to the purpose.

Well, quoth Panurge to the Semiquaver friar, who happened to be by, dear bumbasting, shaking, trilling, quavering cod, what thinkest thou of this fellow? Is he not a rank heretic? FRI. Much.

PAN. Ought he not to be singed? FRI. Well.

PAN. As soon as may be? FRI. Right.

PAN. Should not he be scalded first? FRI. No.

PAN. How then, should he be roasted? FRI. Quick.

PAN. Till at last he be? FRI. Dead.

PAN. What has he made you? FRI. Mad.

PAN. What do you take him to be? FRI. Damned.

PAN. What place is he to go to? FRI. Hell.

PAN. But, first, how would you have him served here? FRI. Burnt.

PAN. Some have been served so? FRI. Store.

PAN. That were heretics? FRI. Less.

PAN. And the number of those that are to be warmed thus hereafter is? FRI. Great.

PAN. How many of them do you intend to save? FRI. None.

PAN. So you would have them burned? FRI. All.

I wonder, said Epistemon to Panurge, what pleasure you can find in talking thus with this

lousy tatterdemallion of a monk; I vow! did I
not know you well, I might be ready to think you
had no more wit in your head, than he has in both
his shoulders.   Come, come, scatter no words,
returned Panurge, every one as they like, as the
woman said when she kissed her cow.   I wish I
might carry him to Gargantua : when I am married
he might be my wife's fool.   And make you one,
cried Epistemon.   Well said, quoth Friar John :
now, poor Panurge, take that along with thee, thou
art even fitted ; it is a plain case thou wilt never
escape wearing the bull's feather ; thy wife will be
as common as the highway, that is certain.

On Chap. **XXIX.**—This chapter is full of reflections upon the
keeping of Lent, occasioned by the answers of the Semiquaver,
who concludes in monosyllables that Epistemon ought to be
burnt for a rank heretic, because he inveighs against it, and the
hypocrisy and tricks of his brother cheats, during that harvest of
theirs.—*M.*

CHAPTER XXX

HOW WE CAME TO THE LAND OF SATIN

Having pleased ourselves with observing that new
order of Semiquaver friars, we set sail, and in three
days our skipper made the finest and most delightful
island that ever was seen ; he called it the Island of
Frize ; for all the ways were of frize.

In that island is the land of Satin, so celebrated
by our court pages.   Its trees and herbage never
lose their leaves or flowers, and are all damask and
flowered velvet.   As for the beasts and birds, they
are all of tapestry work.   There we saw many

beasts, birds on trees, of the same colour, bigness, and shape, of those in our country ; with this difference, however, that these did eat nothing, and never sung, or bit like ours : and we also saw there many sorts of creatures which we never had seen before.

Among the rest, several elephants in various postures ; twelve of which were the six males and six females that were brought to Rome by their governor in the time of Germanicus, Tiberius' nephew : some of them were learned elephants, some musicians, others philosophers, dancers, and showers of tricks ; and all sat down at table in good order, silently eating and drinking like so many fathers in a fratry-room.

With their snouts or proboscises, some two cubits long, they draw up water for their own drinking, and take hold of palm leaves, plums, and all manner of edibles; using them offensively or defensively, as we do our fists ; with them tossing men high into the air in fight, and making them burst with laughing when they come to the ground.

They have joints in their legs, whatever some men, who never saw any but painted, may have written to the contrary. Between their teeth they have two huge horns : thus Juba called them, and Pausanias tells us, they are not teeth, but horns : however, Philostratus will have them to be teeth, and not horns. It is all one to me, provided you will be pleased to own them to be true ivory. These are some three or four cubits long, and are fixed in the upper jaw-bone, and consequently not in the lowermost. If you hearken to those who will tell you to the contrary, you will find yourself damnably mistaken, for that is a lie with a latchet : though it were Ælian, that long-bow man, that told you so, never

believe him, for he lies as fast as a dog can trot.
It was in this very island that Pliny, his brother
tell-truth, had seen some elephants dance on the
rope with bells, and whip over the tables, presto,
be gone, while people were at feasts, without so
much as touching the toping topers, or the topers
toping.

I saw a rhinoceros there, just such a one as Harry
Clerberg had formerly showed me : methought it
was not much unlike a certain boar which I had
formerly seen at Limoges, except the sharp horn on
its snout, that was about a cubit long ; by the means
of which that animal dares encounter with an
elephant, that is sometimes killed with its point
thrust into its belly, which is its most tender and
defenceless part.

I saw there two-and-thirty unicorns. They are
a cursed sort of creatures, much resembling a fine
horse, unless it be that their heads are like a stag's,
their feet like an elephant's, their tails like a wild
boar's, and out of each of their foreheads sprouts a
sharp black horn, some six or seven feet long ;
commonly it dangles down like a turkey-cock's
comb. When a unicorn has a mind to fight, or put
it to any other use, what does he do but make it
stand, and then it is as straight as an arrow.

I saw one of them, which was attended with a
throng of other wild beasts, purify a fountain with
its horn. With that Panurge told me, that his
prancer, *alias* his nimble-wimble, was like the
unicorn, not altogether in length indeed, but in
virtue and propriety ; for as the unicorn purified
pools and fountains from filth and venom, so that
other animals came and drank securely there afterwards ; in the like manner, others might water their
nags, and dabble after him, without fear of shankers,

carnosities, gonorrhœas, buboes, crinkams, and such other plagues, caught by those who venture to quench their amorous thirst in a common puddle ; for with his nervous horn he removed all the infection that might be lurking in some blind cranny of the mephitic sweet-scented hole.

Well, quoth Friar John, when you are sped, that is when you are married, we will make a trial of this on thy spouse, merely for charity sake, since you are pleased to give us so beneficial an instruction.

Aye, aye, returned Panurge, and then immediately I will give you a pretty gentle aggregative pill of God, made up of two-and-twenty kind stabs with a dagger, after the Cæsarian way.   Catso ! cried Friar John, I had rather take off a bumper of good cool wine.

I saw there the golden fleece, formerly conquered by Jason, and can assure you on the word of an honest man, that those who have said it was not a fleece, but a golden pippin, because $\mu\tilde{\eta}\lambda.o\nu$ signifies both an apple and a sheep, were utterly mistaken.

I saw also a chameleon, such as Aristotle describes it, and like that which had been formerly shown me by Charles Maris, a famous physician of the noble city of Lyons on the Rhone : and the said chameleon lived on air, just as the other did.

I saw three hydras, like those I had formerly seen. They are a kind of serpent, with seven different heads.

I saw also fourteen phœnixes.   I had read in many authors that there was but one in the whole world in every century; but, if I may presume to speak my mind, I declare that those who said this had never seen any, unless it were in the land of tapestry ; though it were vouched by Lactantius Firmianus.

I saw the skin of Apuleius' golden ass.

I saw three hundred and nine pelicans.

Item, six thousand and sixteen Seleucid birds marching in battalia, and picking up straggling grasshoppers in cornfields.

Item, some cynamologi, argatiles, caprimulgi, thynnunculs, onocrotals or bitterns, with their wide swallows, stymphalides, harpies, panthers, dorcasses or bucks, cemades, cynocephali, satyrs, cartasans, tarands, uri, monopses, pegasi, neades, cepes, marmosets or monkeys, presteres, bugles, musimons, byturoses, ophyri, screech owls, goblins, fairies, and griffins.

I saw Mid-Lent on horseback, with Mid-August and Mid-March holding its stirrups.

I saw some mankind wolves,[1] centaurs, tigers, leopards, hyenas, camelopardels, and orixes or huge wild goats with sharp horns.

I saw a remora, a little fish called *echineis* by the Greeks, and near it a tall ship, that did not get ahead an inch, though she was in the offing with top and top-gallants spread before the wind. I am somewhat inclined to believe, that it was the very numerical ship in which Periander the tyrant happened to be, when it was stopped by such a little fish in spite of wind and tide. It was in this land of Satin, and in no other, that Mutianus had seen one of them.

Friar John told us, that in the days of yore, two sort of fishes used to abound in our courts of judicature, and rotted the bodies and tormented the souls of those who were at law, whether noble or of mean descent, high or low, rich or poor; the first were your April fish or mackerel,[2] the others

---

[1] Loupgarous or wehrwolves.

[2] *Maquereaulx* in French signifies both mackerel and pimps.

your beneficial remoras, that is, the eternity of law-suits; the needless lets that keep them undecided.

I saw some sphynges, some raphes, some ounces, and some cepphi, whose fore-feet are like hands, and their hind-feet like men's feet.

Also some crocutas and some eali as big as sea-horses with elephants' tails, boars' jaws and tusks, and horns as pliant as an ass's ears.

The leucrocutes, most fleet animals, as big as our asses of Mirabelais, have necks, tails, and breasts like a lion's, legs like a stag's, the mouth up to the ears, and but two teeth, one above and one below; they speak with human voices, but when they do, they say nothing.

Some people say, that none ever saw an aëry, or nest, of sakers; if you will believe me, I saw no less than eleven, and I am sure I reckoned right.

I saw some left-handed halberts, which were the first that I had ever seen.

I saw some manticores, a most strange sort of creatures, which have the body of a lion, red hair, a face and ears like a man's, three rows of teeth which close together, as if you joined your hands with your fingers between each other; they have a sting in their tails like a scorpion's, and a very melodious voice.

I saw some catablepases, a sort of serpents, whose bodies are small, but their heads large without any proportion, so that they have much ado to lift them up; and their eyes are so infectious, that whoever sees them dies upon the spot, as if he had seen a basilisk.

I saw some beasts with two backs, and those seemed to me the merriest creatures in the world: they were most nimble at wriggling the buttocks, and more diligent in tailwagging than any water-wagtails, perpetually jogging and shaking their double rumps.

I saw there some milched craw-fish, creatures that I never heard of before in my life; these moved in very good order, and it would have done your heart good to have seen them.

CHAPTER XXXI

HOW IN THE LAND OF SATIN WE SAW HEARSAY, WHO KEPT A SCHOOL OF VOUCHING

WE went a little higher up into the country of Tapestry, and saw the Mediterranean Sea open to the right and left down to the very bottom; just as the Red Sea very fairly left its bed at the Arabian Gulf, to make a lane for the Jews, when they left Egypt.

There I found Triton winding his silver shell instead of a horn, and also Glaucus, Proteus, Nereus, and a thousand other godlings and sea monsters.

I also saw an infinite number of fish of all kinds, dancing, flying, vaulting, fighting, eating, breathing, billing, shoving, milting, spawning, hunting, fishing, skirmishing, lying in ambuscado, making truces, cheapening, bargaining, swearing, and sporting.

In a blind corner we saw Aristotle holding a lantern, in the posture in which the hermit uses to be drawn near St Christopher, watching, prying, thinking, and setting everything down in writing.

Behind him stood a pack of other philosophers, like so many bums by a head bailiff; as Appian, Heliodorus, Athenæus, Porphyrius, Pancrates, Archadian, Numenius, Possidonius, Ovidius, Oppianus, Olympius, Seleucus, Leonides, Agathocles, Theophrastus, Damostratus, Mutianus, Nymphodorus, Ælian, and five hundred other such plodding dons, who were full of business, yet had little to do ; like Chrysippus or Aristarchus of Soli, who for eight-and-fifty years together did nothing in the world but examine the state and concerns of bees.

I spied Peter Gilles among these, with an urinal in his hand, narrowly watching the water of those goodly fishes.

When we had long beheld everything in this land of Satin, Pantagruel said, I have sufficiently fed my eyes, but my belly is empty all this while, and chimes to let me know it is time to go to dinner : let us take care of the body, lest the soul abdicate it ; and to this effect, let us taste some of these anacampserotes [1] that hang over our heads. Pshaw, cried one, they are mere trash, stark naught on my word, they are good for nothing.

I then went to pluck some myrobolans off of a piece of tapestry, whereon they hung, but the devil a bit I could chew or swallow them ; and had you had them betwixt your teeth, you would have sworn they had been thrown silk ; there was no manner of savour in them.

One might be apt to think Heliogabalus had taken a hint from thence, to feast those whom he had caused to fast a long time, promising them a sumptuous, plentiful, and imperial feast after it; for all the treat used to amount to no more than several sorts of meat in wax, marble, earthenware, painted and figured tablecloths.

While we were looking up and down to find some more substantial food, we heard a loud various

[1] An herb, the touching of which is said to reconcile lovers.

153

noise, like that of paper mills, or women bucking of linen: so with all speed we went to the place whence the noise came, where we found a diminutive, monstrous, misshapen old fellow, called Hearsay. His mouth was slit up to his ears, and in it were seven tongues, each of them cleft into seven parts. However he chattered, tattled, and prated with all the seven at once, of different matters, and in divers languages.

He had as many ears all over his head, and the rest of his body, as Argus formerly had eyes; and was as blind as a beetle, and had the palsy in his legs.

About him stood an innumerable number of men and women, gaping, listening, and hearing very intensely; among them I observed some who strutted like crows in a gutter, and principally a very handsome bodied man in the face, who held then a map of the world, and with little aphorisms compendiously explained everything to them; so that those men of happy memories grew learned in a trice, and would most fluently talk with you of a world of prodigious things, the hundredth part of which would take up a man's whole life to be fully known.

Among the rest, they descanted with great prolixity on the pyramids and hieroglyphics of Egypt, of the Nile, of Babylon, of the Troglodytes, the Hymantopodes or crump-footed nation, the Blemiæ, people that wear their heads in the middle of their breasts, the Pigmies, the Cannibals, the Hyperborei and their mountains, the Egypanes with their goat's feet, and the devil and all of others; every individual word of it by hearsay.

I am much mistaken if I did not see among them Herodotus, Pliny, Solinus, Borosus, Philostratus,

Pomponius Mela, Strabo, and God knows how many other antiquaries.

Then Albert, the great Jacobin friar, Peter Tesmoin, *alias* Witness, Pope Pius the Second, Volaterranus, Paulus Jovius the valiant, Jemmy Cartier, Chaton the Armenian, Marco Polo the Venetian, Ludovico Romano, Pedro Aliares, and forty cart-loads of other modern historians, lurking behind a piece of tapestry, where they were at it, ding-dong, privately scribbling the Lord knows what, and making rare work of it, and all by hearsay.

Behind another piece of tapestry (on which Naboth and Susanna's accusers were fairly represented), I saw close by Hearsay, good store of men of the country of Perce and Maine, notable students, and young enough.

I asked what sort of study they applied themselves to? and was told, that from their youth they learned to be evidences, affidavit-men, and vouchers; and were instructed in the art of swearing; in which they soon became such proficients, that, when they left that country, and went back into their own, they set up for themselves, and very honestly lived by their trade of evidencing; positively giving their testimony of all things whatsoever, to those who fee'd them most roundly to do a job of journey-work for them: and all this by hearsay.

You may think what you will of it, but I can assure you, they gave some of us corners of their cakes, and we merrily helped to empty their hogsheads. Then, in a friendly manner, they advised us to be as sparing of truth as possibly we could, if ever we had a mind to get court preferment.

On Chaps. XXX. and XXXI.—The Island of Satin means more than one thing. First, it signifies such tapestry work as we call arras; in which are represented several histories, fables, and fabulous animals and vegetables, such as are many of those of which the author speaks in these two chapters. He displays a great knowledge of antiquity in the account he gives us of those matters, and an uncommon wit and judgment in his remarks.

This island means chiefly the works of several ancient and modern authors mentioned here, who having often spoken by hearsay, are not to be believed in many things, though their style be as smooth and soft as satin. We may also understand by that land of Satin, the romances of that age, filled with monsters and monstrous tales; and chiefly that of Amadis de Gaul, which was then very much read; the best writers, as I have already said, having chosen to translate that book, to display in it all the beauties, copiousness, and graces, which the French tongue could boast of in the reign of Henry II.—*M.*

CHAPTER XXXII

HOW WE CAME IN SIGHT OF LANTERN-LAND

Having been scurvily entertained in the land of Satin, we went on board, and having set sail, in four days came near the coast of Lantern-land. We then saw certain little hovering fires on the sea.

For my part I did not take them to be lanterns, but rather thought they were fishes, which lolled their flaming tongues on the surface of the sea; or *lampyrides*, which some call *cicindelas* or glow-worms, shining there as ripe barley does o' nights in my country.

But the skipper satisfied us that they were the lanterns of the watch, or more properly, lighthouses, set up in many places round the precinct of the place, to discover the land, and for the safe piloting in of some outlandish lanterns, which, like good Franciscan and Jacobin friars, were coming to make their personal appearance at the provincial chapter.

However, some of us were somewhat suspicious that these fires were the forerunners of some storm, but the skipper assured us again they were not.

————

CHAPTER XXXIII

HOW WE LANDED AT THE PORT OF THE LYCHNOBII, AND CAME TO LANTERN-LAND

Soon after we arrived at the port of Lantern-land, where Pantagruel discovered, on a high tower, the lantern of Rochelle, that stood us in good stead, for it cast a great light. We also saw the lantern of Pharos, that of Nauplion, and that of Acropolis, at Athens, sacred to Pallas.

Near the port, there is a little hamlet inhabited by the Lychnobii, that live by lanterns, as the gulligutted friars in our country live by nuns; they are studious people, and as honest men as ever shit in a trumpet. Demosthenes had formerly lanternised there.

We were conducted from that place to the palace by three obeliscolichnys,[1] military guards of the port, with high-crowned hats, whom we acquainted with the cause of our voyage, and our design; which was to desire the Queen of the country to

[1] A kind of beacons.

grant us a lantern to light and conduct us, during
our voyage to the Oracle of the Bottle.

They promised to assist us in this, and added,
that we could never have come in a better time;
for then the lanterns held their provincial chapter.

When we came to the royal place we had
audience of her highness the Queen of Lantern-
land, being introduced by two lanterns of honour,
that of Aristophanes, and that of Cleanthes.
Panurge, in a few words, acquainted her with
the causes of our voyage, and she received us
with great demonstrations of friendship; desiring
us to come to her at supper-time, that we might
more easily make choice of one to be our guide;
which pleased us extremely. We did not fail
to observe intensely everything we could see —
as the garbs, motions, and deportments of the
Queen's subjects — principally the manner after
which she was served.

The bright Queen was dressed in virgin crystal
of Tutia, wrought damaskwise, and beset with
large diamonds.

The lanterns of the royal blood were clad partly
with bastard-diamonds, partly with diaphanous
stones; the rest with horn, paper, and oiled cloth.

The cresset-lights took place according to the
antiquity and lustre of their families.

An earthen dark-lantern, shaped like a pot, notwithstanding this, took place of some of the first
quality; at which I wondered much, till I was
told it was that of Epictetus, for which three
thousand drachmas had been formerly refused.

Martial's polymix[2] lantern made a very good

---

[2] A lamp with many wicks, or a branched candlestick with
many springs coming out of it, that supply all the branches
with oil.

figure there; I took particular notice of its dress, and more yet of the *icosimyx*, formerly consecrated by Canopa, the daughter of Tisias.

I saw the pensile lantern, formerly taken out of the temple of Apollo Palatinus at Thebes, and afterwards by Alexander the Great carried to the town of Cymos.

I saw another that distinguished itself from the rest by a bushy tuft of crimson silk on its head. I was told it was that of Bartolus, the lantern of the civilians.

Two others were very remarkable for glister-pouches that dangled at their waist. We were told, that one was the greater light, and the other the lesser light of the apothecaries.

When it was supper-time, the Queen's highness first sat down, and then the rest, according to their rank and dignity. For the first course, they were all served with large Christmas candles, except the Queen, who was served with a hugeous, thick, stiff, flaming taper of white wax, somewhat red towards the tip; and the royal family, as also the provincial lantern of Mirebalais, who were served with nut-lights; and the provincial of Lower Poictou, with an armed candle.

After that, God wot, what a glorious light they gave with their wicks: I do not say all, for you must except a parcel of junior lanterns, under the government of a high and mighty one. These did not cast a light like the rest, but seemed to me dimmer than any long-snuff farthing candle, whose tallow has been half melted away in a hot-house.

After supper we withdrew to take some rest, and the next day the Queen made us choose one of the most illustrious lanterns to guide us: after which we took our leave.

On Chaps. **XXXII.** and **XXXIII.**—Lantern-land is the land of Learning, frequented by bachelors of arts, masters of arts, doctors, and professors in various studies, bishops, etc. Thus in the preceding chapter, Aristotle is seen in a blind corner holding a.lantern, watching, prying, cudgelling his brain, and setting everything down, with a pack of philosophasters about him, like so many bums by a head bailiff, because he is lantern of the peripatetics. Here we have Bartolus, the lantern of the civilians; Epictetus, one of the lanterns of the stoics.

The lantern of Rochelle on a high tower, which stood his fleet in good stead, casting a great light, seems to be Geoffrey d'Estissac, bishop and lord of Maillezais, one of Rabelais' best patrons, and even for that never to be forgotten. He would not call him the lantern of Maillezais, for this had been too plain and improper, because Maillezais is an inland town; but as Rochelle was then the chief town in that diocese, insomuch that the Episcopal See was transferred to that seaport town in 1648, he calls him the lantern of Rochelle, which he places on a high tower, because that prelate was eminent for his quality, as well as for his virtue and learning.

He tells us that the lanterns held their provincial chapter: so this may be thought by some to refer to the Council of Trent. Yet I had rather understand it of some meeting of the clergy in France, or more particularly of the University of Paris; some of whose best members may be the lanterns which lighted our travellers, after they had made their application to the Queen for one to conduct them to the Oracle of the Bottle, or rather to the knowledge of truth.

The Lychnobians, who inhabit a little hamlet near the port of Lantern-land, are booksellers. They live by lanterns, that is, by the learned, as the gulligutted friars live by nuns; that is, they grow as fat by buying and selling their works, as the hungry friars do by managing the concerns of nuns, of which they are so greedy. They are studious people; that is, they often study how to get a good copy for little or nothing, contrive a taking title, etc. I believe this needs no comment.—*M*.

CHAPTER XXXIV

HOW WE ARRIVED AT THE ORACLE OF THE BOTTLE

OUR glorious lantern lighting and directing us to our heart's content, we at last arrived at the desired island, where was the Oracle of the Bottle. As soon as friend Panurge landed, he nimbly cut a caper with one leg for joy, and cried to Pantagruel, Now we are where we have wished ourselves long ago. This is the place we have been seeking with such toil and labour. He then made a compliment to our lantern, who desired us to be of good cheer, and not be daunted or dismayed, whatever we might chance to see.

To come to the Temple of the Holy Bottle, we were to go through a large vineyard, in which were all sorts of vines, as the Falernian, Malvesian, the Muscadine, those of Taige, Beaune, Mirevaux, Orleans, Picardent, Arbois, Coussi, Anjou, Grave, Corsica, Vierron, Nerac, and others. This vine-yard was formerly planted by the good Bacchus, with so great a blessing, that it yields leaves, flowers, and fruit, all the year round, like the orange trees at Serene.

Our magnificent lantern ordered every one of us to eat three grapes, to put some vine-leaves in his shoes, and take a vine-branch in his left hand.

At the end of the close we went under an arch built after the manner of those of the ancients. The trophies of a toper were curiously carved on it.

First, on one side was to be seen a long train of flagons, leathern bottles, flasks, cans, glass bottles, barrels, nipperkins, pint-pots, quart-pots, pottles, gallons, and old-fashioned semaises (swingeing wooden pots, such as those out of which the Germans fill their glasses): these hung on a shady arbour.

On another side was store of garlic, onions, shallots, hams, botargos, caviar, biscuits, neats' tongues, old cheese, and such like comfits, very artificially interwoven, and packed together with vine-stocks.

On another were a hundred sorts of drinking glasses, cups, cisterns, ewers, false cups, tumblers, bowls, mazers, mugs, jugs, goblets, tallboys, and such other Bacchic artillery.

On the frontispiece of the triumphal arch, under the zoophore, was the following couplet:

> You, who presume to move this way,
> Get a good lantern lest you stray.

We took special care of that, cried Pantagruel, when he read them; for there is not a better or a more divine lantern than ours in all Lantern-land.

This arch ended at a fine large round alley, covered over with the interlaid branches of vines, loaded and adorned with clusters of five hundred different colours, and of as many various shapes, not natural, but due to the skill of agriculture; some were golden, others blueish, tawny, azure, white, black, green, purple, streaked with many colours, long, round, triangular,[1] cod-like, hairy, great-headed, and grassy. That pleasant alley ended at three old ivy-trees, verdant, and all loaden with rings. Our most illustrious lantern directed us to make ourselves high-crowned hats with some of their leaves, and cover our heads wholly with them, which was immediately done.

Jupiter's priestess, said Pantagruel, in former days, would not, like us, have walked under this arbour.

[1] Read *Torangle*; for that is the word used by Rabelais. It signifies a glass turned angularly. In the author's time they said *tor* for *tour*, *torner* for *tourner*.

There was a mystical reason, answered our most perspicuous lantern, that would have hindered her. For had she gone under it, the wine, or the grapes of which it is made, that is the same thing, had been over her head, and then she would have seemed overtopped and mastered by wine. Which implies, that priests, and all persons who devote themselves to the contemplation of divine things, ought to keep their minds sedate and calm, and avoid whatever may disturb and discompose their tranquillity; which nothing is more apt to do than drunkenness.

You also, continued our lantern, could not come into the Holy Bottle's presence, after you have gone through this arch, did not that noble priestess Bacbuc first see your shoes full of vine-leaves; which action is diametrically opposite to the other, and signifies that you despise wine, and having mastered it, as it were, tread it under foot.

I am no scholar, quoth Friar John, for which I am heartily sorry, yet I find, by my breviary, that in the Revelation, a woman was seen with the moon under her feet, which was a most wonderful sight. Now, as Bigot explained it to me, this was to signify, that she was not of the nature of other women; for they have all the moon at their heads, and, consequently, their brains are always troubled with a lunacy: this makes me willing to believe what you said, dear Madam Lantern.

On Chap. XXXIV. — Being lighted and directed by the lantern—the learned—our travellers at last arrive at the island where was the Oracle of the Bottle—Truth. Their guide desires them not to be daunted whatever they see, because fear disorders the mind, and renders us incapable of discovering truth. They pass through a large vineyard, in which are all sorts of vines, which yield leaves, flowers, and fruits, all the year round. There they eat three grapes, put vine-leaves in their shoes, and take vine-branches in their hands.

The variety of vines in this large vineyard, implies the vast field through which the learned range in the search after truth: some matters, like the leaves, are unprofitable ; some, like the flowers, pleasant; and others, like the fruit, useful. But they must use even the last moderately—which is implied by the three grapes; and at the first entrance into the regions of truth, be soberly wise. The insignificant leaves must be trod under foot : for this reason they put some in their shoes; and also to show they have mastered the rudiments of learning, unless some will say, that the leaves at their feet signify their desire of stepping forward to come to the oracle of truth. Vine-branches (which may well be supposed to have flowers as well as leaves) are held by them in their left hand, in token of their hopes to reap the fruit of their study.—*M.*

CHAPTER XXXV

HOW WE WENT UNDER GROUND TO COME TO THE TEMPLE OF THE HOLY BOTTLE, AND HOW CHINON IS THE OLDEST CITY IN THE WORLD

WE went under ground through a plastered vault, on which was coarsely painted a dance of women and satyrs, waiting on old Silenus, who was grinning on horseback on his ass. This made me say to Pantagruel, that this entry put me in mind of the painted cellar, in the oldest city in the world, where such paintings are to be seen, and in as cool a place. Which is the oldest city in the world? asked Pantagruel. It is Chinon, sir, or Cainon in Touraine, said I. I know, returned Pantagruel, where Chinon lies, and the painted cellar also, having myself drunk there many a glass of cool wine; neither do I doubt but that Chinon is an ancient town—witness its blazon. I own it is said twice or thrice,

> Chinon,
> Little town,
> Great renown,
> On old stone
> Long has stood;
> There's the Vienne, if you look down;
> If you look up, there's the wood.

But how, continued he, can you make it out that 'tis the oldest city in the world? Where did you find this written? I have found it in the sacred writ, said I, that Cain was the first that built a town; we may then reasonably conjecture that from his name he gave it that of Cainon. Thus, after his example, most other founders of towns have given them these names: Athena, that is Minerva in Greek, to Athens; Alexander to Alexandria; Constantine to Constantinople; Pompey to Pompeiopolis in Cilicia; Adrian to Adrianople; Canaan to the Canaanites; Saba to the Sabæans; Assur to the Assyrians; and so Ptolemais, Cæsarea, Tiberias, and Herodium in Judæa got their names.

While we were thus talking, there came to us the great flask whom our lantern called the philosopher, her holiness the Bottle's governor. He was attended with a troop of the temple-guards, all French bottles in wicker armour; and seeing us with our javelins wrapped with ivy, with our illustrious lantern, whom he knew, he desired us to come in with all manner of safety, and ordered we should be immediately conducted to the Princess Bacbuc, the Bottle's Lady of Honour, and priestess of all the mysteries; which was done.

ON CHAP. XXXV.—They go down under ground through a plastered vault, on which is coarsely painted a dance of women and satyrs, waiting on old Silenus, who was grinning on horseback on his ass. This shows, that we must not dwell on the surface or outside of things, but dive to their very centre or

bottom, to come at truth. This also may refer to this work.
The plastered vault, on which is coarsely daubed a dance of
women and satyrs, is, in its literal sense, smutty, drunken, lewd,
and satirical expressions; and our author is the Silenus, who
grins and laughs at every one. He has ingeniously brought in a
discourse about the antiquity of Chinon, his native town; by
which he seems at the same time to ridicule the fables that are
reported in many towns about their founders, whom some make
as ancient as the patriarch of highest pedigree in Wales.—*M.*

CHAPTER XXXVI

HOW WE WENT DOWN THE TETRADIC STEPS, AND OF PANURGE'S FEAR

WE went down one marble step under ground,
where there was a resting, or, as our workmen call
it, a landing-place, then, turning to the left, we
went down two other steps, where there was another
resting-place; after that we came to three other
steps, turning about, and met a third; and the like
at four steps which we met afterwards. There
quoth Panurge, Is it here? How many steps have
you told? asked our magnificent lantern. One, two,
three, four, answered Pantagruel. How much is
that? asked she. Ten, returned he. Multiply
that, said she, according to the same pythagorical
tetrad. That is ten, twenty, thirty, forty, cried
Pantagruel. How much is the whole? said she.
One hundred, answered Pantagruel. Add, continued she, the first cube—that is eight: at the
end of that fatal number you will find the temple
gate; and pray, observe, this is the true psychogony
of Plato, so celebrated by the academics, yet so little
understood; one moiety of which consists of the

unity of the two first numbers full of two square
and two cubic numbers. We then went down those
numerical stairs, all under ground; and I can assure
you, in the first place, that our legs stood us in good
stead; for had it not been for them, we had rolled
just like so many hogsheads into a vault. Secondly,
our radiant lantern gave us just so much light as is
in St Patrick's hole in Ireland, or Trophonius'
cavern in Bœotia; which caused Panurge to say to
her, after we had got down some seventy-eight
steps :—

Dear madam, with a sorrowful, aching heart, I
most humbly beseech your lanternship to lead us
back. May I be led to hell, if I be not half dead
with fear; my heart is sunk down into my hose; I
am afraid I shall make buttered eggs in my breeches.
I freely consent never to marry. You have given
yourself too much trouble on my account; the Lord
shall reward you in his great rewarding-place; neither
will I be ungrateful when I come out of this cave of
Troglodytes. Let us go back, I pray you. I am
very much afraid this is Tænarus, the low way to
hell, and methinks I already hear Cerberus bark.
Hark! I hear the cur, or my ears tingle; I have no
manner of kindness for the dog, for there never is a
greater toothache than when dogs bite us by the
shins: and if this be only Trophonius' pit, the
lemures, hob-thrushes, and goblins will certainly
swallow us alive: just as they devoured formerly one
of Demetrius' halberdiers, for want of luncheons of
bread. Art thou here, Friar John? Prythee, dear,
dear cod, stay by me; I am almost dead with fear!
Hast thou got thy bilbo? Alas! poor Pilgarlic is
defenceless; I am a naked man thou knowest: let
us go back. Zoons! fear nothing, cried Friar John,
I am by thee, and have thee fast by the collar;

eighteen devils shall not get thee out of my clutches, though I were unarmed. Never did a man yet want weapons who had a good arm with as stout a heart; heaven would sooner send down a shower of them; even as in Provence, in the fields of La Crau, near Mariannes, there rained stones (they are there to this day) to help Hercules, who otherwise wanted wherewithal to fight Neptune's two bastards. But whither are we bound? Are we a-going to the little children's limbo? By Pluto, they will bepaw and conskite us all. Or are we going to hell for orders? By cob's body! I will hamper, bethwack, and belabour all the devils, now I have some vine-leaves in my shoes. Thou shalt see me lay about me like mad, old boy. Which way? where the devil are they? I fear nothing but their damned horns: but cuckoldy Panurge's bull-feather will altogether secure me from them.

Lo! in a prophetic spirit I already see him, like another Actæon, horned, horny, hornified. Prythee, quoth Panurge, take heed thyself, dear frater, lest, till monks have leave to marry, thou weddest something thou dost not like, as some quartan ague; if thou dost, may I never come safe and sound out of this hypogeum, this subterranean cave, if I do not tup and ram that disease merely for the sake of making thee a cornuted, corniferous property; otherwise I fancy the quartan ague is but an indifferent bed-fellow. I remember Gripe-men-all threatened to wed thee to some such thing; for which thou calledst him heretic.

Here our splendid lantern interrupted them, letting us know this was the place where we were to have a taste of the creature,[1] and be silent; bidding us not

---

[1] It should be, where we were to observe taciturnity: *favere linguis:* which in the sacrifices, and other religious ceremonies

despair of having the word of the Bottle before we went back, since we had lined our shoes with vine-leaves.

Come on, then! cried Panurge, let us charge through and through all the devils of hell: we can but perish, and that is soon done: however, I thought to have reserved my life for some mighty battle. Move, move, move forwards; I am as stout as Hercules, my breeches are full of courage: my heart trembles a little, I own, but that is only an effect of the coldness and dampness of this vault; it is neither fear nor ague. Come on, move on, piss, pish, push on. My name is William Dreadnought.

On Chap. XXXVI.—Our pilgrims, going down the tetradic stairs, find a resting-place after the first step, another resting-place after the third, another after the sixth, and a fourth resting-place after the tenth step. This implies, that the progress made at first, in the way to truth, is but small; but by degrees a greater is made, the more we get forward: so that on the second day we go twice as far as we did the first; three times as far on the third; and four times as far on the fourth; till at last we come to our journey's end.—*M.*

CHAPTER XXXVII

HOW THE TEMPLE GATES IN A WONDERFUL MANNER OPENED OF THEMSELVES

After we were got down the steps, we came to a portal of fine jasper, of Doric order, on whose front we read this sentence in the finest gold, ΕΝ 'ΟΙΝΩ ΑΛΗΘΕΙΑ: that is, In wine, truth. The two folding doors of the gate were of Corinthian-like brass,[1] of the Romans, signified to keep silence; *favorare* being the same as *favere linguis.* But this word, by the printer's fault, used to be written *savorare*, which occasioned the mistake above.

[1] See Pliny, l. 34, c. 2. Corinthian brass is held to be a mixture of gold, silver, and brass.

massy, wrought with little vine-branches, finely embossed and engraven, and were equally joined and
closed together in their mortise without any padlock,
key-chain, or tie whatsoever. Where they joined,
there hanged an Indian loadstone as big as an
Egyptian bean, set in gold, having two points,
hexagonal, in a right line; and on each side,
towards the wall, hung a handful of scordium.[2]

There our noble lantern desired us not to take it
amiss that she went no farther with us, leaving us
wholly to the conduct of the priestess Bacbuc : for
she herself was not allowed to go in, for certain
causes rather to be concealed than revealed to
mortals. However, she advised us to be resolute
and secure, and to trust to her for the return. She
then pulled the loadstone that hung at the folding
of the gates, and threw it into a silver box fixed for
that purpose : which done, from the threshold of
each gate she drew a twine of crimson silk, about
nine feet long, by which the scordium hung, and
having fastened it to two gold buckles that hung at
the sides, she withdrew.

Immediately the gates flew open [3] without being
touched; not with a creaking, or loud harsh noise,
like that made by heavy brazen gates; but with a
soft pleasing murmur that resounded through the
arches of the temple.

Pantagruel soon knew the cause of it, having
discovered a small cylinder or roller that joined the
gates over the threshold; and, turning like them
towards the wall on a hard well-polished ophites

[2] Wrong: Rabelais says, 'Une poignée de scordon,' *i.e.*, a
handful of garlic ; σκόρδον, in Greek; not σκόρδιον, *scordium*,
which is another herb, ' quæ allii odorem resipit ' (say Robinson's
Lexicon) ; it has indeed the smell of garlic and no more.

[3] This is in imitation of the description of Apolidon's palace
in ch. ii. of b. iv. of Amadis de Gaul.

stone, with rubbing and rolling, caused that harmonious murmur.

I wondered how the gates thus opened of themselves to the right and left, and after we were all got
in, I cast my eye between the gates and the wall, to
endeavour to know how this happened; for one
would have thought our kind lantern had put
between the gates the herb *æthiopis*, which they
say opens some things that are shut; but I perceived
that the parts of the gates that joined on the inside
were covered with steel; and just where the said
gates touched when they were opened, I saw two
square Indian loadstones,[4] of a blueish hue, well
polished, and half a span broad, mortised in the
temple wall. Now, by the hidden and admirable
power of the loadstones, the steel plates were put
into motion, and consequently the gates were slowly
drawn; however, not always, but when the said
loadstone on the outside was removed, after which
the steel was freed from its power, the two bunches
of scordium being at the same time put at some
distance because it deadens the magnet, and robs it
of its attractive virtue.

On the loadstone that was placed on the right
side, the following iambic verse was curiously engraven in ancient Roman characters :

'Ducunt volentem fata, nolentem trahunt.'[5]

Fate leads the willing, and the unwilling draws.

---

[4] Here Rabelais speaks of the Indian loadstone, whose virtue
he believed to be so strong, that in the islands called Manioles,
such ships as had iron pins, or nails in them, stopped short on
their way, without any possibility of proceeding any farther,
because of the loadstone which the adjoining land abounded with.

[5] This verse is none of Seneca's the tragedian, as Erasmus
took it to be in his Adages, at the word *fato non repugnandum.*
The thought is in some of the Greak iambics of the stoic

The following sentence was neatly cut in the loadstone that was on the left :

ALL THINGS TEND TO THEIR END.

CHAPTER XXXVIII

OF THE TEMPLE'S ADMIRABLE PAVEMENT

WHEN I had read those inscriptions, I admired the beauty of the temple, and particularly the disposition of its pavement, with which no work that is now, or has been under the cope of heaven, can justly be compared; not that of the Temple of Fortune at Præneste in Sylla's time; or the pavement of the Greeks, called *asarotum*, laid by Sosistratus in Pergamus. For this here was wholly in compartments of precious stones, all in their natural colours. One of red jasper, most charmingly spotted. Another of ophites. A third of porphyry. A fourth of lycophthalmy, a stone of four different colours, powdered with sparks of gold, as small as atoms. A fifth of agate, streaked here and there with small milk-coloured waves. A sixth of costly chalcedony.[1] And another of green jasper, with certain red and yellowish veins. And all these were disposed in a diagonal line.

At the portico, some small stones were inlaid, and evenly joined on the floor, all in their native colours,

Cleanthes, from whence Epictetus taking it, and putting it into his manual, the other Seneca, who fancied it beautiful enough to make fresh use of it, put into Latin iambics Cleanthes' Greek ones, and inserted them in the CVIIth of his Epistles.

[1] Costly, because the vases made of this stone are very subject to crack or break.

to embellish the design of the figures; and they were ordered in such a manner, that you would have thought some vine-leaves and branches had been carelessly strewed on the pavement; for in some places they were thick, and thin in others. That inlaying was very wonderful everywhere: here were seen, as it were in the shade, some snails crawling on the grapes; there, little lizards running on the branches; on this side, were grapes that seemed yet greenish; on another, some clusters that seemed full ripe, so like the true, that they could as easily have deceived starlings, and other birds, as those which Zeuxis drew.

Nay, we ourselves were deceived; for where the artist seemed to have strewed the vine-branches thickest, we could not forbear walking with great strides, lest we should entangle our feet, just as people go over an unequal stony place.

I then cast my eyes on the roof and walls of the temple, that were all pargetted with porphyry and mosaic work; which from the left side at the coming in, most admirably represented the battle, in which the good Bacchus overthrew the Indians; as followeth.

CHAPTER XXXIX

HOW WE SAW BACCHUS' ARMY DRAWN UP IN BATTALIA IN MOSAIC WORK

At the beginning, divers towns, hamlets, castles, fortresses, and forests were seen in flames; and several mad and loose women, who furiously ripped up, and tore live calves, sheep, and lambs, limb from limb, and devoured their flesh. There we learned how Bacchus,[1] at his coming into India, destroyed all things with fire and sword.

Notwithstanding this, he was so despised by the Indians, that they did not think it worth their while to stop his progress; having been certainly informed by their spies, that his camp was destitute of warriors, and that he had only with him a crew of drunken females, a low-built, old, effeminate, sottish fellow, continually addled, and as drunk as a wheel-barrow, with a pack of young clownish doddipoles, stark naked, always skipping and frisking up and down, with tails and horns like those of young kids.

For this reason the Indians had resolved to let them go through their country without the least opposition, esteeming a victory over such enemies more dishonourable than glorious.

In the meantime, Bacchus marched on, burning everything; for, as you know, fire and thunder are his paternal arms; Jupiter having saluted his mother Semele with his thunder; so that his maternal house was ruined by fire. Bacchus also caused a great deal of blood to be spilt; which, when he is roused and angered, principally in war, is as natural to him as to make some in time of peace.

Thus the plains of the Island of Samos are called Panema, which signifies all bloody, because Bacchus there overtook the Amazons, who fled from the country of Ephesus, and there let them blood, so that they all died of phlebotomy. This may give you a better insight into the meaning of an ancient proverb, than Aristotle has done in his problems; viz., Why, it was formerly said, Neither eat, nor sow any mint[2] in time of war. The reason is, that

[1] This chapter is taken from Lucian's discourse, intituled Bacchus.
[2] The reason of this proverb is not that mint being cold of

blows are given in time of war without any distinc-
tion of parts or persons; and if a man that is
wounded has that day handled or eaten any mint, it
is impossible, or at least very hard, to staunch his blood.

After this, Bacchus was seen marching in battalia,
riding in a stately chariot, drawn by six young
leopards. He looked as young as a child, to show
that all good topers never grow old: he was as red
as a cherry, or a cherub, which you please; and had
no more hair on his chin, than there is in the inside
of my hand: his forehead was graced with pointed
horns, above which he wore a fine crown or garland
of vine-leaves and grapes, and a mitre of crimson
velvet, having also gilt buskins on.

He had not one man with him, that looked like a
man; his guards, and all his forces, consisted wholly
of Bassarides, Evantes, Euhyades, Edonides, Trie-
therides, Ogygiæ, Mimallonides, Mænades, Thyades,
and Bacchides, frantic, raving, raging, furious, mad
women, begirt with live snakes and serpents, instead
of girdles, their dishevelled hair flowing about their
shoulders, with garlands of vine-branches instead of
forehead-cloths, clad with stag's or goat's-skins, and
armed with torches, javelins, spears, and halberts,
whose ends were like pine-apples: besides, they had
certain small light bucklers, that gave a loud sound
if you touched them never so little, and these served
them instead of drums; they were just seventy-nine
thousand two hundred and twenty-seven.

itself, as Aristotle supposed, the using it would be bad for those
whose trade is to fight. Mint has so little of this quality, that,
according to Dioscorides, Hippocrates, and Ætius, it provokes
urine, and causes seed to abound so as to slip away involuntarily
by being too thin. The reason of the proverb is, rather because
by exciting too much to love, those who have exhausted themselves in the wars of Venus, must of necessity be less in a readiness for those of Bellona.

Silenus, who led the van, was one on whom Bacchus relied very much, having formerly had many proofs of his valour and conduct. He was a diminutive, stooping, palsied, plump, gorbellied, old fellow, with a swingeing pair of stiff-standing lugs of his own, a sharp Roman nose, large rough eyebrows, mounted on a well-hung ass; in his fist he held a staff to lean upon, and also bravely to fight, whenever he had occasion to alight; and he was dressed in a woman's yellow gown. His followers were all young, wild, clownish people, as hornified as so many kids, and as fell as so many tigers, naked, and perpetually singing and dancing country dances: they were called tityri and satyrs; and were in all eighty-five thousand one hundred and thirty-three.

Pan, who brought up the rear, was a monstrous sort of a thing: for his lower parts were like a goat's, his thighs hairy, and his horns bolt upright; a crimson fiery phiz, and a beard that was none of the shortest. He was a bold, stout, daring, desperate fellow, very apt to take pepper in the nose for yea and nay.

In his left hand he held a pipe, 'and a crooked stick in his right. His forces consisted also wholly of satyrs, ægipanes, argipanes, sylvans, fauns, lemures, lares, elves, and hobgoblins; and their number was seventy-eight thousand one hundred and fourteen. The signal or word common to all the army was Evohé.

CHAPTER XL

HOW THE BATTLE, IN WHICH THE GOOD BACCHUS
OVERTHREW THE INDIANS, WAS REPRESENTED IN
MOSAIC WORK

IN the next place we saw the representation of
the good Bacchus' engagement with the Indians.
Silenus, who led the van, was sweating, puffing,
and blowing, belabouring his ass most grievously;
the ass dreadfully opened its wide jaws, drove
away the flies that plagued it, winced, flounced,
went back, and bestirred itself in a most terrible
manner, as if some damned gad-bee had stung it at
the breech.

The satyrs, captains, sergeants, and corporals of
companies, sounding the orgies with cornets, in a
furious manner went round the army, skipping,
capering, bounding, jerking, farting, flying out at
heels, kicking and prancing like mad, encouraging
their company to fight bravely; and all the deline-
ated army cried out Evohé!

First, the Mænades charged the Indians with
dreadful shouts, and a horrid din of their brazen
drums and bucklers: the air rung again all around,
as the mosaic work well expressed it. And pray,
for the future do not so much admire Apelles,
Aristides the Theban, and others who drew claps
of thunder, lightnings, winds, words, manners, and
spirits.

We then saw the Indian army, who had at last
taken the field, to prevent the devastation of the
rest of their country. In the front were the
elephants, with castles well garrisoned on their
backs. But the army and themselves were put

into disorder; the dreadful cries of the Bacchides having filled them with consternation, and those huge animals turned tail, and trampled on the men of their party.

There you might have seen gaffer Silenus on his ass, putting on as hard as he could, striking athwart and alongst, and laying about him lustily with his staff, after the old fashion of fencing. His ass was prancing and making after the elephants, gaping and martially braying, as it were to sound a charge, as he did when formerly, in the bacchanalian feasts, he waked the nymph Lottis, when Priapus, full of priapism, had a mind to priapise, while the pretty creature was taking a nap.

There you might have seen Pan frisk it with his goatish shanks about the Mænades, and with his rustic pipe excite them to behave themselves like Mænades.

A little farther you might have blessed your eyes with the sight of a young satyr who led seventeen kings his prisoners; and a Bacchis, who with her snakes, hauled along no less than two-and-forty captains; a little faun, who carried a whole dozen of standards taken from the enemy; and goodman Bacchus on his chariot, riding to and fro fearless of danger, making much of his dear carcase, and cheerfully toping to all his merry friends.

Finally, we saw the representation of his triumph, which was thus: First, his chariot was wholly covered with ivy, gathered on the mountain Meros: this for its scarcity, which you know raises the price of everything, and principally of those leaves in India.[1] In this, Alexander the Great followed his

[1] It is Theophrastus' opinion, in lib. 16, cap. 34, of Pliny, that throughout India there grows no ivy. Thus, we are to read India, in this place, conformable to the old editions, not Ida, as the new ones have it.

example at his Indian triumph.   The chariot was
drawn by elephants joined together, wherein he was
imitated by Pompey the Great, at Rome, in his
African triumph.   In it the good Bacchus was seen
drinking out of a mighty urn, which action Marius
aped after his victory over the Cimbri, near Aix in
Provence.   All his army were crowned with ivy;
their javelins, bucklers, and drums, were also wholly
covered with it; there was not so much as Silenus'
ass, but was betrapped with it.

The Indian kings were fastened with chains of
gold close by the wheels of the chariot; all the
company marched in pomp with unspeakable joy,
loaded with an infinite number of trophies, pageants,
and spoils, playing and singing merry epiniciums,[2]
songs of triumph, and also rural lays and dithyrambs.

At the farthest end was a prospect of the land of
Egypt; the Nile with its crocodiles, marmosets,
ibides,[3] monkeys, trochilos, or wrens, ichneumons,
or Pharaoh's mice, hippopotami, or sea-horses, and
other creatures, its guests and neighbours.   Bacchus
was moving towards that country under the conduct
of a couple of horned beasts, on one of which was
written in gold, *Apis*, and *Osiris* on the other;
because no ox or cow had been seen in Egypt till
Bacchus came thither.

[2] Songs of victory, from the Greek $\nu\iota\kappa\eta$, victory.

[3] A kind of stork, very black, hath the legs of a crane, and a
long crooked bill. See Herodotus, lib. 2, and Pliny, lib. 8,
cap. 27. Cicero, lib. 1, *De Nat. Deor.* and Pliny, lib. 10, cap. 28,
call these storks *ibes;* but our author chose rather to follow the
usual declension of the Latin genitive. [The ibis is meant.]

CHAPTER XLI

HOW THE TEMPLE WAS ILLUMINATED WITH A WONDERFUL LAMP

BEFORE I proceed to the description of the Bottle, I will give you that of an admirable lamp, that dispensed so large a light over all the temple, that, though it lay under ground, we could distinguish every object as clearly as above it at noonday.

In the middle of the roof was fixed a ring of massy gold, as thick as my clenched fist. Three chains somewhat less, most curiously wrought, hung about two feet and a half below it, and in a triangle supported a round plate of fine gold, whose diameter or breadth did not exceed two cubits and half a span. There were four holes in it, in each of which an empty ball was fastened, hollow within, and open at the top, like a little lamp; its circumference about two hands' breadth: each ball was of precious stone; one an amethyst, another an African carbuncle, the third an opal, and a fourth an anthracites; they were full of burning water, five times distilled in a serpentine limbeck, and inconsumptible, like the oil formerly put into Pallas' golden lamp at Acropolis of Athens by Callimachus. In each of them was a flaming wick, partly of asbestine flax, as of old in the temple of Jupiter Ammon, such as those which Cleombrotus, a most studious philosopher, saw; partly of Carpasian flax, which were rather renewed than consumed by the fire.

About two feet and a half below that gold plate, the three chains were fastened to three handles, that were fixed to a large round lamp of most

pure crystal, whose diameter was a cubit and a
half, and opened about two hands' breadth on
the top ; by which open place a vessel of the
same crystal, shaped somewhat like the lower
part of a gourd-like limbeck, or an urinal, was
put at the bottom of the great lamp, with such
a quantity of the afore-mentioned burning water,
that the flame of asbestine wick reached the centre
of the great lamp. This made all its spherical
body seem to burn and be in a flame, because
the fire was just at the centre and middle point,
so that it was not more easy to fix the eye on it
than on the disc of the sun, the matter being
wonderfully bright and shining, and the work
most transparent and dazzling, by the reflection
of the various colours of the precious stones,
whereof the four small lamps above the main lamp
were made, and their lustre was still variously
glittering all over the temple. Then this wandering light being darted on the polished marble and
agate, with which all the inside of the temple was
pargetted, our eyes were entertained with a sight
of all the admirable colours which the rainbow
can boast, when the sun darts his fiery rays on
some dropping clouds.

The design of the lamp was admirable in itself,
but, in my opinion, what added much to the beauty
of the whole, was, that round the body of the crystal
lamp, there was carved in kataglyphic work, a lively
and pleasant battle of naked boys, mounted on little
hobby-horses, with little whirligig lances and shields,
that seemed made of vine-branches with grapes on
them ; their postures generally were very different,
and their childish strife and motions were so ingeniously expressed, that art equalled nature in
every proportion and action.   Neither did this

seem engraved, but rather hewed out and embossed in relief, or, at least, like grotesque, which, by the artist's skill, has the appearance of the roundness of the object it represents; this was partly the effect of the various and most charming light, which, flowing out of the lamp, filled the carved places with its glorious rays.

CHAPTER XLII

HOW THE PRIESTESS BACBUC SHOWED US A FANTASTIC FOUNTAIN IN THE TEMPLE, AND HOW THE FOUNTAIN WATER HAD THE TASTE OF WINE, ACCORDING TO THE IMAGINATION OF THOSE WHO DRANK OF IT

WHILE we were admiring this incomparable lamp, and the stupendous structure of the temple, the venerable priestess Bacbuc, and her attendants, came to us with jolly smiling looks, and seeing us duly accoutred, without the least difficulty, took us into the middle of the temple, where, just under the aforesaid lamp, was the fine fantastic fountain. She then ordered some cups, goblets, and tallboys of gold, silver, and crystal to be brought, and kindly invited us to drink of the liquor that sprung there, which we readily did: for, to say the truth, this fantastic fountain [1] was very inviting, and its materials and workmanship more precious, rare, and admirable than anything Plato ever dreamt of in limbo.

[1] Fantastic, inasmuch as the liquor which flowed from it had the taste of whatever sort of wine the drinker fancied he was drinking, or had a fancy to drink.

Its basis or ground-work was of most pure and
limpid alabaster, and its height somewhat more than
three spans, being a regular heptagon on the outside,
with its stylobates or footsteps, arulets, cymasults or
blunt tops, and doric undulations about it.	It was
exactly round within.	On the middle point of each
angle brink stood a pillar orbiculated, in form of a
circle of ivory or alabaster.	These were seven in
number, according to the number of the angles.

Each pillar's length, from the basis to the architraves, was near seven hands, taking an exact
dimension of its diameter through the centre of its
circumference and inward roundness ; and it was
so disposed, that, casting our eyes ·behind one of
them, whatever its cube might be, to view its
opposite, we found that the pyramidal cone of our
visual light ended at the said centre, and there, by
the two opposites, formed an equilateral triangle,
whose two lines divided the pillar into two equal parts.

That which we had a mind to measure, going
from one side to another, two pillars over, at the
first third part of the distance between them, was
met by their lowermost and fundamental line, which,
in a consult line drawn as far as the universal centre,
equally divided, gave, in a just partition, the distance
of the seven opposite pillars in a right line, beginning
at the obtuse angle on the brink, as you know that
an angle is always found placed between two others
in all angular figures odd in number.

This tacitly gives us to understand, that seven
semi-diameters are in geometrical proportion, compass, and distance, somewhat less than the circumference of a circle, from the figure of which they
are extracted; that is to say, three whole parts, with
an eighth and a half, a little more, or a seventh and
a half, a little less, according to the instructions

given us of old by Euclid, Aristotle, Archimedes, and others.

The first pillar, I mean that which faced the temple gate, was of azure, sky-coloured sapphire.

The second, of hyacinth, a precious stone, exactly of the colour of the flower into which Ajax's choleric blood was transformed; the Greek letters, A I, being seen on it in many places.

The third, an anachite diamond, as bright and glittering as lightning.

The fourth, a masculine ruby-ballais amethystizing, its flame and lustre ending in violet or purple, like an amethyst.

The fifth, an emerald, above five hundred and fifty times more precious than that of Serapis in the labyrinth of the Egyptians, and more verdant and shining than those that were fixed instead of eyes, in the marble lion's head, near King Hermias' tomb.

The sixth, of agate, more admirable and various in the distinctions of its veins, clouds, and colours, than that which Pyrrhus, King of Epirus, so mightily esteemed.

The seventh, of syenites, transparent, of the colour of a beryl, and the clear hue of Hymettian honey; and within it the moon was seen, such as we see her in the sky, full, silent, new, and in the wane.

These stones were assigned to the seven heavenly planets by the ancient Chaldeans; and that the meanest capacities might be informed of this, just at the central perpendicular line, on the chapiter of the first pillar, which was of sapphire, stood the image of Saturn in elutian lead, with his scythe in his hand, and at his feet a crane of gold, very artfully enamelled, according to the native hue of the saturnine bird.

On the second, which was of hyacinth, towards

the left, Jupiter was seen in jovetian brass, and on his breast an eagle of gold enamelled to the life.

On the third, was Phœbus in the purest gold, and a white cock in his right hand.

On the fourth, was Mars in Corinthian brass, and a lion at his feet.

On the fifth, was Venus in copper, the metal of which Aristonidas made Athamas' statue, that expressed in a blushing whiteness his confusion at the sight of his son Learchus, who died at his feet of a fall.

On the sixth, was Mercury in *hydrargyrum;* I would have said quicksilver, had it not been fixed, malleable, and unmoveable; that nimble deity had a stork at his feet.

On the seventh, was Luna in silver, with a greyhound at her feet.

The size of these statues was somewhat more than a third part of the pillars on which they stood, and they were so admirably wrought, according to mathematical proportion, that Polycletus' canon (or rule) could hardly have stood in competition with them.

The basis of the pillars, the chapiters, the architraves, zoophores, and cornices, were Phrygian work of massy gold, purer and finer than any that is found in the rivers Leede,[2] near Montpelier, Ganges in India, Po in Italy, Hebrus in Thrace, Tagus in Spain, and Pactolus in Lydia.

The small arches between the pillars were of the same precious stone of which the pillars next to them were. Thus, that arch was of sapphire which ended at the hyacinth pillar, and that was of hyacinth which went towards the diamond, and so on.

Above the arches and chapiters of the pillars, on the inward front, a cupola was raised to cover the fountain; it was surrounded by the planetary statues,

---

[2] The Lez. From Ledus.

heptagonal at the bottom, and spherical on the top, and of crystal so pure, transparent, well-polished, whole and uniform in all its parts, without veins, clouds, flaws, or streaks, that Zenocrates never saw such a one in his life.

Within it were seen the twelve signs of the Zodiac, the twelve months of the year, with their properties, the two equinoxes, the ecliptic line, with some of the most remarkable fixed stars about the antarctic pole, and elsewhere, so curiously engraven, that I fancied them to be the workmanship of King Necepsus, or Petosiris, the ancient mathematician.

On the top of the cupola, just over the centre of the fountain, were three noble long pearls, all of one size, pear fashion, perfectly imitating a tear, and so joined together as to represent a fleur-de-lis or lily, each of the flowers seeming above a hand's breadth. A carbuncle jetted out of its calix or cup, as big as an ostrich's egg, cut seven square (that number so beloved of nature), and so prodigiously glorious, that the sight of it had like to have made us blind, for the fiery sun, or the pointed lightning, are not more dazzling and insufferably bright.

Now were some judicious appraisers to judge of the value of this incomparable fountain, and the lamp of which we have spoke, they would undoubtedly affirm, it exceeds that of all the treasures and curiosities in Europe, Asia, and Africa put together. For that carbuncle alone would have darkened the pantarbe of Iarchus the Indian magician, with as much ease as the sun outshines and dims the stars with his meridian rays.

Now let Cleopatra, that Egyptian queen, boast of her pair of pendants, those two pearls, one of which she caused to be dissolved in vinegar, in the presence of Anthony the Triumvir, her gallant !

Or let Pompeia Plautina [3] be proud of her dress covered all over with emeralds and pearls curiously intermixed, she who attracted the eyes of all Rome, and was said to be the grave-pit and magazine of the conqnering robbers of the universe.

The fountain had three tubes or channels of right pearl, seated in three equilateral angles already mentioned, extended on the margin, and those channels proceeded in a snail-like line, winding equally on both sides.

We looked on them awhile, and had cast our eyes on another side, when Bacbuc directed us to watch the water; we then heard a most harmonious sound, yet somewhat stopped by starts, far distant, and subterranean, by which means it was still more pleasing than if it had been free, uninterrupted, and near us, so that our minds were as agreeably entertained through our ears with that charming melody, as they were through the windows of our eyes, with those delightful objects.

Bacbuc then said, Your philosophers will not allow that motion is begot by the power of figures; look here and see the contrary. By that single snail-like motion, equally divided as you see, and a five-fold infoliature, moveable at every inward meeting, such as is the vena cava, where it enters into the right ventricle of the heart; just so is the flowing of this fountain, and by it a harmony ascends as high as your world's ocean.

She then ordered her attendants to make us drink; and, to tell you the truth of the matter as near as possible, we are not, heaven be praised! of the nature of a drove of calf-lollies, who (as your

[3] Rabelais, who it is probable wrote from memory, is mistaken here, and had forgot that Pliny calls this lady Lollia Paulina.

sparrows cannot feed unless you bob them on the
tail⁴) must be rib-roasted with tough crab-tree, and
firked into a stomach, or, at least, into an humour to
eat or drink : no, we know better things, and scorn
to scorn any man's civility, who civilly invites us
to a drinking bout. Bacbuc asked us then, how
we liked our tiff. We answered, that it seemed to
us good, harmless, sober Adam's liquor, fit to keep
a man in the right way, and, in a word, mere element; more cool and clear than Argyrontes in
Ætolia, Peneus in Thessaly, Axius in Mygdonia,
or Cydnus in Cilicia, a tempting sight of whose cool
silver stream caused Alexander to prefer the short-
lived pleasure of bathing himself in it, to the inconveniences which he could not but foresee would
attend so ill-timed an action.

This, said Bacbuc, comes of not considering with
ourselves, or understanding the motions of the
musculous tongue, when the drink glides on it in
its way to the stomach. Tell me, noble strangers,
are your throats lined, paved, or enamelled, as formerly was that of Pithyllus,⁵ nicknamed Theutes,
that you can have missed the taste, relish, and
flavour of this divine liquor? Here, said she, turning towards her gentlewomen, bring my scrubbing-
brushes, you know which, to scrape, rake, and clear
their palates.

They brought immediately some stately, swinge-

---

⁴ Here the author has in his eye the *badauds* (cockneys we
call them) of Paris. He before, in l. 2, c. 14, calls them
buvereaux (*i.e.*, sippers, small drinkers, though it may mean
water-drinkers), because, as Budæus observes, l. 5, of his *De Asse*,
the people of Paris, generally, drink but little wine. Rabelais
calls them calves (*veaux*). Now, to play the calf, is properly
to play the cockney (*badaud*). This *badaud* may well enough
come from *vitellus*.

⁵ See Athenæus, l. 1, c. 6.

ing, jolly hams, fine substantial neat's-tongues, good
hung-beef, pure and delicate botargos, venison,
sausages, and such other gullet-sweepers. And, to
comply with her invitation, we crammed and twisted
till we owned ourselves thoroughly cured of thirst,[6]
which before did damnably plague us.

We are told, continued she, that formerly a
learned and valiant Hebrew chief, leading his people
through the deserts, where they were in danger of
being famished, obtained of God some manna, whose
taste was to them, by imagination, such as that of
meat was to them before in reality : thus, drinking
of this miraculous liquor, you will find its taste like
any wine that you shall fancy to drink. Come,
then, fancy and drink. We did so, and Panurge
had no sooner whipped off his brimmer, but he cried,
By Noah's open shop ! it is vin de Baulne, better
than ever was yet tipped over tongue, or may ninety
and sixteen devils swallow me ! Oh ! that to keep
its taste the longer, we gentlemen topers had but
necks some three cubits long or so, as Philoxenus
desired to have, or, at least, like a crane's as Melan-
thus [7] wished his.

On the faith of true Lanterners, quoth Friar John,
it is gallant, sparkling Greek wine; now, for God's
sake, sweetheart, do but teach me how the devil
you make it. It seems to me Mirevaux wine, said
Pantagruel, for, before I drank, I supposed it to be
such. Nothing can be disliked in it, but that it is
cold, colder, I say, than the very ice; colder than
the water of Nonacris and Dircé,[8] or the Contho-

---

[6] The original reads : *nous mangeasmes jusque la que confessions
nos estomachz estre tresbien escurez, de soif nous importunans assez
fascheusement.*

[7] It is Athenæus, who, l. 1, c. 5, relates the story.

[8] Rabelais, who did not narrowly look into the thing, has writ
it Dircé, doubtless misled by honest Nicholas Perrot, whose

porian spring at Corinth, that froze up the stomach and nutritive parts of those that drank of it.

Drink once, twice, or thrice more, said Bacbuc, still changing your imagination, and you shall find its taste and flavour to be exactly that on which you shall have pitched. Then never presume to say that anything is impossible to God. We never offered to say such a thing, said I; far from it, we maintain He is omnipotent.

CHAPTER XLIII

HOW THE PRIESTESS BACBUC EQUIPT PANURGE, IN ORDER TO HAVE THE WORD OF THE BOTTLE

WHEN we had thus chatted and tippled, Bacbuc asked, Who of you here would have the word of the Holy Bottle? I, your most humble little funnel, if it please you, quoth Panurge. Friend, said she, I have but one thing to tell you, which is, that when you come to the Oracle, you take care to hearken and hear the word only with one ear. This, cried Friar John, is wine of one ear, as Frenchmen call it.

She then wrapped him up in a gaberdine, bound his noddle with a goodly clean biggin, clapped over it a felt, such as those through which hypocras is distilled,[1] at the bottom of which, instead of a cowl, she put three obelisks, made him draw on a pair of

words on this passage of Martial, are: 'Dircê et Neme fontes sunt frigidissimi æstate inter Bilbilim et Segobregam, in ripa fere Salonis amnis.' So I have even left it Dircé in the text; though I am satisfied it is wrong.

[1] [It is known to the old distillers as 'the sleeve of Hippocrates.']

old-fashioned codpieces instead of mittens, girded him about with three bagpipes bound together, bathed his jobbernol thrice in the fountain; then threw a handful of meal on his phiz, fixed three cock's feathers on the right side of the hypocratical felt, made him take a jaunt nine times round the fountain, caused him to take three little leaps, and to bump his arse seven times against the ground, repeating I do not know what kind of conjurations all the while in the Tuscan tongue, and ever and anon reading in a ritual or book of ceremonies, carried after her by one of her mystagogues.

For my part, may I never stir if I do not really believe, that neither Numa Pompilius, the second King of the Romans, nor the Cerites of Tuscia, nor the old Hebrew captain, ever instituted so many ceremonies as I then saw performed; nor were ever half so many religious forms used by the soothsayers of Memphis in Egypt to Apis; or by the Euboians, at Rhamnus, to Rhamnusia; or to Jupiter Ammon,[2] or to Faronia.[3]

When she had thus accoutred my gentleman, she took him out of our company, and led him out of the temple, through a golden gate on the right, into a round chapel made of transparent speculary stones, by whose solid clearness the sun's light shined there through the precipice of the rock without any windows or other entrance,[4] and so easily and fully dispersed itself through the greater temple, that the light seemed rather to spring out of it than to flow into it.

The workmanship was not less rare than that or

[2] See Q. Curtius, l. 4.

[3] A Goddess of the Woods; for it is storied, that when her grove in the mountain of Soracte was burned down, the people carried thither her picture, and presently the wood sprang afresh.

[4] An imitation of Pliny's description of the temple of Fortune of Seius, built by Nero, l. 36, c. 22.

the sacred temple at Ravenna,[5] or that in the island of Chemnis in Egypt. Nor must I forget to tell you, that the work of that round chapel was contrived with such a symmetry, that its diameter was just the height of the vault.

In the middle of it was an heptagonal fountain of fine alabaster most artfully wrought, full of water, which was so clear that it might have passed for element in its purity and simplicity. The sacred Bottle was in it to the middle, clad in pure fine crystal, of an oval shape, except its muzzle, which was somewhat wider than was consistent with that figure.

CHAPTER XLIV

HOW BACBUC, THE HIGH-PRIESTESS, BROUGHT PANURGE
BEFORE THE HOLY BOTTLE

THERE the noble priestess Bacbuc made Panurge stoop and kiss the brink of the fountain; then bade him rise and dance three ithymbi.[1] Which done, she ordered him to sit down, between two stools placed there for that purpose, his arse upon the ground. Then she opened her ritual book, and, whispering in his left ear, made him sing an *epileny*, as follows :—

[5] The cathedral church of Ravenna was anciently a temple consecrated to Hercules.
[1] Dances in honour of Bacchus.

BOTTLE! whose mysterious deep
Does ten thousand secrets keep,
With attentive ear I wait;
Ease my mind, and speak my fate.
Soul of joy, like Bacchus, we
More than India gain by thee.
Truths unborn thy juice reveals,
Which futurity conceals.
Antidote to frauds and lies,
Wine, that mounts us to the skies
May thy father Noah's brood
Like him drown, but in thy flood.
Speak, so may the liquid mine
Of rubies or of diamonds shine.
Bottle! whose mysterious deep
Does ten thousand secrets keep,
With attentive ear I wait;
Ease my mind, and speak my fate.

When Panurge had sung, Bacbuc threw I do not
know what into the fountain, and straight its water
began to boil in good earnest, just for the world
as doth the great monastical pot at Bourgueil,[2]
when it is high holiday there. Friend Panurge
was listening with one ear, and Bacbuc kneeled
by him, when such a kind of humming was
heard out of the Bottle, as is made by a swarm
of bees bred in the flesh of a young bull, killed
and dressed according to Aristæus' art, or such
as is made when a bolt flies out of a cross-bow,
or when a shower falls on a sudden in summer.
Immediately after this was heard the word TRINC.
By cob's body, cried Panurge, it is broken, or
cracked at least, not to tell a lie for the matter;
for, even so do crystal bottles speak in our country,
when they burst near the fire.

Bacbuc arose, and gently taking Panurge under
the arms, said, Friend, offer your thanks to indulgent
heaven, as reason requires ; you have soon had the
word of the Goddess Bottle : and the kindest, most
favourable, and certain word of answer that I ever
yet heard her give, since I officiated here at her
most sacred oracle ; rise, let us go to the chapter,
in whose gloss that fine word is explained. With
all my heart, quoth Panurge ; by jingo ! I am just
as wise as I was last year ; light ! where is the
book ? Turn it over, where is the chapter ? Let
us see this merry gloss.

[2] St Peter of Bourgueil, of the order of St Benedict, a royal
abbey in the diocese of Angers.

CHAPTER XLV

HOW BACBUC EXPLAINED THE WORD OF THE GODDESS
BOTTLE

BACBUC having thrown I do not know what into the fountain, straight the water ceased to boil : and then she took Panurge into the greater temple, in the central place, where there was the enlivening fountain.

There she took out a hugeous silver book,[1] in the shape of a half-tierce,[2] or hogshead, of sentences ; and having filled it at the fountain, said to him : The philosophers, preachers, and doctors of your world, feed you up with fine words and cant at the ears ; now, here we really incorporate our precepts at the mouth. Therefore I will not say to you, read this chapter, see this gloss ; no, I say to you, taste me this fine chapter, swallow me this rare gloss. Formerly an ancient prophet[3] of the Jewish nation ate a book, and became a clerk even to the very teeth ; now will I have you drink one, that you may be a clerk to your very liver. Here, open your mandibules.

Panurge gaping as wide as his jaws would stretch,

[1] The monks used to make their drinking-cups in the shape of mass-books and prayer-books, to deceive the world.

[2] It may not be impertinent here to refer to a book called *La Mappemonde Papistique* (Map of Popery), p. 82, which gives an account of a certain sham saint at Venice, who by the help of five or six such books, would spend five or six days together in retirement, and make believe he subsisted all the while by a miracle. At last, these devotional books were found to be no other than so many cases, some filled with march-panes made of the best and fleshiest parts of capons and partridges, and the others so many flagons full of Malmsey wine.

[3] Ezekiel, c. ii. and iii.

195

Bacbuc took the silver book, at least we took it for
a real book, for it looked just for the world like a
breviary ; but, in truth, it was a breviary, a flask of
right Falernian wine, as it came from the grape,
which she made him swallow every drop.

By Bacchus ! quoth Panurge, this was a notable
chapter, a most authentic gloss, on my word. Is
this all that the Trismegistian Bottle's word means ?
In troth I like it extremely, it went down like
mother's milk. Nothing more, returned Bacbuc ;
for *Trinc* is a panomphean word, that is, a word
understood, used, and celebrated by all nations,
and signifies drink.

Some say in your world, that sack is a word used
in all tongues, and justly admitted in the same sense
among all nations ; for, as Æsop's fable hath it, all
men are born with a sack at the neck, naturally
needy, and begging of each other ; neither can
the most powerful king be without the help of
other men, or can any one that is poor subsist
without the rich, though he be never so proud
and insolent ; nay, even were it Hippias [4] the
philosopher, who boasted he could do everything.
Much less can any one make shift without drink
than without a sack. Therefore here we hold
not that laughing, but that drinking is the dis-
tinguishing character of man. I do not say drinking, taking that word singly and absolutely in the
strictest sense : no, beasts then might put in for
a share ; I mean drinking cool delicious wine.
For you must know, my beloved, that by wine
we become divine ; neither can there be a surer
argument, or a less deceitful divination. Your
academics assert the same, when they make the
etymology of wine, which the Greeks call OINOΣ,

4 See Plato in his *Hippias minor.*

to be from *vis*, strength, virtue, and power; for it is in its power to fill the soul with all truth, learning, and philosophy.

If you observe what is written in Ionic letters on the temple gate, you may have understood that truth is in wine.   The Goddess Bottle therefore directs you to the divine liquor; [5] be yourself the expounder of your undertaking.

It is impossible, said Pantagruel to Panurge, to speak more to the purpose than does this true priestess; you may remember I told you as much when you first spoke to me about it.

TRINC then! what says your heart, elevated by Bacchic enthusiasm?

With this quoth Panurge,

Trinc! trinc! by Bacchus let us tope,
And tope again; for, now I hope
To see some brawny, juicy rump
Well tickled with my carnal stump.
Ere long, my friends, I shall be wedded,
Sure as my trap-stick has a red head;
And my sweet wife shall hold the combat,
Long as my baws can on her bum beat.
O what a battle of a—fighting
Will there be! which I much delight in?
What pleasing pains then shall I take
To keep myself and spouse awake!
All heart and juice, I'll up and ride,
And make a duchess of my bride.
Sing Iö pæan! loudly sing
To Hymen, who all joys will bring.

5 Only cheer up your hearts and be merry; and for everything else, so you hold fast your integrity, and maintain the character of a worthy, honest man, whatever state or condition of life may fall to your lot, married or single, God will love you, and be your friend, and all good men will esteem you.

Well, Friar John, I'll take my oath,
This oracle is full of troth :
Intelligible truth it bears,
More certain than the sieve and shears.

CHAPTER XLVI

HOW PANURGE AND THE REST RHYMED WITH POETIC FURY

WHAT a pox ails the fellow? quoth Friar John.
Stark staring mad, or bewitched on my word!
Do but hear the chiming dotterel gabble in
rhyme. What the devil has he swallowed? His
eyes roll in his loggerhead, just for the world like
a dying goat's. Will the addle-pated wight have
the grace to sheer off? Will he rid us of his
damned company, to go shite out his nasty rhyming balderdash in some bog-house? Will nobody
be so kind as to cram some dog's-bur down the
poor cur's gullet? or will he, monk-like, run his
fist up to the elbow into his throat to his very
maw, to scour and clean his flanks? Will he
take a hair of the same dog?

Pantagruel chid Friar John, and said :

Bold monk, forbear; this, I'll assure ye,
Proceeds all from poetic fury;
Warmed by the god, inspired with wine,
His human soul is made divine.

For without jest,
His hallowed breast,
With wine possessed,
Could have no rest,

198

Till he had expressed
Some thoughts at least
Of his great guest.
Then straight he flies
Above the skies,
And mollifies,
With prophesies,
Our miseries.
And since divinely he's inspired,
Adore the soul by wine acquired,
And let the tosspot be admired.

How! quoth the friar, is the fit of rhyming upon you too? Is it come to that? Then we are all peppered, or the devil pepper me. What would I not give to have Gargantua see us while we are in this maggoty crambo-vein! Now may I be cursed with living on that damned empty food, if I can tell whether I shall escape the catching distemper. The devil a bit do I understand which way to go about it: however, the spirit of fustian possesses us all, I find. Well, by St John! I will poetise, since everybody does; I find it coming. Stay, and pray pardon me, if I do not rhyme in crimson;[1] it is my first essay.

Thou, who canst water turn to wine,[2]
Transform my bum, by power divine,
Into a lantern, that may light
My neighbour in the darkest night.

[1] *Cramoisy* (crimson) in French does not so much signify a particular colour as the perfection of any colour whatsoever. Thus, to rhyme in crimson, is, properly speaking, to make as excellent verses in their kind, as crimson is in matter of colours.

[2] It is more profane in the French original a good deal; it is too impious even in the translation: but, we must consider a monk speaks it, as honest Martin Luther used to excuse his rapping out an oath now and then: 'Consider I was bred a monk.'

Panurge then procceds in his rapture, and says :

> From Pythian tripos ne'er were heard
> More truths, nor more to be revered.
> I think from Delphos to this spring,
> Some wizard brought that conjuring thing.
> Had honest Plutarch here been toping,
> He then so long had ne'er been groping
> To find, according to his wishes,
> Why oracles are mute as fishes
> At Delphos : now the reason's clear,
> No more at Delphos they're, but here.
> Here is the tripos, out of which
> Is spoke the doom of poor and rich.
> For Athenæus does relate
> This Bottle is the Womb of Fate ;
> Prolific of mysterious wine,
> And big with prescience divine ;
> It brings the truth with pleasure forth,
> Besides you haven't a pennyworth.
> So, Friar John, I must exhort you
> To wait a word that may import you,
> And to inquire, while here we tarry,
> If it shall be your luck to marry.

Friar John answers him in a rage, and says :

> How, marry ! by St Bennet's boot,
> And his gambadoes, I'll ne'er do't.
> No man that knows me ne'er shall judge
> I mean to make myself a drudge ;
> Or that pilgarlic e'er will doat
> Upon a paltry petticoat.
> I'll ne'er my liberty betray
> All for a little leap-frog play ;
> And ever after wear a clog
> Like monkey or like mastiff-dog :

> No, I'd not have, upon my life,
> Great Alexander for my wife,
> Nor Pompey, nor his dad-in-law,
> Who did each other clapper-claw,
> Not the best he that wears a head,
> Shall win me to his truckle-bed.

Panurge, pulling off his gaberdine and mystical accoutrements, replies :

> Wherefore thou shalt, thou filthy beast,
> Be damned twelve fathoms deep at least ;
> While I shall reign in Paradise,
> Whence on thy loggerhead I'll piss,
> Now when that dreadful hour is come,
> That thou in hell receiv'st thy doom,
> E'en there, I know, thou'lt play some trick,
> And Proserpine sha'n't 'scape a prick
> Of the long pin within thy breeches.
> But when thou'rt using these capriches,
> And caterwauling in her cavern,
> Send Pluto to the farthest tavern,
> For the best wine that's to be had,
> Lest he should see, and run horn mad :
> She's kind, and ever did admire
> A well-fed monk, or well-hung friar.

Go to, quoth Friar John, thou old noddy, thou doddipoled ninny, go to the devil thou art prating of ; I have done with rhyming ; the rheum gripes me at the gullet. Let us talk of paying and going ; come.

———

CHAPTER XLVII

HOW WE TOOK OUR LEAVE OF BACBUC, AND LEFT THE ORACLE OF THE HOLY BOTTLE

Do not trouble yourself about anything here, said the priestess to the friar; if you be but satisfied, we are. Here below, in these circumcentral regions, we place the sovereign good not in taking and receiving, but in bestowing and giving; so that we esteem ourselves happy, not if we take and receive much of others, as perhaps the sects of teachers do in your world, but rather if we impart and give much. All I have to beg of you, is that you leave us here your names in writing, in this ritual. She then opened a fine large book, and as we gave our names, one of her (she) mystagogues, with a gold pin, drew some lines on it, as if she had been writing; but we could not see any characters.

This done, she filled three small leather vessels, with fantastic water, and giving them into our hands, said, Now, my friends, you may depart, and may that intellectual sphere, whose centre is everywhere, and circumference nowhere, whom we call God, keep you in His almighty protection. When you come into your world, do not fail to affirm and witness, that the greatest treasures, and most admirable things, are hidden under ground; and not without reason.

Ceres was worshipped, because she taught mankind the art of husbandry, and by the use of corn, which she invented, abolished that beastly way of feeding on acorns; and she grievously lamented her daughter's banishment into our subterranean regions, certainly foreseeing that Proserpine would meet with more excellent things, more desirable enjoyments, below, than she her mother could be blessed with above.

What do you think is become of the art of forcing the thunder and celestial fire down, which the wise Prometheus had formerly invented ?   It is most certain you have lost it; it is no more on your hemisphere : but here below we have it.   And, without a cause, you sometimes wonder to see whole towns burned and destroyed by lightning and ethereal fire, and are at a loss about knowing from whom, by whom, and to what end, those dreadful mischiefs were sent.   Now they are familiar and usual to us; and your philosophers, who complain that the ancients have left them nothing to write of, or to invent, are very much mistaken. Those phenomena which you see in the sky; whatever the surface of the earth affords you, and the sea, and every river contains, is not to be compared with what is hid within the bowels of the earth.

For this reason the subterranean ruler has justly gained in almost every language, the epithet of rich. Now, when your sages shall wholly apply their minds to a diligent and studious search after truth, humbly begging the assistance of the sovereign God, whom formerly the Egyptians in their language called The Hidden and The Concealed, and invoking Him by that name, beseech Him to reveal and make Himself known to them, that Almighty Being will, out of His infinite goodness, not only make His creatures, but even Himself known to them.

Thus will they be guided by good lanterns.   For all the ancient philosophers and sages have held two things necessary, safely and pleasantly to arrive at the knowledge of God, and true wisdom : first, God's gracious guidance, then man's assistance.

So among the philosophers, Zoroaster took Arimaspes for the companion of his travels ; Æsculapius, Mercury; Orpheus, Musæus ; Pythagoras, Aglaophemus ; and among princes and warriors, Hercules, in his most difficult achievements, had his singular friend Theseus ; Ulysses, Diomedes ; Æneas, Achates : you followed their examples, and came under the conduct of an illustrious lantern ; now, in God's name depart, and may He go along with you ! [1]

On Chap. XXXVII., etc.—The description of the temple, its gates, pavement, walls, lamps, and fountains, is a masterpiece of architecture; by which the author showed, that he knew as well all the beauties of that art, as he did those of every other that deserves the application of a man of sense. If any have a mind to look for mysteries in all this, perhaps they may find many whose discovery will reward their search. As for me, as I have not had leisure to say more in less room, I will only say something of it that may give a general idea of the author's design, and so conclude.

Bacbuc, which is the name of the bottle, and also that of the priestess, who ministers at the oracle, is Hebrew, and, as we have said, signifies a bottle.

Our mysterious author may perhaps be thought to have had a mind to hint, that the Hebrew original, or text of the Bible, is the first spring of truth, that flows out of it into the versions, as wine poured out of a bottle into a glass or cup. Then, as on the portal of the temple, there was written in characters of the finest gold, 'ΕΝ 'ΟΙΝΩ 'ΑΛΗΘΕΙΑ, [2] some may think it implies, that the wine of truth is also to be found in the Greek text of the New Testament, which gives the name of wine to truth : buy wine and honey without money. The two folding gates may be fancied to denote the Old Testament and the New, which must be opened to come to the oracle of truth. Every one will not like this manner of explaining those passages ; but all, I hope, will approve the following way of understanding the rest.

The perspicuous lantern, which lighted and guided our votaries, opens those gates; but desires them not to take it amiss, that she

---

[1] The usual words of the French preachers concluding their sermons.

[2] *In vino veritas.*

does not go into the temple with them, leaving them wholly to
the conduct of the priestess Bacbuc : for the lantern was not
allowed to go in for certain causes, rather to be concealed than
revealed to mortals.   However, she advises them to be resolute
and secure.

This mystical reason is, that as truth is hated in this world,
most of the learned, who know it, are afraid of conversing with
it openly, lest this make many men their enemies, spoil their
preferment, ruin them, and perhaps cost them their lives.   For
this reason, they come to the very portal of truth's temple,
and even open the gates to others; yet do not enter within its
sanctuary.

The greatest men, both of the clergy and laity in France,
acted thus in the reigns of Francis I. and Henry II.

But another cause of that venerable lantern's staying without
the temple, was the piercing glory which flowed out of the in-
extinguishable lamp, which filled the subterranean temple with a
light infinitely quicker and clearer than that of the sun.   So that
this extreme brightness would have utterly dimmed and eclipsed
that of the lantern.

The author could never have concluded better than by saying,
that when our sages shall wholly apply their minds to a diligent
and studious search after truth, beseeching the hidden God to
make Himself known to them, that Almighty Being will do it,
and impart to them also the knowledge of His creatures.—*M*.

[The references to Pliny in the notes of Mr Ozell are innumerable, and often impertinent.   The scholar who may choose to
compare the natural history of Rabelais with the Latin original
may easily do so without this help.]

END OF BOOK V.

PANTAGRUELIAN PROGNOSTICA-TION,

FOR THE YEAR THAT IS TO COME, FOR EVER AND AYE. CALCULATED FOR THE BENEFIT AND NODDIFICA-TION OF THE GIDDY-BRAINED AND WEATHER-WISE WOULD-BE'S. BY MASTER ALCOFRIBAS NASIER, ARCHITRICLIN TO THE AFORE-MENTIONED PANTA-GRUEL

TO THE COURTEOUS READER

GREETING.—Having considered the infinite abuses arising from the whole cart-loads of Louvain Prognostications, made in the shadow of a pot of drink,[1] or so; I have here calculated one of the most sure and unerring that ever was seen in black and white, as hereafter you will find. For, doubtless, considering what the royal prophet says to God in the fifth Psalm, Thou shalt destroy them that speak leasing, it is a heinous, foul, and crying sin to tell a damned wilful lie, thereby to deceive the poor gaping world, greedy of novelties; such as the French, above all others, have been time out of mind, as Cæsar in his

[1] In the shadow of a glass of wine; _à l'ombre d'ung verre de vin._

Commentaries, and John de Gravot in his Gallic Mythologies, have set down. Which is daily observable throughout all France, where the first questions, which you shall put to people newly arrived, are, What news ? Is there no news stirring ? What do they say ? What is the discourse abroad ? And so inquisitive they are, that they will be stark staring mad at those who come out of strange countries, unless they bring a whole budget full of strange stories, calling them dolts, blockheads, ninnyhammers, and silly ouffs.

Since, then, they are so ready to ask after news, and consequently the more glibly swallow down every flim-flam story that is told them, were it not expedient that some people, on whose faith we might depend, should hold offices of intelligence on the frontiers of the kingdom, and have a competent salary allowed them for nothing else but to examine the news that is brought, whether it is true or no ? Yea, verily, friends. Even so did my good master Pantagruel through all the countries of Utopia and Dipsody : whence it comes that his territories are so prosperous, that at present they cannot tell how to make away with their wine fast enough, but are fain to let it run about in waste, if plenty of good fellows from other parts do not come to help them off with it.

Being therefore desirous to satisfy the curiosity of every good companion, I have tumbled over and over all the pantarchs of the heavens, calculated the quadrates of the moon, hooked out whatever all the astrophiles,[2] hypernephelists,[3] anemophylaxes,[4]

---

[2] Star-lovers.
[3] Such as, by their speculations, raise themselves above the clouds.
[4] Those who bend their thoughts to foretell the blowing of the winds.

uranopetes,[6] ombrophorcs,[7] and the devil and all of them, have thought; and then having conferred with Empedocles upon the whole, who, by the way, desires to be kindly remembered to you, I have here crammed the pith, marrow, and matter of the substance of it into a few chapters. Assuring you that I say nothing of it but what I think; and that I think nothing of it, but what it is; and there is no more to be known in those matters, than what you are going to read. As for anything that may hereafter be said over and above, it will come to pass, peradventure aye, and peradventure no.

Take notice, by-the-bye, that if you do not believe every syllable, iota, and tittle of it, you do me a great deal of wrong, for which, either here or elsewhere, you may chance to be clawed off with a vengeance. A good salt-eel, crab-tree, or bull's pizzle, may be plentifully bestowed on your outward man. You may take pepper in the nose, and snuff and suck up the air as you would oysters, as much as you please; it is all one for that.[7]

Well, however, come, snite your noses, my little children; and you old doating father grey-beards, pull out your best eyes, do on your barnacles, and, in the scale of the sanctuary, weigh me every tittle of what I am going to tell you.

[5] Those who scale the heavens.
[6] Those whose application consists in foretelling the rain.
[7] Here M. Motteux should have added: For depend upon it, there will be hot work at the oven, if the baker do not fall asleep. Upon which conclusion of the sentence, and its beginning with the anguillades (*i.e.*, the whippings with an eel, or an eel's skin), M. Duchat observes, that it is a warning to the French Protestants to quit the kingdom betimes, or prepare to be infallibly burned in it, since their enemies had sworn to destroy them root and branch.

Pantagruelian Prognostication

Of the golden number.—The golden number [8] *non est inventus ;* I cannot find it this year by any calculation that I have made. Let's go on ; *verte folium,* turn over leaf.

CHAPTER I

OF THE GOVERNOR AND LORD ASCENDANT THIS YEAR

WHATSOEVER those blindfolded blockheadly fools, the astrologers of Louvain, Nuremberg, Tubing, and Lyons, may tell ye, don't you feed yourselves up with whims and fancies, nor believe there is any governor of the whole universe this year, but God the Creator, Who by His divine word rules and governs all ; by whom all things are in their nature, propriety, and conditions, and without Whose preservation and governance all things in a moment would be reduced to nothing, as out of nothing they were by Him created. For of Him comes, in Him is, and by Him is made perfect every being, and all life and motion, as says the evangelical trumpet, my Lord St Paul, Romans the 11th.

Therefore the ruler of this year, and of all others, according to our authentic solution, will be God Almighty. And neither Saturn, nor Mars, nor Jupiter, nor any other planet, nor the very angels, nor saints, nor men, nor devils, shall have any virtue, efficacy, or influence whatsoever, unless God of His good pleasure gives it them. As Avicen says, second causes have not any influence or action whatsoever, if the first cause did not influence them. Does not the good little mannikin speak truth, think ye ?

[8] It runs thus in the original : Of the golden number, *non dicitur ;* because I cannot find it, etc.

CHAPTER II

OF THE ECLIPSES THIS YEAR

THIS year there will be so many eclipses of the sun and moon, that I fear (not unjustly) our pockets[1] will suffer inanition, be full empty, and our feeling at a loss. Saturn will be retrograde, Venus direct, Mercury as unfixed as quicksilver. And a pack of planets will not go as you would have them.

For this reason the crabs will go side-long and the rope-makers backward; the little stools will get upon the benches, and the spits on the racks, and the bands on the hats; and many a one's yard will hang down and dandle for want of leathern pouches; fleas will be generally black; bacon will run away from pease in Lent; the belly will waddle "before; the bum will sit down first; there will not be a bean left in a twelfth-cake, nor an ace in a flush; the dice will not run as you wish, though you cog them, and the chance that you desire will seldom come; brutes shall speak in several places; Shrovetide will have its day; one part of the world shall disguise itself to gull and chouse the other, and run about the streets like a parcel of addle-pated animals and mad devils; such a hurly-burly was never seen since the devil was a little boy; and there will be above seven-and-twenty irregular verbs made this year, if Priscian[2] do not hold them in. If God do not help us, we

---

[1] By the sun, chemists mean gold; and by the moon, silver.

[2] Priscian is here put for grammar in general, and in particular for the French grammar, so subject to changes, especially in the verbs at that time; some saying *alla*, others *allit*, *allerent*, *allirent*, and *allarent*; *mors* for *mordu*, *querre* for *querir*, and an hundred others, which were used for the most part indifferently.

shall have our hands and hearts full. But on the other side, if He be with us, nothing can hurt us, as says the celestial star-gazer, who was rapt into the third heaven, Romans the 8th. *Si Deus pro nobis, quis contra nos?* If God be for us, who can be against us? In good faith, *nemo Domine*, nobody is not like your worship; for He is as powerful as He is good. Here for the same, praise ye His holy name.

CHAPTER III[1]

OF THE DISEASES THIS YEAR

THIS year the stone-blind shall see but very little; the deaf shall hear but scurvily; the dumb shall not speak very plain; the rich shall be somewhat in a better case than the poor, and the healthy than the sick. Whole flocks, herds, and droves of sheep, swine, and oxen, cocks and hens, ducks and drakes, geese and ganders, shall go to pot; but the mortality will not be altogether so great among apes, monkeys, baboons, and dromedaries. As for old age, it will be incurable this year, because of the years past. Those who are sick of the pleurisy will feel a plaguey stitch in their sides; those who are troubled with the thorough-go-nimble, or wild-squirt, will often prostitute their blind cheeks to the bog-house; catarrhs this year shall distil from the brain on the lower parts; sore eyes will by no means help the sight; ears shall be at least as scarce

[1] This chapter is so like that which Joach. Fortius Rindel-bergius of Antwerp has entitled *Ridicula, sed jucunda, quædam vaticinia* (anno 1529), that I know not which of the two is the original.

and short in Gascony, and among knights of the
post, as ever; a most horrid and dreadful, virulent,
malignant, catching, perverse, and odious malady,
shall be almost epidemical, insomuch that many
shall run mad upon it, not knowing what nail to
drive to keep the wolf from the door; very often
plotting, contriving, cudgelling, and puzzling their
weak shallow brains, and syllogising and prying up
and down for the philosopher's stone, though they
only get Midas' lugs by the bargain. I quake for
very fear when I think on it; for I assure you, few
will escape this disease, which Averroes calls lack
of money; and by consequence of the last year's
comet, and Saturn's retrogradation, a huge drivelling
he-scoundrel, all be-crinkum'd, be-scabbed, and
cauliflowered with the pox, shall die in the spital;
at his death will be a horrid clutter between the
cats and the rats, hounds and hares, hawks and
ducks, and eke between the monks and eggs.

CHAPTER IV

OF THE FRUITS OF THE EARTH THIS YEAR

I find, by the calculations of Albumazar,[1] in his
book of the Great Conjunction, and elsewhere, that
this will be a plentiful year of all manner of good
things to those who have enough: but your hops
of Picardy will go near to fare the worse for the
cold. As for oats, they will be a great help to
horses. I dare say there will not be much more
bacon than swine. *Pisces* having the ascendant,
it will be a mighty year for mussels, cockles, and

[1] An Arabian philosopher and astrologer, who lived about the
year 910 of the Christian era.

periwinkles. Mercury somewhat threatens our parsley beds; yet parsley will be to be had for money. Hemp will grow faster than the children of this age, and some will find there is but too much on't. There will be but a very few bonchretiens, but choke-pears in abundance. As for corn, wine, fruit, and herbs, there never was such plenty as will be now, if poor folks may have their wish.

CHAPTER V

OF THE DISPOSITION OF THE PEOPLE THIS YEAR

IT is the oddest whimsy in the world, to fancy there are stars for kings, popes, and great dons, any more than for the poor and needy. As if, forsooth, some new stars were made since the flood, or since Romulus or Pharamond, at the making somebody king; a thing that Triboulet or Caillette[1] would have been ashamed to have said, and yet they were men of no common learning or fame; and for aught you or I know, this same Triboulet may have been of the kings of Castile's blood in Noah's ark, and Caillette of that of King Priam.[2] Now, mark ye me, those odd notions come from nothing in the world but want of faith: I say, the true Catholic faith. Therefore, resting fully satisfied that the stars care not a fart more for kings than for beggars, nor a jot more for your rich topping fellows, than for the most sorry, mangy, lousy rascal; I will even leave other addle-pated fortune-

[1] Two court-fools.
[2] He jokes upon those writers who very orderly trace the genealogy of the kings of Spain up to Adam, and deduce the descent of the kings of France from King Priam.

tellers to speak of the great folks, and I will only talk of the little ones.

And in the first place, of those who are subject to Saturn; as for example, such as lack the ready, jealous, or horn-mad, self-tormenting prigs, dreaming fops, crabbed eavesdroppers, raving, doating churls, hatchers and brooders of mischief, suspicious distrustful slouches, mole-catchers,[3] close-fisted griping misers, usurers, and pawnbrokers, Christian-Jews, pinch-crusts, hold-fasts, michers, and penny-fathers, redeemers of dipped, mortgaged, and bleeding copyholds and messuages, fleecers of sheared asses, shoe-makers and translators, tanners, bricklayers, bell-founders, compounders of loans, patchers, clouters, and botchers of old trumpery stuff, and all moping melancholic folks, shall not have this year whatever they would have; and will think more than once how they may get good store of the king's pictures[4] into their clutches; in the meantime, they will hardly throw shoulders of mutton out at the windows, and will often scratch their working noddles where they do not itch.

As for those who are under Jupiter, as canting vermin, bigots, pardon-pedlars, voluminous abbreviators, scribblers of breves, copists,[5] Pope's

[3] Avaricious money-hunters, who, in order to come at riches, which the earth contains in its bowels, never cease digging and delving, as it were, like the ancient French miners called *franc-taupin* (from *talpo*, a mole.)

[4] It is, in the original, Will study hard about the invention of the holy cross. The invention (or finding) of the holy cross, is a solemn holiday celebrated by the Church of Rome on the third of May: also, a shift or device to get money; and that is what it means here: a merry allusion to the other. These *double-entendres*, with which our author abounds, are very pretty in the French, but not always capable of being rendered into English.

[5] Petty scribes in the Court of Rome, who copy the bulls in order for engrossing.

bull-makers, dataries, pettifoggers, capuchins, monks, hermits, hypocrites, cushion-thumping mountebanks, spiritual comedians, forms of holiness, pater-noster faces, wheedling gabblers, wry-necked scoundrels, spoilers of paper, stately gulls,[6] notched-cropt-eared[7] meacocks, public register's clerks, clergy-tailors, wafer-makers, rosary-makers, engrossers of deeds, notaries, grave-bubbles, protocoles, prompters to speakers, and deceitful makers of promises, they shall fare according as they have money. So many clergymen will die, that there will not be men enough found on whom their benefices may be conferred, so that many will hold two, three, four, or more. The tribe of hypocrites shall lose a good deal of its ancient fame, since the world is grown a rake, and will not be fooled much longer, as Avenzagel saith.

Those who are under Mars, as hangmen, cut-throats, dead-doing fellows, freebooters, hedge-birds, foot-pads, highwaymen, catch-poles, bum-bailiffs, beadles, and watchmen, reformadoes, tooth-drawers and corn-cutters, pintle-smiths, shavers, and frig-beards, butchers, coiners, paltry quacks, and mountebanks,[8]

[6] So indeed, Cotgrave has Englished Rabelais' word *prelinguans*, but M. Duchat is more particular: a chief in a court of judicature, who (in like manner as a taster (*un preguste*) takes the essay of meats with his tongue) sums up, and presents the opinion of the other judges before he declares his own.

[7] *Esperrucquetz*, which Cotgrave says is one that wears long locks, or curled hair; but it really means as M. M. translates it, what the Italians call *tosato, senza zazzera*, crop-haired, without a perriwig. (*Esperruqué*.)

[8] *Tacuins.* In the edition of 1542, it is *avicennists*. Most of the rest have *taquins*, because they knew not what *tacüin* meant. Buhaylyha Ben-Gezla, an Arabian, physician to Charlemagne, writ a book entitled *Tacüens*; a work which signifies tables, repertories, because they were tables containing an enumeration of all distempers, with their cures. This book was translated

renegadoes, apostates, and marranized miscreants,
incendiaries or boutefeus, chimney-sweepers, boorish
cluster-fists, charcoal-men, alchymists, merchants of
eel-skins and egg-shells, gridiron and rattle-makers,
cooks, paltry pedlars, thrashmongers and spangle-
makers, bracelet-makers, lantern-makers and tinkers,
this year will do fine things; but some of them
will be somewhat subject to be rib-roasted, and
have a St Andrew's cross scored over their jobbernols
at unawares. This year, one of those worthy persons
will go nigh to be made a field-bishop, and, mounted
on a horse that was foaled of an acorn, give the
passengers a blessing with his legs.

Those who belong to Sol, as topers, quaffers,
whipcans, tosspots, whittled, mellow, cupshotten
swillers, merry grigs, with crimson snouts of their own
dyeing; fat, pursy gorbellies, brewers of wine and
of beer; bottlers of hay, porters, mowers, menders
of tiled, slated, and thatched houses, burthen-
bearers, packers, shepherds, ox-keepers, and cow-
herds, swine-herds, and hog-drivers, fowlers, and bird-
catchers, gardeners, barn-keepers, hedgers, common
mumpers and vagabonds, day-labourers, scourers of
greasy thrum caps, stuffers, and bumbasters of pack
saddles, rag-merchants, idle lusks, slothful idlebies,
and drowsy loiterers, smell-feasts and snap-gobbets,
gentlemen generally wearing shirts with neck-bands,
or heartily desiring to wear such; all these will be
hale and sharp set, and not be troubled with the
gout at the grinders, or a stoppage at the gullet,
when at a feast on free cost.

Those whom Venus is said to rule, as punks,
jilts, flirts, queans, morts, doxies, strumpets, buttocks,

from the Arabic into Latin, by a Jew, Farrogut, another physician
of Charlemagne's. The translation is still in being, though the
original is lost. See further in Duchat.

blowings, tits, pure ones, concubines, convenients, cracks, drabs, trulls, light-skirts, wrigglers, misses, cats, rigs, tried virgins, bona-robas, barbers'-chairs, hedge - whores, wag - tails, cockatrices, whipsters, twiggers, harlots, kept-wenches, kind-hearted things, ladies of pleasure, by what titles or names soever dignified or distinguished; bawds, pimps, panders, procurers, and mutton-brokers; wenchers, lechers, shakers, smockers, cousins, cullies, stallions, and bellybumpers; ganymedes, bardachoes, hufflers, ingles, fricatrices, he - whores, and sodomites; swaggering huff-snuffs, bouncing bullies, bragga-docios, tory-rory rakes and tantivy boys; peppered, clapped, and poxed dabblers; shankered, cauli-flowered, carbuncled martyrs, and confessors of Venus; rovers, ruffian-rogues, and hedge-creepers, female chamberlains; *nomina mulierum desinentia in ess, ut,* laundress, sempstress, hostess, etc., and in *er, ut,* mantua-maker, bed-maker, bar-keeper, fruiterer, etc., all these will be famous this year. But when the sun enters Cancer, and other signs, let them beware of the crinkams and its attendants; as shankers, claps, virulent gonorrhœas, cordees, buboes, or running-nags, pock-royals, botches, wens, or con-dyloms, tetters, scabs, nodes, glands, tumours, car-nosities, etc. Nuns shall hardly conceive without carnal copulation; very few virgins shall have milk at the breasts.

As for those who come under Mercury, as sharpers, rooks, cozeners, setters, as sharks, cheats, pickpockets, divers, buttocking foils, thieves, millers, night-walkers, masters of arts, decretists, picklocks, deer-stealers, hedge rhymers, composers of serious doggerel metre, Merry-andrews, Jack-puddings, tumblers, masters in the art of hocus-pocus, legerdemain, and powder of prelinpinpin; such as break Priscian's head, quibblers

and punsters, stationers, paper-makers, card-makers,
and pirates, they will strive to appear more merry
than they will often be: sometimes they will laugh
without any cause, and will be pretty apt to be
blown up, hit in the plum bag, and march off, unless,[9] they find themselves better stored with chink,
and stronger of the cod than they need be.

Those who belong to Madam Luna, as hawkers
of almanacks and pamphlets, huntsmen, ostrich-
catchers, falconers, couriers, salt-carriers, lunatics,
maggoty fools, crack-brained coxcombs, addle-pated
frantic wights, giddy, whimsical foplings, exchange-
brokers, post-boys, foot-boys, tennis-court keepers'
boys, glass-mongers, light-horse, watermen, mariners,
messengers, rakers, and gleaners, will not long stay
in a place this year. However, so many swagbellies
and puff-bags will hardly go to St Hiacco,[10] as there
did in the year 524.[11] Great numbers of pilgrims[12]
will come down from the mountains of Savoy and

9 Wrong. Read, if they find themselves, etc., not, unless
they find themselves, etc., ' S'ils se trouvent plus d'argent,' etc.,
not ' S'ils ne se trouvent plus d'argent,' etc. It means, that
nothing can hinder them from running away with your money,
but your not trusting them with it. Again, instead of, need be,
read, should be.

10 St James in Galicia.

11 There had been published many predictions, which on
account of the grand conjunction of Saturn, Jupiter, and Mars,
in the sign of Pisces in 1524, did declare there would be in
February that year a second universal deluge : there needed no
more to send the Germans, at that time very much addicted to
pilgrimaging, in shoals to St James in Galicia. This is what is
here meant by Rabelais, who by lifrelofres means the German
pilgrims, who began to grow scarce after the reformation had got
good footing among them.

12 *Miquelots* in the original. Young people who were wont to
go on pilgrimage to St Michael—thence their name *miquelots*, I
suppose. These occasioned the proverb, Little beggars go to St
Michael, great ones to St James.

Auvergne; but Sagittarius sorely threatens them with kibed heels.

———

CHAPTER VI

OF THE CONDITION OF SOME COUNTRIES

THE noble kingdom of France shall prosper and triumph this year, in all pleasures and delights,[1] so that foreign nations shall willingly retire thither. Presents of nosegays, and feasts on birthdays and saints'-days, treats, pastimes, and a thousand sports, shall keep up the mirth. There will be plenty of delicious wines; many radishes in Limosin; a store of chestnuts in Perigord and Dauphiné; a deal of olives in Languedoc; whole shoals of sand in Olone; a world of fish in the sea; swarms of stars in the firmament; abundance of salt at Brouage; and prodigious quantities of corn, pulse, kitchen-herbs, flowers, fruit, butter, cheese, milk, and other dairy goods. No plague, no war, no vexation. A fart for poverty; hang sorrow, cast away care. Old gold, such as your double ducats, rose-nobles, angels, spankers, spur-royals, and well-wooled sheep of Berry, will once more be in fashion, and plenty of seraphs and crowns with a sun upon them. However, about midsummer, you are threatened with an invasion by black fleas, and weevils of la Deviniere. *A Deo, nil est ex omni parte beatum;* nothing is yet found that is perfectly happy; but care must be taken to curb them with store of evening nunchions.

[1] France enjoyed peace from the treaty concluded at Cambray, 1529 ; but the famine which happened in that kingdom about that time occasioned the plague, and both those scourges continued therein till the beginning of 1534. Therefore, either this prognostication was not published till 1534, at soonest, or Rabelais was much out in his guessing.

Italy, Romania, Naples, and Sicily will remain where they stood last year. People will be very thoughtful[2] there towards the latter end of Lent, and sometimes will rave and dream at noonday.[3]

Germany, Switzerland, Saxony, Strasburg, Antwerp, etc., will thrive upon it, if they do not fail to do so. Woe be to pardon-pedlars, if they come among them: I dare engage that there will not be many yearly[4] obits, trentals, and services for the dead founded there.

Spain, Castile, Portugal, and Arragon will be subject to sudden thirst,[5] and young and old will be woefully afraid of dying: for which reason they will be sure to keep themselves warm when it is cold;[6] and will often tell over their money, if they have any.

England, Scotland, and the Easterlings,[7] will be but indifferent Pantagruelists.[8] Wine would at least prove as wholesome to them as beer, provided it

[2] Will think of their sins, which they are to confess at Easter.

[3] In the original there is no rave, but only dream, and M. Duchat says, Rabelais alludes to the constant custom of the people of Rome to take a nap of two hours immediately after dinner; not in bed, but in easy leather chairs made on purpose, with backs and springs to move higher or lower. See Misson's Travels, let. 33.

[4] Wrong: read there will not be many obits, etc., founded there this year, ceste année (not yearly). For now the reformation had taken deep root.

[5] No sudden in Rabelais: great thirsts, if you will: alterations in French, not altercations, as some editions have it. M. Duchat's note here is two-fold: these countries are very hot, and the inquisition there spares nobody.

[6] It is only warm in the original: that is, says M. Duchat, people there should keep close and snug, not only because the evening dews are mortal there, but that they may give the inquisition no advantage over them.

[7] Otherwise Osterlins. See Commines, 1. 5, c. 18.

[8] Will not always have wine to drink when they have a mind to it.

were good and delicious. When they sit at table, their best hopes will be the after-game. St Traignant of Scotland will work miracles and wonders like mad; but the devil-a-bit will he see the better for all the candles that will be offered him, if Aries [9] ascending does not fumble, and rumble, tumble, stumble, and be humble, though he grumble, and be scorned, and unhorned.

The Muscovites, Indians, Persians, and Troglodytes, will often be troubled with the bloody flux, because they will not be ridden, tupped, and rammed by the Romanists, considering the ball of Sagittarius ascendant. The Bohemians, Jews, and Egyptians, will not be brought this year to conform with the said Romanists, as they expect; Venus bitterly threatens them with wens at the throat, [10] if they do not condescend to the will of the King [11] of the Papillons.

Escargots [12] (snails), Sarabouytes, [13] cauquemares [14]

---

[9] The Pope, and his power.

[10] Gibbets.

[11] The King of France: in the original, *roy de parpaillons*—see this explained elsewhere. What Rabelais seems to hint at here is the Bohemians, etc., who by an edict were banished the kingdom, on pain of being hanged. [*Bœmien* likewise means a gipsy.]

[12] This does not mean snails strictly, in this place at least, but, as M. Duchat observes, monks and other religions, to whom the discipline (whip) seems to be instead of a fly-flap to drive away those troublesome insects. Rabelais calls them escargots (snails), because that being covered with the cowl, they resemble snails in their shells.

[13] Or rather *sarabaites*, spoken of in the last ch. of l. 2, and ch. liv. of l. 4, were, in old times, a certain sort of religious, who lived in the utmost licentiousness and dissolution.

[14] From *calcare mares*. These are the same religious whom elsewhere Rabelais calls *farfadets*, a name by which he likewise calls the hobgoblins, and raw-head and bloody-bones. To these, and the preceding, our author declares that the discipline they

(nightmares), cannibals shall be pestered with ox-
flies (informers, promoters), and will have but little
heart to play on the cymbals, and tongs, and keys
(or, to lecher), unless guaiacum be in request.

As for Austria, Hungary, and Turkey, by my troth,
my dainty lads, I cannot tell how they will do;
neither does pilgarlic trouble his head a jot about it,
considering the sun's brave entrance into Capricornus;
and, if you chance to know more of the matter than
I do, pray scatter no words, keep it to yourselves, but
stay for the lame post.

OF THE FOUR SEASONS OF THE YEAR

CHAPTER VII

OF THE SPRING

In all this year's revolution there will be but one
moon, neither will it be new. I dare warrant, you
are damnably down in the mouth about it; you who
do not believe in God,[1] and persecute His holy and
divine Word, as also those that stand up for it. But
you may even hang yourselves out of the way; I
tell you there will never be any other moon than

will give themselves will reduce them to the same condition with
cannibals, and other nations of America, who, not knowing how
to make themselves clothes (at least, not caring to do it), suffer
great inconveniences from the flies, when the Europeans do not
come and fetch their guaiacum, in return for which they generally
give them clothes to cover them.

[1] No Lutheran could have expressed himself in stronger terms.

that which God created in the beginning of the
world, and which was placed in the sky to light and
guide mankind by night. But, in good sooth, I will
not infer thence that it never shows to the earth and
earthly people a decrease or increase of its light,
according as it is nearer the sun or further from it.
No, no; why should I say this? for, wherefore,
because, however, notwithstanding, that, etc., and let
none of you hereafter pray that heaven may keep her
from the wolves; for they will not meddle with her
for this twelve months, I will warrant you. Apropos,
now I think on it, you will see as many flowers again
this season, as in all the other three; neither shall
that man be thought a fool, who will have wit
enough to lay by money, and get together more of it
this quarter than he will do of cobwebs [2] in the whole
year. The griffons [3] and marrons (men who make
the ways passable in great snows, and dwell on the
mountains of Savoy and Dauphiné), and the hyper-
boreans, that are perpetually furred with snow, are
to miss this season, and have none on it: for
Avicenna tells us, it is not spring till the snow does
melt away on the mountains. Believe the liar. [4] I
have known the time when men reckoned ver, or
the spring, to begin when the sun entered into the
first degree of Aries. If they reckon it otherwise
now, I knock under, and mum is the word.

[2] It should be herrings, *arancz:* though some editions have it
araignes. M. Duchat says, Rabelais here means, that in the
spring people had better keep their money, than lay it out in
herrings, which are good for nothing in that season of the year.

[3] *Gryphons:* men, who, like true griffins, climb up the sharpest
and steepest rocks.

[4] *Croyez ce porteur,* in the original; believe the bearer: *i.e.,* I
stand to what he says about the matter.

CHAPTER VIII

OF SUMMER

In the summer I cannot justly tell you what kind of
wind will blow; but this I know, that it ought to be
warm weather then, and now and then a sea-breeze.
However, if things should fall out otherwise, you
must be sure not to curse God; for He is wiser than
we, and knows what is fit for us far better than we
ourselves: you may take my word for it, whatever
Haly [1] and his gang may have said. It will be a
delicious thing to be merry, and drink cool wine;
though some have said there is nothing more contrary
to thirst. I believe it; and indeed *contraria contrariis
curantur*.

CHAPTER IX

OF AUTUMN

In autumn men will make wine, or before or after
it; it is all one to me, so we have but good bub and
nippitati enough: foul mistakes will then be in season;
for many a one will think only to burst at the broad-
side by the way of a fizzle-cum-funk, and will foully
give their breeches a clyster with a fæcal decoction.
As for those men and women who have vowed to
fast till the stars be in the heavens, they may even
from this present hour begin to feed like farmers by
my particular grant and dispensation. Neither do
they begin of the soonest; for those pretty twinkling
things have been fixed there above sixteen thousand
and I cannot tell how many days, and stuck in to the

[1] An Arabian philosopher and mathematician.

purpose too, let me tell you. Nor would I have
you for the future hope to catch larks when the sky
falls: for on my honour that will not happen in
your time. Legions of hypocritical church-vermin.
cucullated sham saints, pedlars and hawkers of
pardons, perpetual mumpers [1] and mumblers of
orisons, and other such gangs of rascally scoundrels
will come out of their dens. [2] 'Scape that 'scape can,
say I. Harkee me! take heed also of the bones
whenever you eat fish, and God preserve you from a
dose of ratsbane too.

CHAPTER X

OF WINTER

In winter, in my silly opinion, those men will not
be overwise, who will sell their furred gowns, swans'
skins, and other warm clothes, to buy fuel; neither
did the ancients use to do so, says Avenzouart. If
it chance to rain, do not fret yourselves; so much
the less dust you will have when you go abroad.
Keep yourselves as hot as toasts, do you hear? beware of catarrhs; drink of the best, till the other
sort mend; and pray henceforth shite no more a-
bed. Oh, oh! poultry, [1] do you build you nests
so high ?

[1] In the original it is *perpetuons*, and means all monks; whose
communities never die, but are perpetual.

[2] With a purpose to catch from the countryfolks all they can
of their harvest.

[1] A mere joke, or trivial pleasantry, put here by Rabelais out
of the gaiety or wantonness of his humour, without any relation
to what went before. Other noted authors, both comical and
serious, have used the very same words at the winding up of their
works. Philip d'Alcippe for one, John Edouard du Monin for
another, *cum multis aliis.*

AN EPISTLE BY PANTAGRUEL'S LIMOSIN

GRAND EXCORIATOR OF THE LATIALE TONGUE; MENTIONED BOOK II. CHAP. VI

To his own Amicissim, residing at the Inclite ana Famosissim Urb of Lugdun

Our auricles, percuss'd by fame sonorous,
Your mirabundous acts have brought before us.
Your placid life, here inaudite before,
Repletes the town of Lugdun o'er and o'er:
Where nymphs convening three times thrice divine,
Prostrate themselves as vot'ries at your shrine.
Some voluntarily fly into your arms,
For your opiparous or aureous charms:
Some, tender souls! on you themselves obtrude,
Mov'd by your tongue's most melleous dulcitude.
Yous phrase, robustly propp'd, with ease produces
Fractions in many weak virgineous cruises:
When you're placientated, the fort is won;
Id est, whene'er y'impel the matter on.

You therefore, if your appetite desires
New dapes each hour, pursue what that requires.
If sated with your urban stale fruitions,
Or with your half unnatural coitions,
You to your neighb'ring rural fund migrate,
And there your lassate corps reanimate.
There ev'ry joy to you is an oblation,
In which your ingeny finds delectation.
The gay Merul and warbling Philomel,
To please you, strive each other to excel.
Their pleasant notes tristitious thoughts confound,
And wake your soul with their letating sound.

An Epistle

To that amæne recess the rural quire,
Sylvanus, satyrs, fauns, and Pan retire:
Gods, demigods, nymphs, dryads, naiads meet,
And leave their mansions for your dulcior seat;
And when the turb is once accumulate,
Jocund jocundity's immensurate.
With sumptuous cates divine ambrosia joins,
And nectar there exuperates all your wines.
With this each dry esuriant guest replete is,
As at the feast of Peleus and his Thetis.
Then all arise; the tables here sublate;
In arbours, some themselves refocillate;
Some in ferine venation take delight;
For coney-caption some have appetite:
In fine, ludes omniform are there invented,
And every indoles and sense contented.
Pleasure invades, pain abdicates the mind:
What more in heaven can its grand tenants find!

While we, alas! must still obambulate,
Sequacious of the court and courtier's fate;
O most infaust who optates there to live!
An aulic life no solid joys can give.
We've been cruciated since your last migration,
With an indesinent obequitation:
Our boots and legs have not been separated,
While we the Burgadelands have conculated.
Lute, unds, and sands did long our march oppose,
And asp'rous rocks, the bulwarks of our foes.
But now I'll not too many verbs effund,
Nor with our ills your auricles obtund:
Nor all our martial conflicts represent,
Obscesses, storms, and fights sanguinolent:
When angry Mars Burgundia cicatris'd,
And friend with friend in dolours sympathis'd;

Rabelais' Works

Desp'rate of conquest, thro' dire accidents,
Apert we jac'd to th' æther without tents.
At last the kind, tho' rigid brume came on;
The camp was derelict, and all are gone.
For when hybernal evils appropinque,
The legions on their hybernacles think.

So, when the bellic season was expir'd,
Wisely the regal majesty retired.
To Fonsbellaqueus now the monarch's come,
The noblest master to the noblest dome:
No more had Nero's match'd its noble pride,
Than with the king, the tyrant could have vied.
Where ev'n Diana's temple rais'd again,
The regal palace would eclipse the fane.
'Tis true, you've ocull'd it in times præterit,
But ev'ry day 't has meliorated merit;
And those who supervis'd it *noct hestern*,
In *hodiern hores*, will major things discern.
Opining to revise a structure new,
Where are surpass'd itself, and nature too.

Now to apply my primary ingredient,
That you move *huc* I think it not expedient:
For, should you come before the brume's abated,
Th' opime you'd linquish for the macerated:
Since, thanks to Jove's benignity, you're valid,
Choose not a frigid state, while yours is calid;
Unless salubrity you vilipend,
And from your own become your medic's friend;
For in veracity, these times denote
Morbs to the sane, and obits to th' ægrote;
And alterate the suavest pulchritude
To the complexion of its native mud.

Incluse with silves behind, and lakes before us,
Our outward man wants something that's calorous.

An Epistle

Scarce one poor fascicle can we acquire;
In fine all solaces from us retire.
And were it not (in this extremity)
Juvated by the town's proximity,
To which we equitate with maturation,
And to kind nature make sacrification,
Soon in our sepulchres we should all hide us;
For, sure, one hebdomad would here occide us.

By this imparity you plainly see
Our life's distress, and yours jocundity;
Our state's naufrageous and periclitating:
If then you sape, as we are cogitating,
Hither, till spring return, make no transition,
Though you were stimulated by ambition.
What though honoribilities it offers,
Large heaps of numms to fill your largest coffers,
Imperial favour too, and what not else?
Ample munificence, and office celse,
Such as you execute when here? yet these
Have no intrinsic valour, though they please.
Our means of life are pote, and cibe, and vest;
Who jugulates himself for wealth's a beast.

To this epistle finis now we'll fix,
Which to your school a transit does adnix;
Where rules to prolix loquels are prescribed,
And doct verbocination is imbibed:
Excoriating the language latiale,
To make reply let not your calam fail;
But atrament at large the candid chart,
With corresponding rhymes transcending art;
Which will to him be the altest obligation
Who is your serv. with maxim veneration,

Desbride Gousier.

AN EPIGRAM

ALL strive of late to bring to purity
Our tongue that once lay in obscurity;
And profligating all barbarity,
With th' Attic set the French in parity;
So, to revive its old nobility,
They shun the phrase of our mobility;
But this disguised, by a fatality
'Tis mere excoriated latiality.

FRANCISCO RABELÆSIO

POETA SITIENS, PONEBAT

Vita,[1] Lyæe, sitis; liquisti, flebis, adures;
Membra, hominem, tumulum; morte, liquore, face.

THE PHILOSOPHICAL CREAM OF ENCYCLOPEDIC QUESTIONS

BY PANTAGRUEL

WHICH WERE SORBONICOFICABILITUDINISSELY DEBATED
IN THE SCHOOLS OF THE DECREE NEAR ST DENYS
DE LA CHARTRE AT PARIS

UTRUM, a platonic idea, hovering to the right on the orifice of the chaos, might drive away the squadrons of democratical atoms?

[1] ' Vita, liquisti membra morte:
Lyæe, flebis hominem liquore;
Sitis, adures tumulum face.'
So it is to be read according to the editions of 1567, 1573, 1584, and 1600, not *foco* as in that of 1596.

The Philosophical Cream

Utrum, the flickermice [1] flying through the translucidity of the cornered gate, might, spy-like, discover the morphean visions twirling and unwinding in a circular manner the thread of the *rete admirabile* that wraps up the *attili* [2] of ill-caulked brains?

Utrum, the atoms turning about at the sound of the hermagorical harmony, might make a compaction or a dissolution of a quintessence, by the subtraction of the pythagorical numbers?

Utrum, the hybernal frigidity of the antipodes, passing in an orthogonal line, through the homogeneous solidity of the centre, might warm the superficial connexity of our heels by a soft antiperistasis?

Utrum, the tassels of the torrid zone might so far be dipped and wetted at the cataracts of the Nile, as to moisten the most caustic parts of the imperial heaven?

Utrum, by reason of the long hair that was bestowed on the bear at her metamorphosis, if her breech were but shaved the Italian way *à la bougarone*, to make Triton a beard, she might not be keeper of the arctic pole'?

Utrum, an elementary sentence might allege a decennal prescription against amphibious animals and *è contra* the other respectively put in her petition in case of seizure and novelty?

Utrum, an historical grammar, and posteriority, by the triad of articles, might find some line or character of their chronicle on the zenonian palm? (open hand, *i.e.* eloquence).

Utrum, the *genera generalissima*, by a violent elevation over their predicaments, might crawl and

---

[1] Bats.
[2] A certain fish in the river Po, which sometimes weighs 1000 lb. [so says M. M. but not Torriano].

clamber up to the stories of the transcendants, and consequently let the special and predicable species follow, to the unspeakable loss and damage of poor masters of arts?

Utrum, Proteus, that transformed himself into all manner of shapes, turning himself into a cigale [3] and musically trying his voice in the dog-days, might make a third concoction with the morning dew carefully bottled up in May, before the full resolution of a zodiacal girdle?

Utrum, the black scorpion might bear a solution of the continuum in his substance, and, by the effusion of his blood, darken and blacken the milky-way, to the great loss and grief of the swagbellied Jacobites? [4]

———

TWO EPISTLES

TO TWO WOMEN OF DIFFERENT HUMOURS

To the first old woman

OLD, toothless, pox'd, mischievous hag of night;
Old graceless witch, who liv'st in virtue's spite;
Old treacherous beldam, burthen to the earth;
Plots, broils, and wars, from thee derive their birth.

[3] A thick, broad-headed flying insect, which sits on trees in hot countries, and sings after a shrieking fashion: it is called *cicada*, in Latin, and therefore mistaken by some here for the grasshopper.

[4] German Jacobites in the original. It alludes from these pilgrims of St James in Galicia, to the philosophers, the followers of the Jacobin Albertus Magnus. 'Albertistæ dicunt quòd galaxia est naturæ cœlestis, Thomistæ dicunt quòd galaxia est naturæ elementaris,' says Dr Gerlam (all-sheep) in part 2nd of Epist. Obs. Viror.

Old arrant bawd, by whose destructive trade
The lewd are sold, the modest are betray'd:
Honour thou never knew'st, thou living tomb,
Whor'd with thy father, in thy mother's womb.
Thy charity does like the devil's prove,
And damns the wretches who thy lewdness love.
Thy livid blood with pois'nous rage is swell'd;
Thy breast with gall, thy head with mischief fill'd.
Thou ne'er of any but thyself spok'st well,
And for detraction e'en surpassest hell.
Old brimstone-bawd, with brandy flaming red,
That mak'st a curst rank brothel of thy bed;
Propitious to all malice and ill-luck,
That hast a teat to give the devil suck:
Damn'd witch, thou dost in magic far excel
Medæa, and the blackest fiends of hell:
Thou mak'st thy hideous phiz more dreadful still;
But when thou dost, we should thy hagship kill,
Lest thy redoubled ugliness affright,
And, like Medusa's, ruin us at sight.
Thou, scarlet whore, ne'er mourn'st for doing ill;
Thy only tears are rheums, and wines distill'd;
Thy only sighs are vented at thy bum,
Outstink a carrion, and outroar a drum.
Old monstrous hag, of matchless, dreadful kind,
Thou the three furies in one body join'd;
Satan, outdone by thee, does envious grow,
And longs to burn thee in revenge below.
Dissembling witch, whose tongue, still muttering, dares
Mock frowning heav'n with thy unhallow'd pray'rs.
Thou, bold bad sprite, with Satan's borrow'd force,
Pretend'st to turn a rapid river's course;
With spells to paleness fright the astonish'd moon,
And darken quite the blushing sun at noon.

Rabelais' Works

Base murd'ring sorceress, with relentless heart,
On innocence thou try'st thy cursed art;
Bewitching infants in their mother's arms,
And death alone can end the painful charms.
No God thou own'st, but thy insatiate gut;
Thou mak'st each trull turn up her filthy scut.
Pity thou slight'st, by pity thou'rt abhorr'd,
And more deserv'dst a faggot than a cord.
Thy cruel heart with rancour has its load,
Natural to thee as poison to a toad.
Thou worst of mischiefs, guide to endless death,
Who scatter'st plagues with thy contagious breath,
Canst thou expect unpunished to remain,
And for each crime to escape a double pain?
Millions in judgment will against thee rise,
And loudly call for vengeance to the skies.
Those whom thy arts to lawless flames decoyed,
Shall be below to burn thy soul employed.
But thou'rt the worst of hells for impious deeds,
T'other perhaps in punishments exceeds.
Prepare, prepare for its revenging pains,
There to be rack'd in everlasting chains.
Tremble, and loudly to the mountains call,
That they may gape, and crush thee with their
    fall!
For still thy latter sins the first excel,
And, living on, thou'lt grow too bad for hell.
Damn'd harridan, with reeking lust more drunk
Than Messaline that great imperial punk:
Ne'er tired, or sated, thou out-dost her more
Than she out-did the utmost stint of whore.
Thy sweaty carcase (which kind heaven con-
    found!)
With noisome steams offends us all around.
Old drunken chambriere, sink of filth and sin,
Plaister without and rottenness within;

Two Epistles

Curst lump of lees; thou universal sore;
Thou putrid product of the common-shore;
Thou lowest, last degree of infamy;
Thou very highest top of villainy;
Repent, or know I'll double every curse:
But no, thou canst not mend, nor e'er be worse.

An Epistle to another Woman of a quite different humour

HAIL! reverend matron, virtuous as you're fair;
Hail! you, whose autumn may with spring compare;
Matron, adorn'd so richly in your mind,
That in your looks the treasures we may find.
With pious doctrine you your faith improve,
Shun idle talk, and books of idler love,
And setting vice and needless forms apart,
Your suffering God engrave within your heart:
While you on earth a heavenly saint commence,
Your charity is, like the world, immense;
Ready to ease the afflicted of their load,
At awful distance ye imitate your God.
So sweet, so modest, and so void of pride,
That e'en that God does own you for his bride.
You to all folly wisely shut your eyes,
And dare the world's alluring joys despise.
That sacred writ alone is your delight,
Which saves the soul from everlasting night.
You temper still, yet never to a fault,
Your wine with water, and your words with thought;
And never cherish'd an unchaste desire,
Or could be warm'd but by the nuptial fire;
But, waiting for your Saviour, pass away
In prayers the night, in pious acts the day.

235

Rabelais' Works

In faith, in piety alone extreme,
You shun applause, yet best deserve esteem.
The prophet's great inspirer fills your breast;
Your head, your heart, by the whole God possest:
While some unthinking virgins are betray'd,
And made proficients in hell's thriving trade,
Your wise advice, your great example draws
The thoughtless wretches out of Satan's jaws.
Matron, in wedlock faithful and sedate,
An honour to that honourable state;
Not weakness made you wed, but piety,
Thus to increase the saint's society.
Those wanton toys could ne'er your heart entice;
Which stifle virtue, and encourage vice.
Matron, whom all the Christian Pallas term,
Wise in your conduct, and your courage firm.
I prize, admire, and love your matchless store,
Your outward beauties much, your inward graces
  more.
From heaven you came, and to that heaven are
  born;
Virtue adorns you, virtue you adorn.
Oh that I may, e'en till my latest hours,
Advance in knowledge, contemplating yours!
May you obtain below what earth can crave!
What heaven can grant, above, you're sure to have.[1]

[[1]The best critics ascribe the two foregoing poems to François Habert.]

236

LETTERS WRITTEN BY FRANCIS RABELAIS

LETTER I

TO MY LORD BISHOP OF MAILLEZAIS

My Lord,—I writ to you at large on the nine-and-twentieth of November, and sent you some Naples grain for your salads, of every sort that is eaten on this side, except pimpernell, which then I could not procure. I have sent you no great quantity at present, because it had been too much for the courier at one time ; but if you please to have more, either for your gardens, or to dispose of otherwise, I will send it you upon notice. I had written to you before, and sent to you the four signatures concerning the benefices of Friar Dom. Philippe, obtained in the name of those whom you have set down in the instructions you gave me. I have not received since any letter from you that mentions the receipt of the aforesaid signatures. I received only one dated from l'Ermenaud, when my Lady d'Estissac came thither, in which you let me know that you had received two packets from me; one from Ferrara, the other from this city, with the cypher which I writ to you; but for aught I understand, you had not yet received the

237

packet where the signatures were enclosed. I can now give you an account, that my business has been granted and dispatched better, and with more certainty, than I could have wished; and I have had therein the assistance and advice of worthy men, particularly of the Cardinal de Genutiis, who is judge of the palace, and of the Cardinal Simonetta, who was auditor of the chamber, a very knowing man, and well versed in such matters. The Pope was of opinion that I should proceed in my business *per cameram:* the above-mentioned cardinals were of a mind that it should be by the court of contradicts: because, that in *foro contentioso*, it cannot be revocable in France, and quæ per contradictoria transiguntur transeunt in rem judicatam: quæ autem · per cameram, et impugnari possunt, et in judicium veniunt.' Those things which are transacted by contradictories, pass as determined; but those things which are done by the chamber, may be called into question, and tried over again.

Upon the whole, I have nothing more to do, than to take up the bulls *sub plumbo.*

My Lord Cardinal du Bellay, as likewise my Lord Bishop of Mascon, have assured me that the charges shall be remitted me, though the Pope by old custom remits nothing, except of what is despatched *per cameram.* There will remain to be paid, only the referendaries, proctors, and other such like scribblers and blotters of parchment. If my money falls short, I will recommend myself to your lordship's alms; for I do not think to leave this place till the Emperor goes.

He is at present at Naples, whence, as he has written to the Pope, he will depart on the sixth of January. This town is already full of Spaniards; and he has sent an extraordinary ambassador to the Pope, besides him who constantly resides at this court, to give him notice of his coming. The Pope leaves him half the palace, and all the borough of St Peter for his retinue, and has ordered three thousand beds to be prepared, according to the Roman custom, that is to say, with quilts; for the city has been unprovided of them ever since it was sacked by the Lanskenets. He has got together as much hay, straw, oats, spelt-corn, and barley, as he could find; and of wine, as much as is arrived *in ripâ*. I fancy he will be at no small charge, which cannot be very easy to him in this his great poverty, so apparent in him, more than in any Pope for these three hundred years past. The Romans have not yet resolved how to behave themselves upon this occasion, and have had many meetings, by order of the senators, conservators, and governor; but they cannot agree in their opinions. The Emperor has declared to them, by said ambassador, that he does not design his people shall be entertained at free cost, but as the Pope shall think fit to entertain them, which does the more sensibly touch the Pope; for he understands well enough, that by this saying the Emperor means to see how, and with what affection, he will treat him and his people.

The holy father has sent two legates to him by the choice of the consistory; to wit, the Cardinal of Sienna, and Cardinal Cæsarini. Since which, the Cardinals Salviati and Rodolph are also gone to him, and with them my Lord de Xaintes. I understand it is about the affair of Florence, and concerning the difference between the Duke Alexander de Medicis, and Philip Strozzi, whose estate, which is considerable, the duke had a mind to confiscate. Next to the Fourques of Auxbourg, in Germany, he is counted the richest merchant in Christendom; and the duke has set people here to poison or kill him, whatever came on it. Being advertised of this attempt, he obtained of the Pope to go armed. And he commonly went attended with thirty soldiers, armed at all points. The said Duke of Florence having noticed (I suppose) that Strozzi, with the above-mentioned cardinals, was gone to the Emperor, and that he offered to the Emperor four hundred thousand ducats, only to give commissions to people who might inform against the tyranny and baseness of the said duke, left Florence, constituted Cardinal Cibo his governor, and came to this city the morrow after Christmas day, the twenty-third hour, entering at St Peter's gate, followed by fifty light horse, in white armour, with lances, and about a hundred harquebusiers. The rest of his train was but little, and in no very good order. And no soul went to see him, but the Emperor's ambassador, who met him at the same gate. As soon as he was in town, he came to the palace, and had a short audience of the Pope; and had lodgings in St George's palace. The next morning he went away, attended as before.

Eight days since, news came to this town, and his holiness has received letters from divers parts, that the Sophy, King of Persia, has defeated the army of the Turks. Yesterday night arrived here the nephew of Monsieur de Vely, the King's ambassador, to the Emperor, who assured my Lord Cardinal du Bellay, that the thing was true; and that this had been the greatest slaughter that has been heard of these four hundred years; for above forty thousand horse were killed on the Turk's side.

Consider what a number of foot fell there! As likewise on the Sophy's side. For among people that do not willingly fly, *non solet esse incruenta victoria;* the victory does not use to be without blood.

The principal defeat was near a little town called Coni, not far distant from the great city of Tauris, for which the Sophy and the Turk contend; the other action was near a place called Betelis. The manner was thus: the Turks had divided their army, and one part was sent to take Coni, of which the Sophy having intelligence, he, with his whole army, rushed upon this separated part, before they could stand upon their guard.

See here the effect of ill counsel, in dividing his army before he had gotten the victory. The French can give a good account of this, when the Duke of Albany drew out the strength and flower of the camp before Pavia. Upon the news of this rout and defeat, Barbarossa is retired to Constantinople to secure the country, and says, by his good gods, that this is nothing, considering the mighty power of the Turk. But the Emperor is eased of the fear that he had of the Turk's coming into Sicily, as he had threatened in the beginning of the spring. And this may give repose to Christendom for some considerable time; and those who would lay tithes upon the church, *eo pretextu,* that they would fortify themselves against the approach of the Turk, are but ill furnished with demonstrative arguments.

LETTER II

My Lord,—I have received letters from Monsieur de Sanct Cerdos, dated from Dijon, in which he

tells me of a process that he has depending in the
Court of Rome. I dare not answer him, without
running the hazard of incurring a great deal of dis-
pleasure. But I understand he has the greatest
right in the world, and that he suffers a manifest
injury, and that he ought to come hither in person.
For there is no such affair, how equitable soever,
that is not lost for want of a man's own soliciting
in it; especially when he has a strong party, who
can overawe with threats those who solicit for him.
The want of a cypher prevents my writing to you
more at large. But it troubles me to see so much
as I do, particularly, being sensible of the great
kindness you have for him; and likewise because
he has of a long time loved and favoured me. In
my opinion Monsieur de Basilac, counsellor (one of
the judges' assistants) in the Parliament of Toulouse,
came hither this winter on a less occasion, and is
older and more infirm than he, and yet has had a
quick dispatch to his content.

LETTER III

My Lord,—The Duke of Ferrara, who went to
the Emperor at Naples, returned hither this morning. I know not yet how he has determined
matters relating to the investiture and homage of
his lands: but I understand he is come back not
well satisfied with the Emperor. I fear he will be
forced to empty his coffers of those crowns his
father left him, and that the Pope and Emperor
will fleece him at pleasure; considering also that it
was for above six months before he refused to
espouse the King's interest, notwithstanding all the
Emperor's remonstrances and threats. My Lord

Bishop of Limoges, who was the King's ambassador at Ferrara, seeing the said duke, without acquainting him with his design, was retired to the Emperor, is returned to France. It is feared that Renée [1] will receive no little ·displeasure by it; the duke having removed Madam de Soubise, her governess, and ordered her to be served by Italians, which does not look well.

LETTER IV

MY LORD,—Three days since arrived here a post from Monsieur de Crissé, who brings an account that some of the Lord Rancé's men, who went to the relief of Geneva, were defeated by a party of the Duke of Savoy's. With him came a courier from Savoy, who brought the news of it to the Emperor. This may unhappily prove *seminarium futuri belli*, the cause of an ensuing war. For these little wilful broils draw after them great battles, which is demonstrable from ancient history, as well Greek and Roman as French, as appears by the battle at Vireton.

LETTER V

MY LORD,—About fifteen days since, Andrew Doria, who went with stores to those who hold the Gouletta near Tunis, for the Emperor, as likewise to supply them with water (for the Arabians of the country make continual war upon them, and they dare not stir out of their garrison), is arrived at Naples, where he stayed not above three days with the Emperor, since when, he is sailed hence with nine-and-twenty galleys; it is said in quest of Judeo

[1] Renée of France, Duchess of Ferrara.

and Cacciadiavolo, who have burnt a great deal of the country of Sardinia and Minorca. The grand master of Rhodes, who was born in Piedmont, is lately dead, in whose room the commander of Forton, between Montauban and Toulouse, is chosen.

LETTER VI

My Lord,—I here send you a book of Prognostications, which busies this whole town : it is entitled, ' *De Eversione Europæ*,' of the overturning of Europe. For my part, I give no credit at all to it. But Rome was never so wholly given over to vanities and prophecies as it is at present. I am apt to think the reason is, because *mobile mutatur semper cum principe vulgus ;* the giddy multitude always change with the prince. I have also sent you an almanack for the ensuing year 1537. I send you besides, the copy of a brief which his holiness has lately decreed for the arrival of the Emperor : as likewise the Emperor's entry into Messina and Naples, and the funeral oration at the interment of the deceased Duke of Milan.

My lord, I humbly recommend myself to your good favour, praying to our Lord for your good health and long life.

Rome, *Dec.* 30*th*, 1536.

LETTER VII

To the Lord de Maillezais

My Lord,—I have received the letters you were pleased to write to me, dated the second of

December : by which I understand that my two packets are come to your hands; one of the 18th, the other of the 22d of October, with the four signatures which I sent you. I writ since to you more at large, on the ninth and twentieth of November, and thirteenth of December. By this time, I believe, you have received the said packets. For Mr Michael Parmentier, bookseller, living at the arms of Basil, writ to me the fifth of this instant, that he had received and sent them to Poictiers. You may assure yourself, that the packets which I shall send you will be safely delivered at Lyons : for I put them into the great sealed packet, which is for the King's affairs ; and when the courier comes to Lyons, he is despatched by the governor; then his secretary, who is much my friend, takes the packet, which I subscribe on the first sheet, to the aforesaid Michael Parmentier. Afterwards there is no difficulty, unless from Lyons to Poictiers, which is the reason that obliges me to set an extraordinary postage upon it, that the greater care may be taken of it by the messengers at Poictiers, in hopes to get a spill by it. For my part, I constantly encourage the said Parmentier with some small presents which I send him of novelties on this side, or to his wife, that he may be the more diligent to engage merchants or messengers at Poictiers to deliver the packets to your lordship. And I very much approve of the advice which you gave me in your letter, that I should not trust them to the hands of the bankers, for fear they should be picked and broken open. I think it will not be amiss, the first time you write to me, especially if it be business of consequence, that you write a line to the said Parmentier, and enclose a piece of gold to him in your letter, in consideration of the care he takes to send your

packets to me, and mine to you. A small matter
sometimes highly obliges honest men, and makes
them more diligent for the time to come, when the
case requires a speedy dispatch.

LETTER VIII

My Lord,—I have not as yet presented your
letters to my Lord Bishop de Xaintes; for he is
not yet returned from Naples, whither he went with
the Cardinals Salviati and Rodolph. He will return in two days; then I will give him your letters,
and desire an answer of them, which I will send
you by the first courier that goes hence. I understand their affairs have not had that success with
the Emperor which they hoped for: and that the
Emperor had positively answered, that at their request and instance, as likewise at the late Pope
Clement's, he had created Alexander de Medicis,
Duke of the territories of Florence and Pisa, which
he never thought to do, nor would have done:
meanwhile to depose him, would be the trick of
some stage-player, which does and undoes the same
thing. However, that they should resolve to acknowledge him as their duke and lord, and obey
him as his vassals and subjects, and be sure they did
so. As to the complaints they made against the
said duke, he would take cognisance of them when
he came to Florence.

For he designs, after some stay at Rome, to pass
through Sienna, and thence to Florence, to Bolonia,
to Milan and Genoa. Thus the aforesaid cardinals,
together with the Bishop of Xaintes, Strozzi, and
some others, returned, *re infectâ*, as wise as they
went.

The thirteenth of this month came back hither the Cardinals of Sienna and Cæsarini, who had been elected by the Pope, and the whole college, legates to the Emperor. They have so negotiated the matter, that the Emperor has deferred his coming hither to the latter end of February. If I had as many crowns as the Pope would give days of pardon, *proprio motu de plenitudine potestatis*, of his own free will, out of the plenitude of his power, and other such like favourable circumstances, to any one that could defer it for five or six years to come, I should be richer than ever was Jacques Cœur. Here are great preparations made in this city for his reception; and a new way is made by the Pope's command, by which he is to make his entry: that is, through St Sebastian's gate towards Champidoli *Templum Pacis* (the Temple of Peace), and the amphitheatre, and he is to pass under the ancient triumphal arches of Constantine, Vespasian, and Titus, of Numetianus, and others: then on one side of St Mark's palace, by Campo de Fiore, and by the palace Farnese, where the Pope used to reside; then by the banks, and below St Angelo's castle. To make and level which way, above two hundred houses, and three or four churches, are pulled down to the ground, which most people take for an ill omen. On the day of the conversion of St Paul, his holiness went to St Paul's to hear mass, and made a feast to all the cardinals. After dinner he returned, passing through the above-mentioned way, and looked at St George's palace. But it is a sad sight to behold the ruins of the demolished houses that are not paid for: nor have the landlords any recompense made them.

To-day arrived here the Venetian ambassadors, four brave old grey-headed gentlemen, who are

going to the Emperor at Naples. The Pope has
sent all his family before them; his bed-chamber-
men, chamberlains, janisaries, lanskenets; and the
cardinals have sent their mules in pontificalibus.

Likewise the 7th of this month, the ambassadors
of Sienna were introduced in good order, and after
they had made their speech in open consistory, and
that the Pope had answered them in fine Latin, they
suddenly parted for Naples. I believe ambassadors
will be sent from all parts of Italy to the Emperor;
and he knows well enough how to play his game,
to get money out of them, as it has been discovered
about ten days since. But I am not yet fully
acquainted with the subtility, which, it is said, he
made use of at Naples; hereafter I may give you an
account of it.

The Prince of Piedmont, the Duke of Savoy's
eldest son, died at Naples fifteen days ago; the
Emperor ordered him a very honourable interment,
at which he assisted in person.

The King of Portugal, six days since, commanded
his ambassador at Rome, that immediately upon
receipt of his letter, he should return to him in
Portugal; which he did the same hour, and came
ready booted and spurred to take his leave of the
most reverend the Lord Cardinal du Bellay. Two
days after, was killed near the Bridge of St Angelo,
in open day, a Portuguese gentleman, who solicited
here for the whole body of the Jews that were
baptised under King Emanuel of Portugal, that he
might succeed to their estates when they died.
The King has also exacted several things of them
against the edict and ordinance of the said King
Emanuel. I doubt we shall hear of some sedition
at Portugal.

LETTER IX

MY LORD,—In the last packet I sent you, I gave you an account, that part of the Turk's army was defeated by the Sophy, near Betelis. The Turk did not very long delay his revenge: for two months after, he fell upon the Sophy with the greatest fury imaginable; and, after having put to fire and sword a great part of the country of Mesopotamia, he has driven back the Sophy on the other side of Mount Taurus. In the meantime, he causes a great number of galleys to be built upon the river Tanais, by which they may come to Constantinople. Barbarossa is still at Constantinople, to secure the country, and has left several garrisons at Bona and Algiers, lest the Emperor should by chance attack him. I have sent you his picture, drawn to the life; as also a map of Tunis, and of the seaport towns adjacent. The lanskenets, whom the Emperor sent into the duchy of Milan, to keep the strong places, are all drowned and lost at sea, to the number of fifteen hundred, in one of the biggest and stoutest ships belonging to the Genoese; and it was near to a port belonging to the commonwealth of Lucca, called Lerza. The occasion was, because they being weary of the sea, and desirous to get ashore, which they could not for the tempest and stress of weather, imagined that the pilot of the ship would still keep them off at sea, longer than he needed; for which cause they killed him, with some other of the officers of the said ship, after whose death the ship remained without a command; and instead of taking in their sails, the lanskenets hoisted them, as being unpractised in sea affairs, and in this confusion they perished within a stone's throw of the aforesaid port.

My Lord, I understand that my Lord Bishop de Lavaur, who was the King's ambassador at Venice, has had his audience of leave, and is returning to France. The Bishop of Rhodes goes in his place, and is now at Lyons with all his retinue, ready to go, when the King has given him his instructions.

My Lord, I humbly recommend myself to your favour, praying to our Lord to give you long life in good health.—Your most humble servant,

FRANCIS RABELAIS.

ROME, *Jan.* 28, 1536.

LETTER X

MY LORD,—I writ to you at large all the news I could learn, the 28th of January last past, by a gentleman, servant to Monsieur de Montreuil, called Tremeliere, who returned from Naples, where he had bought some horses of that kingdom for his lord, and was returning to him with all speed. The same day I received the packet that you were pleased to send me from Legugé, dated the 10th of the said month, in which you may see the method I have taken for the delivery of your letters, by which they are safely and suddenly brought to me here. Your said letters and packets were delivered at the Arms of Basle, on the one-and-twentieth of the same month; the eight-and-twentieth they were delivered to me here. And to encourage at Lyons (for that is the point and principal place) the bookseller at the Arms of Basle to be diligent in this affair, I repeat what I writ to you in my aforementioned packet, if you chance to write to me about anything of consequence: that it is my advice, that on the first occasion of writing to me, you write a word or two to him in a letter, in which be pleased to inclose some gold crowns, or some other piece of old gold, as a royal, an angel, or salutation, in consideration of the pains and care he takes of them; so small a matter will more and more endear him to your service.

Now, to answer your letters, I have diligently searched the registers of the palace, since the time that you commanded me, that is, the years 1529, 1530, and 1531, to see if Dom. Philippe's act of resignation to his nephew were to be found, and have given the clerks of the register two gold crowns, which is but a small recompense for the great and tedious trouble in it. In short, they have found nothing of it, nor ever heard news of his procurations; wherefore, I doubt there is some foul play in his case, or the instructions you writ to me were not sufficient to find them. And that I may be more certified in it, you should tell me, *cujus diocesis*, of what diocese the said Friar Dom. Philippe was; and if you have heard nothing to give more light in the matter, as if it was *purè et simpliciter*, or *causâ permutationis*.

LETTER XI

My Lord,—What I writ to you of my Lord Cardinal du Bellay's answer, when I presented him your letters, ought not to displease your lordship. My Lord of Mascon has sent you an account of the whole matter, and we are not yet like to have a legate in France. It is certain, that the King has presented the Cardinal of Lorrain to the Pope. But I believe, that the Cardinal du Bellay will endeavour by all means possible to get it for himself. The old proverb is true, which says, *Nemo sibi secundus*. And

I shrewdly suspect, by certain signs that I see, that my Lord Cardinal du Bellay will engage the Pope on his behalf, and thus be made acceptable to the King. Nevertheless, be not uneasy, if his answer be a little ambiguous in your concern.

LETTER XII

My Lord,—The grains which I sent you, I can assure you, are the best of Naples, of the same which his holiness has caused to be sowed in his privy garden of Belvedere. There are no other kind of salads on this side but those of Nasidord and Arroussa; but those of Legugé seem to me altogether as good, and somewhat more sweet and grateful to the stomach, and particularly better for you; for those of Naples, in my opinion, are too hot and tough.

As for the season for sowing them, you must caution your gardeners not to sow them altogether so early as they do on this side, for it is not warm weather so soon without as here. They may very well sow your salads twice a year, that is to say, in Lent, and in November; and they may sow the white cardes or thistles in August and September; melons, pompions, and the others in March; fencing them for some days with mats, and a thin layer of horse-dung, not altogether rotten, when they fear it will freeze. Many other grains besides are sold here, as Alexandria gilliflowers, matronal violets, and shrubs, with which they refresh their chambers in the summer, called Belvedere, and other physical herbs. But this would be more for my Lady d'Estissac's turn. If you please to have of all sorts, I will send you without fail. But I am forced to have recourse again to your alms; for the thirty crowns which you ordered to be paid me here are almost gone: yet I have converted none of them to any ill use; nor for eating; for I eat and drink at my Lord Cardinal du Bellay's, or at my Lord Mascon's. But a great deal of money goes away in these silly postage letters, chamber rent, and wearing apparel, though I am as frugal as I can be. If you will be pleased to send me a bill of exchange, I hope I shall make use of it wholly to your service, and not remain ungrateful. I see in this city a thousand pretty cheap things, which are brought from Cyprus, Candia, and Constantinople. If you think fit, I will send what I think fittest of them to you and my Lady d'Estissac. The carriage from hence to Lyons will cost nothing.

Thanks be to God I have made an end of my business, and it has cost me no more than the taking out of the bulls; his holiness, having of his own good nature, given me the composition. And I believe you will find the proceedings right enough, and that I have obtained nothing by them, but what is just and lawful. But I have been obliged to advise very much with able counsel, that everything might be according to due form; and I dare modestly tell you, that I have in a manner hardly made use of my Lord Cardinal du Bellay, or my lord ambassador; though, out of their own kindness, they not only offered me their own good word and favour, but absolutely to make use of the King's name.

LETTER XIII

My Lord,—I have not as yet presented your first letter to the Bishop of Xaintes, for he is not yet returned from Naples, whither he went, as I writ to you before. He is expected here within these three days: then I will give him your second, and entreat an answer of it. I understand, that neither he, nor the Cardinals Salviati and Rodolph, nor Philip Strozzi with his money, have done anything with the Emperor in their affair, though they were willing to pay him a million of gold upon the nail, in the name of all the foreigners and exiles of Florence, also to finish la Rocca [the fortress] begun at Florence, to maintain a sufficient garrison in it for ever in the name of the Emperor, and to pay him yearly 100,000 ducats, provided and upon condition he restored them to their former goods, lands, and liberty.

On the contrary, the Duke of Florence was most honourably received by him at his arrival. The Emperor went out before him, and, *post manus oscula*, he ordered him to be attended to the Castle of Capua in the same town, where his natural daughter has an apartment; 'she is affianced to the said Duke of Florence, by the Prince of Salerne, Viceroy of Naples, the Marquis de Vast, the Duke d'Alva, and other principal lords of his court. He held discourse with her as long as he stayed; kissed her, and supped with her: afterwards the above-mentioned cardinals, the Bishop of Xaintes and Strozzi, never left soliciting. The Emperor has put them off for a final resolution to his coming to that town, to the Rocca, which is a place of prodigious strength, that the duke has built at Florence. Over the portico he has caused an eagle to be painted, with wings as large as the sails of the windmills of Mirebalais, thereby declaring and insinuating, that he holds of nobody but the Emperor. And, in fine, he has so cunningly carried on his tyranny, that the Florentines have declared before the Emperor, *nomine communitatis* [in the name of the commonalty], that they will have no other lord but him. It is certain, that he has severely punished the foreigners and exiles. A pasquil has been lately set up, wherein it is said,

To STROZZI—

Pugna pro patria. Fight for thy country.

To ALEXANDER, DUKE of FLORENCE—

Datum serva. What is given thee, keep.

To THE EMPEROR—

Quæ nocitura tenes quamvis sint cara relinque.
Quit what will hurt thee, though it is ne'er so dear.

To THE KING.—

Quod potes id tenta. Dare what thou canst.

To THE CARDINALS SALVIATI AND RODOLPH—

Hos brevitas sensus fecit conjungere binos.

Pure want of sense unites these blocks,
As petty tradesmen join their stocks.

LETTER XIV

MY LORD,—I writ to you, that the Duke of Ferrara is returned from Naples, and retired to Ferrara. Her highness, the Lady Renée, is brought to bed of a daughter : she had another fine daughter before, between six and seven years of age, and a little son of three years old. He could not agree with the Pope, because he demanded an excessive sum of money for the investiture of his lands. Notwithstanding he had abated fifty thousand crowns for the love of the said lady, and this by the solicitations of my lords the Cardinals du Bellay and Mascon, still to increase the conjugal affection of the said duke towards her. This was the occasion of Lyon Jamet's coming to this town, and they only differed for fifteen thousand crowns : but they could not agree, because the Pope would have him acknowledge, that he held and possessed all his lands entirely in fee of the Apostolical See, which the other would not. For he would acknowledge no more than his deceased father had acknowledged, and what the Emperor had adjudged at Bolonia, by a decree in the time of the deceased Pope Clement.

Thus he departed, *re infectâ* (without doing anything), and went to the Emperor, who promised him, at his coming, that he would easily make the Pope consent, and come to the point contained in his said decree ; and that he should go home, leaving an ambassador with him to solicit the affair, when he came on this side ; and that he should not pay the sum already agreed upon, before he heard further from him. The craft lies here, that the Emperor wants money, and seeks it on all hands, and taxes all the world he can, and borrows it from all parts. When he come hither, he will demand some of the Pope, it is a plain case. For he will represent to them, that he has made all these wars against the Turk and Barbarossa, to secure Italy and the Pope, and that he must of necessity contribute to it. The Pope will answer that he has no money, and will manifestly prove his poverty to him. Then the Emperor, without disbursing anything, will demand the Duke of Ferrara's of him, which he knows he may command at a word : and this is the mystery of the matter. Yet it is not certain whether things will be managed thus or no.

LETTER XV

My Lord,—You ask whether the Lord Pietro Ludovico is the Pope's legitimate son or bastard: be assured the Pope was never married, which is as much as to say, that the aforesaid gentleman is certainly a bastard. The Pope had a very beautiful sister. There is to be seen to this day, at the palace, in that apartment where the Summists reside, built by Pope Alexander, an image of Our Lady, which, it is said, was drawn after that gentlewoman: she was married to a gentleman, cousin to the Lord Rancé, who being in the war, in the expedition of Naples, the said Pope Alexander ****: now the Lord Rancé having certain knowledge of the thing, gave notice of it to his cousin, telling him, that he ought not to suffer such a wrong done to their family by a Spanish Pope; and that if he would endure it, he himself would not. In short, her husband killed her; for which fact the present Pope grieved; and to assuage his sorrow, Alexander made him a cardinal, being yet but very young, and bestowed several other marks of his favour upon him.

At that time the Pope kept a Roman lady, of the house of Ruffina, and by her had a daughter, who was married to the Lord Baugé, Count of Sancta Fiore, who died in this town since I came hither. By her he has one of the two little cardinals, who is called the Cardinal of Sancta Fiore. The Pope likewise had a son, who is the said Pietro Ludovico, concerning whom you inquire, who has married the daughter of the Count de Cervelle, on whom he has got a whole house full of children, and among others the little Cardinacule Farnese, who was made vice-

chancellor by the death of the late Cardinal de
Medicis. By what is said you may judge why the
Pope did not very well love the Lord Rancé, and
vice versâ (on the other side) the Lord Rancé put
no great confidence in him: whence arises a great
quarrel between my Lord John Paul de Cere, son to
the said Lord Rancé, and the above-named Pietro
Ludovico, for he is resolved to revenge the death of
his aunt.

But he is quit of it on the part of the said Lord
Rancé, for he died the 11th day of this month, going
a-hunting, in which he extremely delighted, old as
he was. The occasion was this: he had got some
Turkish horses from the fairs of Racana, and as he
was hunting on one of them that was very tender-
mouthed, it fell, tumbled over him, and bruised him
with the saddle-bow so severely, that he did not live
above half-an-hour after the fall. This was a great
loss to the French, for the King in him has lost a
good servant for his affairs in Italy. It is rightly
said that the Lord John Paul his son will be no less
hereafter. But it will be a long time ere he gets
such experience in feats of arms, or so great a
reputation among the commanders and soldiers, as
the late brave man had. I wish with all my heart,
that my Lord d'Estissac, by his death, had the county
of Pontoise; for, it is said, it brings a good revenue.

To assist at the funeral, and to comfort the
Marchioness, his wife, my Lord Cardinal has sent to
Ceres, near twenty miles from this town, my Lord
de Rambouillet, and the Abbot of St Nicaise, who
was a near kinsman to the deceased. (I believe you
have seen him at Court.) He is a little man, all
life; who was called the Archdeacon of the Ursins:
besides, he has sent some others of his prothonotaries;
which, likewise my Lord of Mascon has done.

LETTER XVI

My Lord,—I defer to my next to give you more at large, the news concerning the Emperor; for his design is not yet perfectly discovered. He is still at Naples, but is expected here by the end of this month. Great preparations are made for his coming, and abundance of triumphal arches. His four harbingers have been a good while here in town; two of them Spaniards, one Burgundian, and the fourth a Fleming.

It is a great pity to see the ruins of the churches, palaces and houses, which the Pope caused to be demolished, and pulled down, to make and level him a way. For the charges of his reception, he has laid a tax on the college of cardinals, on those who have places at court, and the artificers of the town, as much as the very aquarols. The town is already full or foreigners.

On the 5th of this month, the Cardinal of Trent (Tridentinus) arrived, being sent here by the Emperor. His train is very numerous, and more sumptuous than the Pope's. He had with him above a hundred Germans, all dressed alike: their gowns were red, with a yellow galloon; and on their right sleeve was embroidered a wheat-sheaf tied close, and round it was written *unitas*.

I hear he is much for peace, and reconciling all the Christian princes. He eagerly desires a general council, whatever is done in other matters. I was present when he said to my Lord Cardinal du Bellay: 'His holiness, the cardinals, bishops, and prelates of the Church, are against a council, and will by no means hear anything of it, though they are pressed by secular princes on that subject; but I see the time at hand, when the prelates of the Church shall be reduced to demand a council, and the laity will not hearken to it. This will be when the latter have taken from the Church all the wealth and patrimony which they had given, while ecclesiastics, by the means of frequent councils, maintained peace and unity among the laity.' Andrew Doria came to this town on the 3d of this month, in no very good equipage. No manner of particular respect was shown him at his arrival, save only the Lord Pietro Ludovico conducted him as far as the palace of the Cardinal Camerlingo, who is a Genoese, of the house of Spinola. The next day he saluted the Pope, and the day after went away for Genoa, on the Emperor's behalf, to inform himself underhand, concerning the disposition of the French about the war. We have had here a positive account of the old Queen of England's death; and they add that the princess, her daughter, lies very ill. However, the bull that was issued out against the King of England to excommunicate him, and to interdict and proscribe his kingdom, did not pass at the consistory, because of the articles 'De commentibus externorum et commerciis mutuis,' of the passages of foreigners and mutual intercourses, which my Lord Cardinal du Bellay and the Bishop of Mascon opposed, in the King's name, on account of the interest which he pretends to have in it. It has been put off till the Emperor's arrival.

My lord, I most humbly recommend myself to your kind favour, praying God that it may please him to keep you long in health and prosperity. —Your Lordship's most humble servant,

FRANCIS RABELAIS.

ROME, *Feb.* 15, 1536.

260

On the Pantagruelian Prognostication and other short Pieces.—Our author, who was a learned astronomer, has chiefly ridiculed astrologers in his Prognostication. He published an Almanack, printed at Lyons in 1553; and perhaps this was printed with it. However, we cannot be sure of this; for it is not to be procured, no more than some of his letters, besides his sciomachy, and festivals at Rome, in Cardinal du Bellay's palace at the Duke of Orleans' birth. I am told, that something of the nature of these predictions has been printed here in Poor Robin's Almanack. I do not wonder at it; for as there is wit and satire in this piece, even one of the most learned men in Germany has not been ashamed to borrow a great deal of it; I mean Joachim Fortius Rindelbergius, who begins a small piece of this nature with the very beginning of the second chapter of this.

Thus he has it in Latin: 'Proximo anno cæci parum aut nihil videbunt, surdi malè audient, muti non loquentur. Ver erit calidum ac humidum, æstas calida et sicca, autumnus frigidus et siccus, hyems frigida et sicca. Æstate erunt quandoque pluviæ, interdum fulmina et tonitrua. Bellum erit inter aucupes et aves, inter piscatores et pisces, inter canes et lepores, inter feles et mures, inter lupos et oves, inter monachos et ova. Multi interibunt pisces, boves, oves, porci, capræ, pulli, et capones; inter simias, canes et equos, mors non tantoperè sæviet. Senectus eodem anno erit immedicabilis propter annos qui præcesserunt. Non pauci inopiâ laborabunt,' etc., p. 556.

There runs a vein of Protestantism through most of this work, which is undoubtedly Rabelais', though it is said to be calculated by Alcofribas Nasier; for that name is only an anagram of the author's, François Rabelais.

The Epistle, said to be written by the Limosin, partly in an affected Frenchified Latin, is to ridicule that way of writing, as appears by the epigram after it. The Cream of Encyclopedic Questions is a trifle, which, like many other insignificant things of other great men, has been kept from oblivion merely for the sake of its author, and added to his works, with the epistles, after his death, as appears by the titlepage of some old editions of the fifth book. The Epistle to the Old Hag, seems to be a sharp invective against the Church of Rome. The Epistle to the Wise Matron, seems to be an encomium on the reformed church.

THE END.

Colston & Coy. Limited, Printers, Edinburgh.

www.ingramcontent.com/pod-product-compliance
Lightning Source LLC
Chambersburg PA
CBHW020352030726
47496CB00007B/2115